BLOOD ON THE LINE

The year is 1857, and on the LNWR train to London, a criminal is being escorted to his appointment with the hangman. But Jeremy Oxley, conman, thief and murderer, has one last ace up his sleeve: a beautiful and ruthless accomplice willing to do anything to save her lover. Inspector Robert Colbeck is dreaming of his wedding as he enters Superintendent Tallis's office. When he learns that Oxley, his nemesis, has once again escaped. No matter the cost, he must bring the murderous Oxley to justice once and for all.

BLOOD ON THE LINE

BLOOD ON THE LINE

by

Edward Marston

Magna Large Print Books
Long Preston, North Yorkshire,
BD23 4ND, England.

British Library Cataloguing in Publication Data.

Marston, Edward
     Blood on the line.

     A catalogue record of this book is
     available from the British Library

     ISBN   978-0-7505-3481-9

First published in Great Britain in 2011 by Allison & Busby Ltd.

Copyright © 2011 by Edward Marston

Cover illustration by arrangement with Allison & Busby Ltd.

The moral right of the author has been asserted

Published in Large Print 2012 by arrangement with
Allison & Busby Ltd.

Magna Large Print is an imprint of Library Magna Books Ltd.

Printed and bound in Great Britain by
T.J. (International) Ltd., Cornwall, PL28 8RW

This one is for Judith. Choo-choo!

CHAPTER ONE

1857

'Are you *serious?*' asked Dirk Sowerby, eyebrows aloft in disbelief.

'Never more so,' replied Caleb Andrews. 'I'm starting to feel my age, Dirk. It's time to think of retirement.'

'But you've got more energy than the rest of us put together.'

Andrews laughed. 'That's not saying much.'

'What does your daughter think of the idea?'

'To be honest, it was Maddy's suggestion. Now that she's about to get married, she doesn't need her old father to support her anymore. She feels that I've earned a rest.'

The two men were on the footplate of the locomotive they'd just brought into Wolverhampton station. The engine was still hissing and wheezing but at least they were now able to have a conversation without having to shout at each other. Andrews was not just one of the senior drivers on the London and North Western Railway, he was an institution, a grizzled veteran who'd dedicated himself to rail transport and achieved an almost iconic status among his work colleagues. He was a short, wiry man in his fifties with a wispy beard flecked with coal dust. Sowerby, by contrast, was tall, big-boned, potato-faced and well over twenty years younger. He idolised Andrews and – even though he sometimes felt the sharp edge of his friend's tongue – was always glad to act as his fireman.

The LNWR train was on its way back to London but it did not have a monopoly on the route. As the two men chatted, a goods train belonging to the Great Western Railway steamed through the recently opened Low Level station nearby and left clouds of smoke in its wake. Andrews curled his lip in disgust.

'We were here first,' he declared. 'Why does Wolverhampton have two stations? We can see to all of the town's needs.'

'Tell that to Mr Brunel.'

'I wish I could, Dirk. There's a lot of other things I could say to him as well. The man's an idiot.'

'That's unfair,' said Sowerby, defensively. 'Brunel is a genius.'

'A genius at getting things wrong,' snapped Andrews, 'such as the ridiculous broad gauge on the GWR. If he's so clever, why did he get involved in that stupid atmospheric railway in Devon? He lost a pretty penny on that. Yes,' he added, warming to his theme, 'and don't forget the battle of Mickleton when Brunel tried to use force to remove the contractors building the Campden Tunnel, even though the Riot Act had already been read.'

'Everyone makes some mistakes, Caleb.'

'He's made far too many for my liking.'

'Well, I think he's a brilliant engineer.'

'He might be if he stuck to one thing and learnt to do it properly. But that's not good enough for Brunel, is it? He wants to design *everything* – railways, bridges, tunnels, stations, docks and harbour improvements. Now he's building iron ships. You wouldn't get me sailing on one of those, I can tell you.'

'Then we have to disagree,' said Sowerby with a wistful smile. 'I'd love to go on a steamship to some faraway country. It's something I dream about.'

'You should be dreaming about taking over my job when I give it up. That should be your ambition, Dirk. The quickest and safest way to travel is by rail. It's also the most enjoyable way.' Andrews glanced down the platform. 'Unless you happen to be *that* poor devil, of course.'

Sowerby craned his neck. 'Who do you mean, Caleb?'

Andrews indicated three people walking towards the train.

'Look at that prisoner being marched between two policemen. See the look on his face?' He gave a grim chuckle. 'Somehow I don't think *he's* going to enjoy travelling by rail.'

The arrival of the newcomers caused some commotion on the platform. Most of the passengers had boarded the train by now but there were several relatives and friends who'd come to see them off. They were diverted by the sight of a prisoner being hustled towards a carriage by two uniformed policemen. The older and brawnier of the policemen was handcuffed to the prisoner. What caused people to stare was the fact that the person under police escort was not the kind of ugly and uncouth villain they might expect but a handsome, well-dressed man in his thirties. Indeed, it was his taller companions who looked more likely to commit terrible crimes.

One of them, Arthur Wakeley, was a stringy individual with a gaunt face darkened by a menacing scowl. The other, Bob Hungerford, had the unmistakable appearance of a thug who prowled fairgrounds in search of easy targets, far more inclined to attack a policeman than become one. Tugging on his handcuffs, he pulled the prisoner along like an angry owner with a badly behaved dog. In spite of themselves, the onlookers felt an instinctive sympathy for the man, wondering

14

what he could possibly have done to justify such harsh treatment and to be compelled to suffer such public humiliation. When the three of them disappeared into a compartment, the small crowd drifted slowly over to it.

There was more drama to come. As the whistle signalled the train's departure, a young woman dashed onto the platform with a valise in her hand and ran to the nearest carriage. A porter was on hand to open the door and, as the train started to move, she flung herself into the compartment. The door clanged shut behind her. There was a collective gasp from the crowd as they imagined how she'd react when she realised she'd be travelling in the company of two intimidating policemen and their prisoner.

'Dear me!' exclaimed Irene Adnam, seeing the trio on the seat opposite her. 'I seem to have got into the wrong compartment. I do apologise.'

'No apology is needed,' said Wakeley, running an approving eye over her. 'You're most welcome to join us. Bob and I are pleased to have you with us. I can't speak for *him*, mind you,' he went on with a nudge in the prisoner's ribs. 'And I doubt if he'll speak for himself at the moment. He's gone very quiet. It often happens that way. Put a pair of handcuffs on them and they lose their tongue.'

'Until then,' said Hungerford, 'this one was talking nineteen to the dozen. I was glad to shut him up.'

Irene smiled nervously. 'I see.'

She glanced at the man sitting between them but he didn't raise his eyes to meet her gaze. He seemed to be ashamed, embarrassed and overwhelmed by the situation. The policemen, however, were eager to catch the eye of such an attractive and smartly attired young woman and they clearly found her a more rewarding spectacle than the fields scudding past the windows. Irene stared at the handcuffs.

'Does he have to be chained to one of you?' she asked.

Hungerford smirked. 'Would *you* rather be handcuffed to him?

'No, no, of course not – it's just that he can hardly escape when the train is in motion. Besides, there are two of you against one of him.'

'In other words,' said Wakeley, 'you're sorry for him.'

'Well, yes, I suppose that I am.'

'Don't be, miss. He deserves to be handcuffed, believe me. In fact, if it was my decision, I'd have him in leg irons as well.'

'That would be dreadful.'

'He's a criminal. He has to be punished.'

'So you won't remove the handcuffs?'

'Not for a second.'

Irene stifled the rejoinder she was about to make and opened her valise instead. Putting a hand inside, she brought out an object that was covered by a piece of cloth. The policemen watched with interest but their curiosity turned to amazement when she whisked the cloth away and was seen to be holding a pistol. Irene's face hardened and her gentle voice now had some steel in it.

'You have one last chance to release him.'

'What are you doing?' cried Hungerford, shrinking back in fear.

'She's only bluffing,' said Wakeley with a confident chuckle. He extended a palm. 'Now, give me that gun before somebody gets hurt.'

'Do as I say!' she ordered. 'Release Mr Oxley.'

Hungerford was mystified. 'You *know* him?'

'They're in this together, Bob,' decided Wakeley, 'but they won't get away with it.' He gave Irene a challenging glare. 'I don't think this lass has the guts to pull that trigger. The weapon is only for show. In any case, she could only kill one of us. Where would that get her?'

Irene was calm. 'Why don't we find out?'

Aiming the barrel at Wakeley, she pulled the trigger and there was a loud report. The bullet hit him between the eyes and burrowed into his brain, knocking his head backwards. The prisoner suddenly came to life. Before he could recover from the shock of his friend's death, Hungerford was under attack. He not only had to grapple with Oxley, there was the woman to contend with as well. Irene did not hold back. Knocking off the policeman's top hat, she used the butt of the weapon to club him time and again. Hungerford was strong and fought bravely but he was no match for two of them. His head had been split open and blood gushed down over his face and uniform. Oxley was trying to strangle him while his accomplice was delivering more and more blows to his head. It was only a matter of time before Hungerford began to lose consciousness.

The moment the policeman slumped to the floor, Oxley searched Hungerford's pocket for the key to the handcuffs. He found it, released himself, then stole a quick kiss from his deliverer.

'Well done, Irene!' he said, panting.

'What will we do with these two?' she asked.

'I'll show you.'

Opening the door, he grabbed Wakeley under both arms and dragged him across to it. The train then plunged into a tunnel, its rhythmical clamour taking on a more thunderous note and its smoke thickening in the confined area. With one heave, Oxley hurled the dead man out of the compartment. Since Hungerford was bigger and weightier, it took

18

the two of them to shove him out into the tunnel. Oxley closed the door and gave a laugh of triumph.

'We did it!' he shouted, spreading his arms. 'Come here.'

'Not until you've taken that coat off,' she said, looking at it with distaste. 'It's covered in his blood. You can't be seen wearing that.' She opened the valise. 'It's just as well that I thought to bring you another one, isn't it? I had a feeling that you might need to change.'

When Caleb Andrews brought the train to a halt under the vast iron and glass roof over New Street station in Birmingham, his only interest was in lighting his pipe. He puffed away contentedly, blithely unaware that two of his passengers had been murdered during the journey from Wolverhampton and that the killers had just melted unseen into the crowd.

CHAPTER TWO

Nothing upset Edward Tallis more than the murder of a policeman. As a superintendent at the Detective Department in Scotland Yard, he had devoted himself to law enforcement and felt personal grief whenever one of

19

his officers was killed in the line of duty. Even though the latest victims had not been members of the Metropolitan Police Force, Tallis was consumed by a mingled sadness and fury. He waved the telegraph in the air.

'I want this villain caught and caught quickly,' he announced. 'He has the blood of two policemen on his hands.'

'We need more details,' said Victor Leeming.

'It's up to you to find them, Sergeant.'

'What exactly does the telegraph say?'

'It says enough to get you off your backside and on the next train to Wolverhampton. Apart from anything else,' said Tallis, 'your help has been specifically requested by the London and North Western Railway. This has just arrived by messenger.' He picked up a letter with his other hand. 'They are mindful of the fact that we served them well in the past.'

'That was Inspector Colbeck's doing,' argued Leeming.

Tallis bristled. 'It was a joint effort,' he insisted.

'The superintendent is correct, Victor,' said Colbeck, stepping in to rescue the sergeant from the ire of his superior. 'Whatever we've achieved must be ascribed to the efficiency of this whole department. Cooperation is everything. No individual deserves to be singled out.'

Tallis was only partially mollified. It was a source of great irritation to him that he did not get the credit to which he felt he was entitled. Newspaper reports of their triumphs invariably picked out Inspector Robert Colbeck as their unrivalled hero. It was the Railway Detective who claimed all the attention. Tallis could only smoulder impotently in his shadow.

The three men were in the superintendent's office, blissfully free from cigar smoke for once. Seated behind his desk, Tallis, a former soldier, was seething with outrage at the latest news. He wanted instant retribution. The detectives sat side by side in front of him. Leeming, always uneasy in the presence of the superintendent, wanted to leave at once. Colbeck pressed for more information.

'Did the telegraph give the name of the escaped prisoner?' he asked, politely.

'No,' snapped Tallis.

'What about the letter from the LNWR?'

'I think there was a mention in that – though, shamefully, the two murder victims were not named. The villain takes precedence over them, it seems.' He put down the telegraph and looked at the letter. 'Yes, here we are. The killer's name is Oxley.'

Colbeck was stunned. 'Would that be Jeremy Oxley, by any chance?'

'No Christian name is given, Inspector.'

'But it *could* be him.'

'Presumably.'

'Do you know the man?' asked Leeming.

'If it's Jeremy Oxley, I know him extremely well,' said Colbeck, ruefully. 'And this will not be the first time that he's committed a murder.' He rose to his feet. 'We must leave immediately, Victor. I have a copy of *Bradshaw* in my office. That will tell us which train we can catch.' As Leeming got up from his chair, Colbeck turned to Tallis. 'Is there anything else we need to know, Superintendent?'

'Only that I'll be watching you every inch of the way,' said Tallis. 'And so will the general public. They must not be allowed to think that anyone can kill a representative of law and order with impunity. I want to see Oxley dangling from the gallows.'

'So do I,' said Colbeck, teeth gritted. 'So do I.'

Madeleine Andrews was working at her easel when she heard the familiar footsteps outside on the pavement. She was surprised that her father had returned so early and her first thought was that he might have been injured at work. Putting her brush aside, she rushed to open the door. When she saw that Andrews was apparently unharmed, she heaved a sigh of relief.

'What are you doing home at this hour,

Father?' she asked.

'If you let me in, I'll tell you.'

Madeleine stood aside so that Andrews could step into the house. As she closed the door behind him, another fear surfaced.

'You haven't been *dismissed,* have you?'

He cackled. 'They'd never dare to sack me, Maddy.'

'Then why are you here?'

'It's because I was the driver of the death train.'

She gaped. 'What do you mean?'

'Sit down and you'll hear the full story.'

Madeleine lowered herself into a chair but she had to wait while her father filled and lit his pipe. He puffed on it until the tobacco glowed and gave off a pleasing aroma.

'What's this about a death train?' she asked.

'Two policemen were murdered on it,' he explained, taking a seat. 'Not that I knew anything about it at the time. We picked them and their prisoner up at Wolverhampton station. Somewhere between there and Birmingham a shot was fired. Dirk Sowerby and I didn't hear a thing above the roar of the engine, of course, but passengers in the next carriage did. They told the guard and he found blood all over the seat. There was a blood-covered coat in there as well.'

'What about the policemen?'

'They'd been thrown out of the carriage, Maddy.'

She recoiled at the thought. 'Oh – how dreadful!'

'It really upset Dirk.'

'It upset both of you, I daresay.'

'I've got a stronger stomach than my fire-man,' boasted Andrews. 'And it's not the first time a crime has been committed on one of my trains. That's how we came to meet Inspector Colbeck in the first place, so you might say that I was seasoned.'

'Your train was robbed and you were badly injured,' recalled Madeleine, 'but – thank God – nobody was actually killed on that occasion. Let's go back to Wolverhampton. You say that you picked up two policemen and a prisoner.'

'That's right. He was handcuffed to one of the peelers. I saw them on the platform and pointed them out to Dirk.'

'Was the prisoner a big strong man?'

'Not really.'

'Then how could he get the better of two policemen?'

'That's what we'll have to decide.'

'*We?*' she repeated.

'Inspector Colbeck and me,' he said, airily. 'I'm a witness, so I'll have to be involved. In fact, the investigation won't get anywhere without me. What do you think of that, Maddy? Your father is going to be a detective in his own right. I'll wager that the inspector will be tickled pink to work alongside me.'

Victor Leeming was so enthralled at the prospect of hearing the full story that he forgot all about his dislike of rail transport. He was a stocky man with the kind of unsightly features designed to unsettle rather than reassure anyone meeting him for the first time. Colbeck knew his true worth and – even though they differed markedly in appearance, manner and intelligence – they were a formidable team. The two of them had boarded a train at Euston and shared an empty carriage as it steamed off. Colbeck, an elegant dandy, was known for his aplomb yet he was now very animated.

'It *has* to be Jeremy Oxley,' he said, slapping his knee. 'It's too great a coincidence.'

'Who is this man?' asked Leeming.

'He's the reason I joined the police force.'

'Yet you always say that you gave up your other work as a barrister because you only came along *after* a crime was committed. What you wanted to do was to prevent it happening in the first place.'

'That's true, Victor. When I was called to the bar, I had grandiose notions of making wonderful speeches about the need for justice as the bedrock of our society. I was soon robbed of that delusion. Being a barrister was not as lofty a profession as I'd imagined. To be frank, there were times when I felt as if I was taking part in a comic opera.'

'How did you come across Oxley?'

'He broke into a jewellery shop and collected quite a haul,' said Colbeck. 'When the owner of the premises chased him, Oxley shot the man dead in cold blood.'

'Were there any witnesses?'

'There were several.'

'That was helpful.'

'Alas, it was not. They lost their nerve when they received death threats from Oxley's accomplice. Only one of them had the courage to identify him as the man who'd fired the fatal shot.'

'Was he convicted on the strength of the evidence?'

'Unfortunately, no – the case never came to court.'

'Why not?'

'He escaped from custody.'

Leeming sighed. 'He's an old hand at doing that, then.'

'There was worse to come, Victor,' said Colbeck, jaw tightening. 'He hunted down the witness who was prepared to identify him and showed no mercy.'

'He *killed* the man?'

'The victim was a woman – Helen Millington.'

Colbeck spoke her name with a sorrow tinged with something more than mere affection. For a moment, his attention drifted and a distant look came into his eye. Old and very painful memories flitted across his mind. Leeming waited patiently until his friend was ready to continue.

'I'm sorry,' said Colbeck, making an effort to concentrate. 'It's just that it made a deep impression on me at the time. I was only a junior counsel in the case but it fell to me to persuade Miss Millington to come forward. In doing so,' he added, biting his lip, 'I inadvertently caused her death.'

'You weren't to know that Oxley would murder her, sir.'

'Death threats had been sent.'

'Yes, but that sort of thing happens all the time. Criminals will often try to scare a witness or a jury by issuing dire warnings. It doesn't mean that they'll actually carry out their threats.'

'That's what I keep telling myself but the guilt remains. I felt so *helpless*, Victor. She was a beautiful young woman in the prime of life. She didn't deserve such a fate. I was desperate to avenge her death in some way, but what could I do as a barrister except make eloquent speeches in court?' He took a deep breath and composed himself before continuing. 'It was then I decided to join the fight against crime instead of simply dealing with its consequences.'

'That was very brave of you, sir.'

'The real bravery was shown by Helen Millington.'

'What I meant was that you must have given up a good income to work for a lot less money.'

'There are other kinds of rewards, Victor.'

'Yes,' said Leeming with a grin, 'there's nothing to touch the satisfaction of arresting a real villain and watching him get his punishment in court. You can't *buy* something like that.'

'It's just as well. I don't think we could afford it on police pay.'

They shared a laugh. Colbeck glanced through the window and realised that they were just passing Leighton Buzzard station. They were not far from the spot where Caleb Andrews had been tricked into stopping his train so that it could be boarded and robbed of the gold coin it was carrying. As a result of the robbery, during which Andrews had been wounded, Colbeck had first met Madeleine, the driver's anguished daughter. What had started as a chance meeting had slowly matured into a friendship that had grown in intensity until it became a love match. He and Madeleine were now engaged to be married. Colbeck at last felt that his private world was complete. Thinking fondly of their future together, he let his thoughts dwell on her for a few luxurious minutes. As he pictured her face, however, and longed to see it again in the flesh, it was suddenly replaced in his mind's eye by that of the equally lovely

Helen Millington. Taken aback, Colbeck gave an involuntary start.

Leeming was worried. 'Is something wrong, Inspector?'

'No, no. I'm fine.'

'You seemed to be miles away.'

'Then I apologise. It was rude of me to ignore you.'

'Tell me more about this Jeremy Oxley.'

'His friends call him "Jerry" and he has a long criminal record. He's a thief, confidence trickster and ruthless killer. Most of his victims have fallen for his charm. Oxley is very plausible.'

'Let's see how plausible he is at the end of a rope.'

'We have to find him first, and that,' conceded Colbeck, 'will not be easy. He's as slippery as an eel.'

'So it seems. How would you describe him?'

'He's rather different from the villains we normally pursue. In fact, you wouldn't take him for a criminal at all. Oxley, by all accounts, is good-looking, personable and educated. He has the talent to succeed in most professions. The tragedy is that he chose to make his living on the wrong side of the law.'

Leeming regarded him shrewdly. 'Catching him means a lot to you, doesn't it, sir?'

'Yes, it does,' admitted Colbeck. 'I've been after him for years and this is the first time he's crossed my path again. I'm going to make sure that it's the last time as well. It's a debt I have to pay to Helen Millington. This is not just another investigation to me, Victor,' he stressed. 'It's a mission. I won't rest until we have this devil in custody.'

It was several hours later but Irene's hands were still shaking slightly. Oxley enfolded them in his own palms and held them tight.

'You're still trembling,' he observed.

'I can't help it, Jerry. When I shot that policeman, I felt as cool as a cucumber. It was only afterwards that I realised what I'd done.'

'Yes – you rescued me from disaster.'

'I killed a man,' she said with a shudder. 'I never thought I'd be able to do that. I hoped that they'd release you when I pulled out the gun. It never crossed my mind that I'd have to pull the trigger.'

'But you *did*, Irene,' he said, kissing her on the forehead. 'I knew that you wouldn't let me down.'

She gave a shrug. 'I love you. That's why I did it.'

'And because you did it – I love *you*.'

He squeezed her hands then sat back in his chair. They were in a public house in Stafford, sitting in a quiet corner where they could talk freely. Oxley had already changed his appearance so that any description of him would be misleading. He'd shaved off his neat moustache, combed his hair in a different way and put on a pair of spectacles with clear glass in them. He looked quite different. In the interests of evading suspicion, Irene had also made adjustments to her hair and to her clothing. Witnesses who saw her diving onto the train in Wolverhampton would not recognise her now. After calmly leaving the train at Birmingham, they had bought tickets to Stafford and travelled there in separate carriages. Nobody on the same journey would have connected them.

While Oxley was in a state of euphoria after his escape, she remained anxious and preoccupied. She took out a handkerchief and blew her nose. Looking up at him, her eyes were moist.

'Was it like this for you, Jerry?' she asked, nervously.

'What are you talking about?'

'The first time you killed someone. Did you have this terrible feeling in the pit of your stomach? Did your hands shake? Were you haunted by remorse?'

'Not in the slightest,' he said, coldly.

'You must have had some regrets.'

'I put them out of my mind.'

'I can't do that somehow. I keep seeing his face at the moment I actually shot him.' She shook her head. 'I just can't believe I did that.'

'Would you rather have seen me put on remand?'

'No, no – I'd have hated that.'

'Then you did the right thing.'

'Did you feel that *you* did the right thing when you killed a man for the first time?'

'Of course – he was foolish enough to chase me when I robbed his jewellery shop. It was the right thing to kill him and the right thing to kill her as well.'

She was shocked. 'You killed a *woman?*'

'She was going to bear witness against me.'

'When was this – and how did you do it?'

'That doesn't matter,' he said, dismissively. 'It was a long time ago and I've put it all behind me. That's what you must do. All I can tell you is that I felt proud.'

'Proud?' she echoed. 'How can you be proud of taking a life?'

'It showed I had the courage to do so. Most people don't have that courage. They never know that sense of power you get. That's what I had, Irene, and – when you get over the initial shock – you'll enjoy remembering that same thrill as well.'

She was unconvinced. 'I doubt that, Jerry.'

'There's nothing quite like it.'

They had been together almost a year now and it had been a very fruitful partnership. Her air of innocence and wholesomeness belied the fact that she was an accomplished thief and had long since abandoned any claim to respectability. Oxley had used her time and again to distract people while he stole things from their premises. As the more experienced criminal, he was able to teach her the tricks of the trade. Drawn ever closer to him, Irene became so besotted that she did not realise that Oxley was manipulating her emotions. She was utterly devoted to him. When his luck finally ran out and he was captured, all that she could think about was setting him free. Her audacious plan had worked. It had involved killing one man and helping to hurl a second one to his death, but her lover was back with her again. Irene just wished that she could relish his company instead of being assailed by regrets over what she'd done.

Taking her hands again, he looked deep into her eyes.

'Are you happy, Irene?'

'Of course I'm happy,' she said, forcing a smile.

'You don't have to do this, you know. You're under no compulsion. If you'd rather go your own way, we can part here and now. You're not at my beck and call.'

'But I *want* to be, Jerry.'

'I sense that you're getting cold feet.'

'That's not true,' she asserted, sitting up straight. 'I was a little troubled about it, that's all. It's past now. I feel much better, honestly. The only thing I want is to be with you.'

'Then we have something in common,' he said, leaning forward to whisper in her ear, 'because the only thing I want is to be with you. Let's find somewhere to spend the night, then I can tell you why.'

'I thought we were going to Manchester.'

'That can wait until tomorrow. Given what we did today, I think we're entitled to celebrate.'

'Yes, we are!'

'Are you ready to be my wife for another night?'

Irene laughed. 'I'm ready tonight and *every* night.'

They got up from their table and headed for the door. As they came out of the pub, they were elated. With Irene on his arm, Oxley strode purposefully along, distributing smiles to everyone he passed and making the most of his freedom. He then pulled Irene gently into an alleyway so that he could confide something to her.

'Remember this, my love,' he told her. 'You didn't shoot a human being on that train this morning.'

'But I did, Jerry,' she said, earnestly. 'You saw me.'

'All you killed was a policeman.'

'So?'

Oxley beamed. 'They don't count.'

CHAPTER THREE

As soon as they arrived in the town, they hired a cab to take them to Garrick Street, home of the Wolverhampton Borough Police Force. Roland Riggs, the duty sergeant, was a big, beetle-browed man with an instinctive dislike of anyone who tried to take over an investigation he felt should be carried out by his own men. Colbeck and Leeming were given a frosty welcome. Accustomed to such treatment, they asserted their authority and drew all the relevant information out of Riggs. They learnt the names of the two murdered policemen and heard how the both of them had been hit by a train coming in the opposite direction. What Riggs could not explain was how two of his best officers had been unable to stop the prisoner from escaping.

'Jeremy Oxley didn't look like a dangerous man,' he argued.

'I *knew* it was him,' said Colbeck

'The inspector has had a brush with Oxley before,' explained Leeming. 'That's why he was so eager to take on the case.'

'By rights, it falls within our jurisdiction,' insisted Riggs. 'Bob Hungerford and Arthur

Wakeley were good friends of mine. It's the reason I volunteered to tell their wives what had happened. You can imagine how I felt doing that.'

'You have my sympathy, Sergeant,' said Colbeck 'It must have been a harrowing assignment. The only consolation is that they heard the appalling news from an experienced officer who knew how to soften their grief. They're not the kind of tidings you want a young and unschooled policeman blurting out on the doorstep.'

Riggs was solemn. 'I'd agree with you there.'

'Where was the prisoner being taken?' wondered Leeming.

'It was only as far as Birmingham. We had information that a man fitting his description had robbed a pawnshop there at gunpoint. The way that Oxley resisted arrest was a confession in itself. Our colleagues in Birmingham were delighted to hear that we had him in custody.'

'They must have been surprised to hear of his escape.'

Riggs rubbed his chin. 'I'd still like to know how the bugger managed that.'

'I think there's only one logical explanation,' said Colbeck. 'He must have had an accomplice. I feel sure that you'd never have let him leave here until he'd been thoroughly searched. He would not have been carrying a concealed weapon.'

'We know our job, Inspector.'

'Then another person was involved.'

'That's an obvious assumption,' said Riggs, gruffly, 'yet the only passenger who got into the same compartment was a young woman. A number of witnesses recalled her, jumping on the train at the very last moment.'

'There's your accomplice,' concluded Colbeck.

Riggs was dubious. 'Could someone like that shoot one policeman and help to overpower another? I think not, Inspector.'

'Then you don't know Jerry Oxley. He has a strange power over women and can get them to do almost anything for him. Believe me, I've had dealings with this fellow. His accomplice then was the woman with whom he'd been living. The likelihood is that the one in question this time is his latest mistress.'

'So he's *corrupted* her,' said Leeming with disapproval.

'Oh, I suspect that she was not entirely without corruption beforehand, Victor. How else could she meet him in the first place without frequenting the sorts of places he tends to visit? All that he did was to draw her deeper into the criminal fraternity.'

'Where could she have got hold of a gun?'

'She and Oxley would travel with a weapon all the time.'

'He was carrying a pistol when we arrested him,' noted Riggs.

'Then his accomplice could have bought a second one. It's not difficult if you have enough money, and they'd just committed a robbery in Birmingham, remember. No,' Colbeck went on, 'I don't think we should waste time speculating on how she acquired the weapon. The first thing we must do is to unmask the second accomplice.'

Riggs blinked. 'There were *two* of them?'

'Yes, Sergeant, and I'm afraid to tell you that one of them wears a police uniform. Oxley's mistress had help from one of your men.'

'That's a disgraceful allegation!' shouted Riggs, banging his desk. 'I can vouch for every one of my constables. None of them would dream of being party to a plot to murder two of their fellow officers.'

'I'm sure that's true,' said Colbeck, 'but, then, the man I'm after would have had no idea that such dread consequences would ensue. It probably never occurred to him that he was aiding and abetting the escape of a desperate criminal.'

Riggs folded his arms. 'Explain yourself, Inspector.'

'Very few people must have known when Oxley was being transferred from here to Birmingham. Is that agreed?'

'Yes – only a handful of us had the details.'

'I need the name of every man who knew the exact train on which the prisoner would be taken this morning. You, presumably, are one of them.'

'Are you accusing *me?*' howled Riggs, reddening.

'Of course not,' said Colbeck with a soothing smile. 'You are evidently far too sensible to let such vital information slip. It must have been someone else. How many people knew?'

'And where can we get in touch with them?' added Leeming.

'Let me see now,' said Riggs, thinking hard and using his fingers to count. 'Including me, there'd only be four of us – but I have complete faith in the other three. They're all decent, reliable, upright men who'd never dare to be involved in anything like this.'

'Would you care to put money on that?' said Leeming.

'I'm not a gambling man, Sergeant.'

'It's just as well because you'd certainly lose.'

Riggs fell back on pomposity. 'My men are above suspicion.'

Colbeck was impassive. 'Give us their names.'

Though she was pleased to see her father, Madeleine did find him a distraction while she was trying to paint. He kept coming up behind her to look at her latest railway scene and to offer unwanted advice. It was Colbeck who'd discovered her talent as an artist and encouraged her to develop it to the point where she was able to sell her work. There were other female artists in London but none specialised in pictures of locomotives in the way that Madeleine did. Landscapes and seascapes had no appeal for her and she lacked the eye for figurative painting, but there were few people who could bring a train so vividly to life on a canvas in the way that she did. It was a gift.

'I'm surprised that he hasn't been in touch with me,' said Andrews, looking over her shoulder. He nudged her elbow. 'You've got the wrong colour on that carriage, Maddy.'

'I haven't finished painting it yet.'

'I thought the inspector would be banging on my door by now.'

'Why on earth should he do that, Father?' she asked. 'In the first place, Robert may not even be responsible for the investigation. And even if he is, how could he possibly know that you drove the train on which murder was committed?'

He gave a grudging nod. 'There is that, I suppose.'

'You'll just have to wait.'

'Well, it won't be for long,' he said, 'because I'm certain that he'll be in charge of the case. The LNWR would be mad not to ask for him. It's only a matter of time before he discovers that I was on the footplate this morning. That will bring him running.'

'But you didn't see anything of interest.'

'Yes, I did. I saw those two policemen with their prisoner.'

'Can you describe him?'

'Well, he wasn't young but, then again, you couldn't call him an old man. As for the villain's face, I must have been thirty-odd yards away, Maddy, so I can't really help you.'

'Then you won't be able to help Robert either.'

Andrews was deflated, fearing that his offer of assistance might be turned down by Colbeck. Slumping into his chair, he racked his brains for any tiny details that he might be able to pass on in the hope of ingratiating himself with the Railway Detective. When none came to mind, he was tempted to invent some. Madeleine, meanwhile, had resumed work at her easel. He looked across at her.

'Have you set a date yet, Maddy?'

'You know that we haven't,' she replied.

'Then it's high time that you did.'

'There's no real urgency.'

'There may not be for you,' he complained, 'but what about me? How can I retire when I still have you to support? I told Dirk Sowerby about it this morning. He

41

refused to believe that I'd finally turn my back on the railway but I can't wait to do it.'

'You could retire tomorrow, if you wished.'

'Not while I've got a daughter to feed and clothe.'

'I don't need you to support me anymore, Father,' she said. 'Now that I can sell my work, I have a fair amount of money coming in. You can't use me as an excuse.'

It was true. Madeleine's income – albeit irregular – had enabled them to buy all kinds of additional items for their little house in Camden. It had also transformed her wardrobe. When she and Colbeck went out together, she always dressed well and did not look out of place on his arm. It would be a wrench to leave the house in which she was born and brought up, but she was confident that her father could cope now that he'd finally got over the death of his wife. How he would fill his day during his retirement was another matter. Madeleine did not want him spending too much time at the marital home. She and Colbeck would value their privacy.

'There's lots of things I can do when I leave the LNWR,' he said, giving his imagination free rein. 'I could take an interest in gardening, learn to paint just like you, travel the country by train, get married again, have a stall in the market, write my life story, go to church more often or decorate the house. My real ambition, of course, is to work side by side with my son-in-law.'

'You're too old to join the police force, Father,' she pointed out.

'We'd have an unofficial arrangement. Whenever he had a tricky case, he'd tell me the full details and I'd advise him what to do. I think I'd make a wonderful detective, Maddy. Why don't you mention that to the inspector? He might be grateful for my help.'

Madeleine suppressed a grin. 'Then again, he might not.'

'But my instincts are sharp.'

'Robert is well aware of your instincts, Father,' she said, turning to offer a gentle smile. 'If he felt he could make use of them, I'm sure that he would. You'll just have to wait. In the meantime, I think that you should just let him get on with his job.'

Two of the policemen who'd been aware of the exact train on which the prisoner would be travelling were on duty together. Colbeck and Leeming met them on their beat and interviewed them. Like Riggs, they were not receptive to the idea of detectives from London taking over the search for the killers of their former colleagues. When they realised why they were being questioned, they became indignant at the suggestion that they might unwittingly have given away the information that told Oxley's accomplice when and where to strike. Their language became ripe. Roused by their aggressive attitude, Leeming had to control an urge to hit one of the men. Colbeck calmed all three of them down before apologising to the policemen. It was clear to him, he told them, that they were in no way implicated. After ridding themselves of some more bad language, they stalked off to continue their beat.

'That leaves only one man,' noted Leeming.

'Yes,' said Colbeck, 'Constable Toby Marner.'

'I hope he's a little more helpful than those two.'

'Nobody likes to be accused of a crime, Victor, even if it's an unintentional one. Their intemperate reaction was forgivable.'

'I'd have forgiven them with a punch on the nose.'

'Save your strength for the real villain – Jerry Oxley. The one thing we can guarantee is that he'll put up a fight.'

They went to the address they'd been given and knocked on the door of a shabby house in one of the rougher districts of the town. The woman who answered the door was Toby Marner's landlady. She told them that they might find him at the Waterloo, a nearby public house. Colbeck asked her some questions about her lodger and was told that he'd been a good tenant.

When they located the seedy pub, they had no difficulty in picking out the man they were after. Sitting alone in a corner, the tall, rangy Marner was wearing his uniform and hat but he was not the image of sobriety expected of a law enforcement officer. His eyes were glazed, his cheeks red and he was quaffing a pint of beer as if his life depended on it. The detectives joined him and introduced themselves. It took Marner a few moments to understand what they were saying.

'What do you want with me?' he asked, slurring his words.

'We need your assistance,' said Colbeck. 'According to Sergeant Riggs, you were told on which train the prisoner would be travelling this morning. Is that true?'

Marner was defensive. 'I wasn't the only one.'

'We've spoken to the others. We're satisfied that none of them passed on the information to anyone else.'

'Neither did I.'

'Are you sure?' pressed Leeming.

'I'm very sure.'

'Well, *somebody* let the cat out of the bag.'

Marner tensed. 'Are you calling me a liar?'

'We just want to solve this mystery,' said Colbeck, adopting a quieter tone. 'As you're well aware, two of your fellow policemen were murdered this morning on a train. You must have known them well.'

'I did, Inspector.' There was a sob in his voice. 'Bob Hungerford was my brother-in-law. We joined the police force together.'

'Then you have a special reason to want his killers arrested.'

'Yes, I do.'

'Is there any chance that you might accidentally have divulged the details of Oxley's transfer to anyone?'

'None at all,' said Marner, emphatically.

'Not even to your landlady, for instance?'

'I told nobody.'

'What about other policemen?'

Marner became truculent. 'I've given you my answer, so you can leave me alone. Go back to London and let us deal with this. Arthur Wakeley and Bob Hungerford were Wolverhampton lads through and through. This is our case.'

He was slurring his words even more now and almost keeled over at one point. When Marner reached for his tankard, Colbeck moved it out of the way. The policeman was outraged.

'Give me my beer.'

'I think you've had enough already,' said Colbeck. 'You can't hold your beer because you're not a drinking man.'

'Who can afford to be on police pay?' moaned Leeming.

'Your landlady said that you very rarely go

46

to a pub. That's why she was so surprised when she saw you heading in this direction. Do you know what that tells me, Constable Marner? It tells me that you're a man with a need to drown his sorrows.'

'You're right,' said Marner. 'I'm mourning the death of two good friends. Is there anything wrong in that?'

'No,' replied Colbeck, fixing him with a piercing stare. 'I'd expect it – especially if you are somehow connected with those deaths. And I'm inclined to think that you are.'

'That's a filthy lie!'

'You're the one who's lying and you know it.'

'I want my beer back.'

'It's no good trying to block out the truth,' said Colbeck, sternly. 'It will always come out in the end. Do you know what I believe we should do? Instead of talking to you here, I think we should have this conversation at Constable Hungerford's house. Your sister will be present then.' He leant in close. 'You'd never dare to tell lies in front of her, would you?' Marner swallowed hard. 'You wouldn't be cruel enough to add to her grief by trying to deceive us.' He stood up and gestured towards the door. 'Shall we go?'

Marner remained in his seat, staring anxiously ahead of him as he thought about what might lay ahead. He chewed his lip and wrung his hands. They could see the terror in his eyes. When Leeming took him by the elbow, Marner let out a yelp and burst into tears.

'Don't take me to my sister,' he begged. 'Please don't make me go there. After what I did, I just can't face Mary. I'd die of shame.'

'And what exactly did you do?' asked Leeming.

Colbeck resumed his seat. 'Let's give him time to clear his mind, Victor,' he advised, 'then he'll tell us the whole story. That's right, isn't it, Constable Marner?'

'Yes, Inspector,' murmured the other.

'I fancy that you're in possession of information that will help in the search for those who murdered your colleagues. To hold it back would be a crime in itself.'

'I know.'

'Then you should get it off your chest.'

Marner needed a couple of minutes to compose his thoughts and to confront the horror of what had occurred. Colbeck let him have another sip of beer. Clearing his throat, Marner was about to confess when he started to weep again. Colbeck put a consoling hand on his shoulder and prompted him.

'You didn't think you were doing anything wrong, did you?'

'No, Inspector,' replied Marner.

'Was any money involved?'

'He offered me five pounds.'

'Are you talking about Oxley?'

'Yes,' said Marner. 'At first I refused, but five pounds is a lot of money to a man like me.'

'And me,' Leeming interjected. 'What did you do to earn it?'

'It seemed like a simple favour. All that I had to do was to tell the prisoner's wife what train he'd be on and she'd give me five pounds. Oxley said she'd be there to wave him off.'

'Instead of which,' said Colbeck, 'she caught the same train and helped him to escape.'

'I wasn't to know that,' bleated Marner. 'His wife was so pleased when I spoke to her. I felt sorry for her. I could see that she was carrying her husband's child.'

'She played on your emotions, Constable. To begin with, I doubt very much if she was his wife. I'm certain they cohabit but theirs is not a union blessed in the sight of God. As for being pregnant, that was another lie. What woman in that condition can run to catch a train then help to commit a murder?'

'You were tricked,' said Leeming with disgust. 'You betrayed your friends. Because you took those five pounds, two policemen are going to their grave.'

Marner was in despair. 'You think I don't realise that, Sergeant? Ever since I heard the news, I've been in torment. What I did was terrible. If I had a gun, I swear to God that I'd have used it on myself by now.' He put his head in his hands. 'I feel like a murderer.

'Stop thinking about yourself,' said Colbeck, 'and try to help us instead. You met this so-called wife and had the opportunity to take her measure. We need you to remember every single thing about her that you can. Each detail is important.' Marner looked up at him through bleary eyes. 'What was your first impression of her?'

'She was a … very appealing young lady.'

'At what age would you put her?'

'I think she was not much more than twenty,' said Marner.

'What about her build, height and colouring?'

'She was slim, of medium height and dark-haired.'

'Can you recall any significant feature about her?'

'Yes,' replied Marner, thinking about his encounter. 'I'll wager that she came from Manchester. She tried to hide her accent but I could hear it nevertheless. I lived in the city for a couple of years and you get to know the sound of a Manchester voice. That's where Mrs Oxley – or whatever her real name is – hailed from. I'd stake every penny I have on it.'

CHAPTER FOUR

To avoid being seen together, they travelled
north to Manchester next morning in
separate railway carriages. It gave each of
them time to reflect on what had happened.
For his part, Oxley was still excited. Twenty-
four hours earlier, he'd been in custody and
destined for certain imprisonment or – if his
criminal record was unveiled – even a death
sentence. Only a daring plan had rescued
him. The fact that two policemen had died in
the process did not disturb him in the
slightest. They were expendable in his view.
What stuck in his mind was the extraordinary cunning and audacity shown by Irene. It
had drawn him closer than ever to her. None
of his other mistresses – and there had been
several over the years – would have had the
nerve to devise and carry through such a
plan. Irene Adnam was indeed exceptional.
Oxley resolved that she would continue to
pose as his wife for a long while yet.

Ensconced in the corner of another carriage, Irene ignored the lascivious glances
she was attracting from the elderly man
opposite her and tried to confront the
enormity of what she had done. She had

51

killed one man and helped to throw another to a hideous death in the tunnel. Had he known the truth about her, the passenger would not be running such covetous eyes over her. Irene was still shaken. A night in Oxley's arms had stilled her fears but they'd returned now that she was alone. Thieving was a way of life for her. It left her conscience untroubled. Murder, however, was a very different matter. Impelled to shoot one man out of love for another, she was unable to dismiss it from her mind. What if her victim had been married and had children? What kind of misery had she inflicted on them? The same could be asked of the policeman she'd struck with her pistol until he lost consciousness. His family would be suffering dreadfully. Friends of both men would be bereft. Such thoughts made her feel almost dizzy with remorse.

Irene tried to tell herself that it had all been a means to an end. She was infatuated with Oxley. The idea of his being locked away for several years was unbearable. Whatever extreme steps it took, he had to be saved from imprisonment. He was amazed at her bravery and overcome with gratitude. In the course of their frantic lovemaking, he'd even talked of marriage for the first time. If she did become his wife in reality as well as in name, she would have paid a high price for it, but she convinced herself that it would have been worthwhile. Two dead Wolverhampton policemen would fade into the past; Jeremy Oxley was her future.

As the train chugged into Manchester station, she got ready to leave. By the time she alighted onto the platform, Oxley was well ahead of her. He bought a newspaper from the bookstall then went out through the exit. Irene followed him. By prior arrangement, they were well clear of the station before they met up.

'What did you buy?' she asked.

'A copy of *The Times*,' he said, opening the newspaper. 'It's reached Manchester already. I wanted to see what they had to say about us.' He spotted a headline. 'Here we are – POLICEMEN MURDERED DURING ESCAPE BID. We're famous at last, Irene. I shall enjoy reading this.' His laughter died instantly and his smile became a grimace. 'I don't like this,' he admitted

She was worried. 'What is it, Jerry?'

'We have a problem. According to this report, the detective in charge of the case is Inspector Colbeck of Scotland Yard. He and I have crossed swords before, though he wasn't in the police force at the time. We have to be very careful, Irene.'

'Why is that?'

'Colbeck has a score to settle with me. He's very determined. Once he picks up our scent, he'll stay on our tail until he catches

53

up with us. This is bad news, Irene,' he said, folding up the newspaper. 'The last person in the world I want after me is Robert Colbeck.'

After spending the night in Wolverhampton, the two detectives began the day by walking to the railway station. The town was still in a state of shock after the turn of events. People were grim, silent and fearful. They moved about as if in a daze. Posters had already been put up at the station, offering a reward for information leading to the arrest of Jeremy Oxley. A brief description was given of him. Colbeck and Leeming interviewed the clerk in the booking office. He remembered the young woman who'd arrived late for a train the previous morning and said that he'd issued her with a single ticket to Birmingham. Since he saw so many passengers in the course of a day, he could give only the sketchiest details about her. Like all the employees at the station, he was very apprehensive. Murder on the LNWR was a very bad advertisement for the company. It would inevitably deter some passengers from travelling by rail.

'I hope that you catch him soon, Inspector,' said the clerk.

'We'll do our best,' promised Colbeck.

'Until he's under lock and key, nobody will feel safe when they travel on the railway.'

'I *never* feel safe on a train,' said Leeming under his breath.

Hiring a cab, the detectives were driven to the tunnel where the murder victims had been tossed onto the line. They climbed a fence and walked across the track. A railway policeman emerged from the tunnel and ordered them to leave at once. His manner became more respectful when he heard that he was talking to detectives from Scotland Yard. His job was to guard that end of the tunnel to prevent those of ghoulish disposition from seeking out the exact point at which the policemen had been mangled by an oncoming train. The other end of the tunnel was also under supervision.

Lighting a lamp, the man used it to guide his way into the gloom of the tunnel. Colbeck and Leeming walked in single file behind him, their footsteps echoing in the void. When they heard a distant train approaching, they swiftly flattened themselves against the dank wall. The noise got closer and closer, then there was an explosion of sound as the locomotive plunged into the tunnel. The train was only feet away when it shot past, deafening them momentarily and creating a gust of wind that scooped up the dust from the ground. Colbeck and the policeman took it in their stride but Leeming was scared.

'That was too close for comfort,' he complained.

'You'd never make a railwayman, Victor,' said Colbeck.

'It's dangerous being in here.'

'Yes, it is.' Colbeck brushed dust from his sleeves. 'My coat will get filthy if that happens again.'

Their guide led them eventually to the spot where the corpses had been found. He held up the lantern so that they could see that there was still blood on the line. The bodies had been sliced apart by a speeding train. Bob Hungerford, alive when hurled out of the compartment, had died under the wheels of a locomotive. Anxious to get away from the place, Leeming kept glancing up and down the tunnel, wondering from which direction a train would come next. Colbeck, meanwhile, crouched beside the track and ran a hand across it. He did not envy Sergeant Riggs the task of breaking the bad news to the two wives. Reporting a death of any kind to family members was a dismal undertaking and Colbeck had done it many times. Having to pass on details of a horrific murder made it far more disturbing for all concerned. The visit to the tunnel served to reinforce his vow to catch the killers.

'Right,' said Colbeck, standing up. 'There's nothing more we can do here. We have to get to Birmingham.'

'Why?' asked Leeming.

'I want to look at the compartment in which the crime took place.'

'What can that tell us, Inspector?'

'I don't know until we get there.'

They retraced their steps and were grateful that no other trains powered their way through the tunnel. When they got back to their cab, Colbeck asked the driver to take them to the nearest railway station. At Bescot Junction, they caught a local train to Birmingham and got out at New Street. On their last visit to the city, they had arrested a silversmith and his female accomplice, both of whom had later been hanged for their part in a gruesome murder. The place also held happier memories for Colbeck. It was in the wake of the arrest in the Jewellery Quarter that he had proposed to Madeleine and sealed their betrothal by buying her an engagement ring.

There was no occasion to venture into the city this time. What they wanted was the carriage that had been detached from the train driven by Caleb Andrews a day earlier and shunted into a siding. It was guarded by a railway policeman who had less respect for London detectives than the man who'd taken them into the tunnel. Surly and uncooperative, he had to be put firmly in his place by Colbeck. Still glaring at them mutinously, he pointed out the relevant compartment. Colbeck climbed up into it with ease then offered a hand to pull Leeming in after him.

'There we are, Victor,' he said, pointing to a bloodstained coat. 'There's evidence here, after all. This must have been discarded by Oxley before he fled.' He picked the coat up by the collar and looked at the name inside it. 'This was made by a reputable tailor and you can see its quality. Oxley makes a point of dressing well.'

Leeming looked at the garment. 'That coat gives me a good idea of his size. He's about my height but somewhat slimmer.'

'He couldn't be seen wearing this when he left the train. That means his accomplice probably brought another one for him to wear. She's obviously a thoughtful lady.'

'She's thoughtful and she's murderous,' said Leeming as he studied the bloodstains on the seat.

Putting the coat down, Colbeck sat on the other side of the compartment. 'She must have been here when they set off,' he ventured. 'Oxley and the two policemen were opposite. Even if she had no experience of firing a gun, she could hardly have missed from such close range. But I suspect that most of this blood was shed by Constable Hungerford. My guess is that she hit him with the butt of the pistol. He must have been knocked out before they could heave him off the train.'

'We're dealing with a very desperate

woman, sir.'

'Yet one who must have looked unthreatening at the time. She caught the policeman completely off guard. Had their suspicions been aroused by her appearance, they might still be alive now.'

Colbeck went through an elaborate mime, shooting someone opposite then getting up and pretending to take part in a struggle with an invisible assailant. He then opened the door and dragged a body across to it. Satisfied that he had reconstructed the crime with some accuracy, he shut the door again.

'What do we do now, Inspector?' asked Leeming.

'We go our separate ways, Victor.'

'Oh?'

'You can return to London to report to the superintendent. Rehearse what you're going to say beforehand. That way, he won't unsettle you so much.'

Leeming rolled his eyes. 'Mr Tallis was born to unsettle me.'

'Console yourself with the thought that you can see your wife and family again this evening. I know how much you hate to spend a night away from Estelle and the children.'

'I miss them, Inspector. Wait until you get married. You'll begin to understand then.'

Colbeck smiled. 'I already do, I assure you.'

'Where will you be?'

'I'll be searching for Oxley's accomplice.'

'But you have no idea where to start.'

'Yes, I do,' said Colbeck. 'You heard what Constable Marner told us. She's a Manchester girl.'

'It's a big city, sir. You could spend a lifetime hunting for her there. And that's assuming that she's actually in Manchester.'

'It doesn't matter if she is or if she isn't, Victor.'

Leeming was baffled. 'I don't follow.'

'If she's working with Jerry Oxley, the chances are that she's no novice. He'd always choose someone with experience.'

'So?'

'She'll have a criminal record,' said Colbeck. 'The police up there will know of her even if they've never managed to arrest the woman. I want to put a name to her face, then we can start looking for her in earnest. *She's* the person who'll lead us to Oxley,' he added, holding up the coat once more. 'Find her and we'll find the man who used to wear this.'

Jeremy Oxley had learnt to travel light. When he'd committed a crime, he immediately moved away from the area and went to ground for a while before selecting his next target. In the course of his travels, he would either stay in hotels under an assumed name

60

or in the homes of criminal associates. Since he was an expert at his trade, he always had plenty of money to buy whatever he needed and to indulge the latest women in his life. Irene had lasted much longer than any of her predecessors. She had never stayed at hotels of such quality before but quickly adapted to her good fortune. Oxley was impressed by the fact that she was the least acquisitive of his mistresses. While others had demanded jewellery and other gifts, Irene was content simply to be with him and to take part in his exploits. The thrill of acting as his accessory was enough for her.

After almost a year of uninterrupted success, their luck had finally run out in Wolverhampton and Oxley had been arrested. His faith in Irene had been justified. Taking risks and displaying careful forethought, she'd rescued him on a train and earned his profound admiration. What pleased him was that she was no longer agonising over the murder of two policemen. She had not mentioned them all morning.

'Tell me about this Inspector Colbeck,' she said.

'If you read the newspapers, you wouldn't need to ask me that. Colbeck has built up a reputation for solving crimes on the railways. He never fails,' warned Oxley. 'At least, he doesn't seem to have done so thus far. His nickname is the Railway Detective.'

'What sort of man is he?'

'I never actually met him. He used to be a barrister.'

'They make lots of money, don't they?'

'The best ones certainly do.'

'Why did he give up his job to become a policeman?'

Oxley smirked. 'I like to think that I might have something to do with that,' he bragged. 'Colbeck is prepared to accept much lower pay for the sheer pleasure of catching people like me.'

They were in their room at a hotel not far from the station. Now that they were alone, Irene wanted to hear more details. She glanced at the report in *The Times*.

'It says here that the inspector is a master at what he does.'

'The same is true of me, Irene. I've managed to stay several steps ahead of Colbeck for a decade now. Not that I've been involved in a railway crime before, mind you. That singles me out. He'll have been delighted to have an excuse to stalk me.'

'How do we keep out of his way?'

'Leave that to me.'

She put the newspaper aside. 'Tell me about the woman – the one that you killed.'

'You don't want to hear about her,' he said, flicking a hand.

'Yes, I do. What was her name?'

'I'm not even sure that I can remember it.

Let me see. It was Helen something. Middleton? No – that wasn't it, but it's close.' He snapped his fingers. 'I have it – Millington. Her name was Helen Millington. She was looking in the window of the shop when I came running out, so she had a clear view of me. Lots of other people did as well,' he went on, 'but we managed to frighten the majority of them off with a warning of retribution. Miss Millington was stupid enough to ignore the warning.'

'What happened?'

'When I escaped from prison, I paid her a visit.'

'So you didn't have to appear in court.'

'No, Irene – I was free.'

'Then this woman wouldn't have been able to give evidence against you, would she? Why didn't you just ignore her?'

'I wanted to send a message to the other people who'd seen me shoot the jeweller. The letters they'd received from a friend of mine were not made up of empty threats. I honoured my promise to kill anyone who spoke against me. Helen Millington had to die.'

'But her death was unnecessary.'

His eyes blazed. 'Not to me.'

Irene was upset. During his time with her, Oxley had avoided any gratuitous violence. He only struck out when – as in the train – it was vital to do so. His ideal crime was one in which nobody got hurt. He'd threatened people with a gun on occasion but she'd never seen him fire it. The thought that he'd hunted down a woman who was no longer a danger to him was unnerving. It revealed an innate brutality that Irene had never discerned before.

'How did you kill her?' she asked.

'Does it matter?'

'I'd like to know, that's all.'

'I strangled her with my bare hands,' he said, calmly. 'I choked the life out of Helen Millington. It was no more than she deserved. Her family had begged her not to give evidence against me but she was persuaded by Robert Colbeck that it was her duty to do so. If you ask me, he was rather more than just a barrister involved in the case. I fancy that he and Miss Millington became close friends. In killing her, therefore, I gained myself a bitter enemy. Colbeck is the type of man who never forgets.'

Irene had never felt afraid of him before but she did now. His attitude to his victim was callous and uncaring. Being a member of the fairer sex had not saved Helen Millington. When his temper was roused, it seemed, Oxley would murder indiscriminately. There was blood on Irene's hands as well, but she took no pride in the fact. Deep down, she was still mortified by what she'd done, wishing there had been an easier way to liberate Oxley. She had been compelled to kill someone, whereas he had done it for the pleasure of revenge.

'I thought you were going to see your father,' he said. 'That's why we came to Manchester, isn't it?'

'Yes, Jerry – I'll go now.'

'Would you like me to come with you?'

'No,' she replied, feeling that she'd like some time apart from him for a while. 'I can manage on my own.'

For once in his life, Leeming managed to deliver a report to Tallis without repeating himself or stumbling over his words. He was as nervous as ever in front of the superintendent but he'd taken Colbeck's advice and made notes of what he was going to say. Tallis was pleased with the lucidity of his account but disappointed in their apparent lack of progress.

'You seem to have made little headway in the case,' he said.

'We are still gathering evidence, sir.'

'What are your orders?'

'I'm to remain here until Inspector Colbeck returns. He's making enquiries in Manchester today. One thing is clear already,' he pointed out. 'This is going to be a complicated investigation. The case is not going to be solved in five minutes.'

'I realise that, man,' said Tallis. 'There'll be

travelling involved and you and Colbeck will be at full stretch. I've decided that you need some assistance.'

Leeming blenched. 'You're not to take charge of the case yourself, are you, sir?'

'I wish that I could, Sergeant, but I'm fettered to this desk. Someone has to stay in control here. London, as you well know, is the capital city of crime. My job is to police it effectively.'

'You do it so well, Superintendent.'

It was not exactly true but Leeming felt obliged to say it. He was relieved that Tallis would not take an active role in the investigation. Neither he nor Colbeck could work properly with their superior breathing down their necks. They'd had experience of his interference during a case that took them to a village in Yorkshire. Because an old army friend of Tallis had been involved, he had insisted on making a personal intervention. It had been unfruitful. Only when the detectives had got rid of him were they able to move forward. When the villain was finally unmasked, Tallis was – helpfully – a long way away.

Steepling his fingers, the superintendent sat back in his chair.

'I propose to assign Detective Constable Peebles to you.'

'I've never heard of the fellow,' said Leeming.

'That's because he's new to the department.'

'I see, sir.'

'He joined the police force when he left
the army,' explained Tallis. 'The one is an
excellent preparation for the other. Nobody
appreciates that more than I do. Ian Peebles
comes to us highly recommended. It's up to
you and the inspector to make full use of his
proven talents.'

'We'll endeavour to do so, Superintendent.'

'I expect no less.' There was a tap on the
door. 'Ah, that will be Peebles now.' His
voice became a rasp. 'Come in!'

The door opened and the newcomer
stepped into the office. Leeming goggled at
him. Ian Peebles was not at all what he had
expected. The detective was tall, skinny and
straight-backed. Though he was now in his
twenties, he looked as if he was still in his
teens. Peebles was youthful, fresh-faced and
buck-toothed. Leeming simply could not
imagine him in some of the perilous
situations in which they were likely to find
themselves.

For his part, Peebles gazed at the sergeant
with a respect that bordered on veneration.
It was the uncritical look of a son for a
father. His buck-toothed grin broadened.

Tallis waved a hand. 'Allow me to introduce Constable Peebles.'

'I'm pleased to meet you,' said Leeming,

struggling to smile.

'It will be a privilege to work with you, Sergeant,' said Peebles with a light Scots accent. 'You and Inspector Colbeck have been my exemplars for much more than a wee while.'

Leeming's heart sank. At a time when they needed expert help, they were being saddled with an immature and wholly inexperienced detective. Blinded by hero worship, Peebles was far more likely to hinder the investigation than provide any useful assistance. They would have to teach him his trade as they went along and that would be fatal. It was like trying to build a locomotive while it was actually speeding along the track. Because of Peebles' army background, Tallis might favour him, but Leeming could see no advantage coming from his addition to the team. Catching someone as elusive as Jeremy Oxley was a huge challenge for even the best detectives. Leeming now felt that he and Colbeck would be doing it with their hands tied behind their backs. The only beneficiary of the arrival of the new detective was the man they were actually pursuing.

Peebles was a walking guarantee of Oxley's continued freedom.

CHAPTER FIVE

Manchester was a vast, sprawling, densely populated city forever shrouded in an industrial haze. Its factory chimneys belched out smoke and its mills poured effluent into rivers and canals. The stink of manufacture was everywhere. Colbeck had visited the city before and knew that its criminal underworld was every bit as vibrant and dangerous as that in London. One advantage that Manchester had over Wolverhampton was that it could offer a cordial welcome to a senior detective from Scotland Yard.

'Robert!' exclaimed Zachary Boone, pumping his hand. 'How good it is to see you again! What brings you to this den of iniquity?'

'What else but the pleasure of seeing you again?'

Boone laughed. 'You always did have a smooth tongue.'

'It comes in useful when dealing with superior officers who try to blame me for everything.'

'I've got people like that on *my* back as well.'

'Soothe them with words. Talk them into a

better mood.'

'You might be able to do that but I can't and I'm not mad enough to try. I'm a rough-and-ready man. It's the only way to survive in this police force.'

Colbeck was pleased to see Inspector Zachary Boone again. They had first met when Boone had been an enterprising young sergeant in pursuit of a man who'd murdered his wife and children in a drunken rage. The killer had fled to London and – with Colbeck's help – Boone had caught and arrested him. He'd been a detective then but, at his own request, Boone had gone back into uniform and risen to the rank of inspector. He was a stout man in his forties with a florid face half-hidden beneath a greying beard. There was a merry twinkle in his eye that even a close acquaintance with the dregs of Manchester society had failed to remove.

They were in Boone's office, a small, stuffy, cluttered room that made Colbeck grateful for the amount of space he enjoyed at Scotland Yard. While the Railway Detective's office was scrupulously tidy, his friend's was in a state of mild chaos, the desk and shelves piled high with multifarious papers and documents. Boone indicated a seat.

'Take a pew, Robert,' he invited, sitting down, 'and before you ask, yes, I do know where everything is. It may look disorganised in here but I know exactly where to put my hand on what I want.'

'I'd expect no less of you, Zachary,' said Colbeck, settling into a creaky chair. 'But it's not your paperwork I've come to inspect. I need some help from that famous brain of yours.'

Boone guffawed. 'I didn't know I had one.'

'You've got an encyclopaedic memory for criminals on your patch. I noticed it the first time we had a discussion together. You had instant recall of all the people you'd arrested.'

'Not to mention the ones I *failed* to arrest – I remember those as well. They slipped through my fingers. It's very easy to do in a city like Manchester. Villains commit a crime then vanish into the rookeries. It's like trying to catch a single fish in a shoal of thousands. There's simply no way that we can search all the lodging houses here, and the sight of a police uniform in some districts is like a red rag to a bull, especially among the Irish.'

'I thought that several of your constables were Irish.'

'They are, Robert, but they tend to be Protestants and that only inflames the Roman Catholic communities. Religion causes us so many problems here. Talking of which,' he continued with barely concealed derision, 'do you know what the city's Watch

71

Committee decided last year? In its supposed wisdom, it brought in a rule that all constables should attend church or chapel regularly.'

'How can they do that when they work most Sundays?'

'That was my argument. Police are police, not saints-in-waiting. Some of my best men have never seen the inside of a church. It doesn't make them less effective at their job. Anyway,' said Boone, raising an apologetic palm, 'you didn't come here to listen to my complaints. It was the escape of Jeremy Oxley that brought you, wasn't it?'

Colbeck was surprised. 'You know about that?'

'We do get the London papers here. Besides, the story was picked up in the *Manchester Guardian*. I read that less often because it's always attacking us for one thing or another. Read the *Guardian* and you'd think that Manchester was awash with prostitutes, thugs and thieves. It's a city without any law enforcement, apparently.' He became serious. 'I always take a close interest in any case where policemen are killed, Robert. I saw that you'd been put in charge of the investigation. Have you picked up Oxley's scent yet?'

'Actually, it's his accomplice who interests me at the moment.'

Colbeck explained that the woman might

well have links to Manchester and he told his friend about his earlier encounter with Jeremy Oxley and how there was unfinished business between them. After listening to him with care, Boone went through a number of names in his head. He needed clarification.

'You say that this young woman is beautiful.'

'At the very least, she's appealing,' said Colbeck. 'Oxley has high standards where his female accomplices are concerned. And he has sufficient money to be able to maintain those standards.'

'Then I think we're looking at one of three possible suspects,' said Boone, scratching his beard. 'Annie Pardoe is the first who comes to mind. Any man would find her appealing on sight, though less so when she gives him a mouthful of abuse. Annie was brought in here once. She might look like a lady but she had the foul tongue of a fishwife. Then again, it could be Nell Underwood. She comes from a good family but it didn't stop her from getting drawn into the wrong company. Even a spell in prison hasn't had any effect on her. We're still looking for Nell in connection with the theft of some items from a haberdasher's shop. She's very light-fingered.'

'Do either of these women have a local accent?'

'Nell does but Annie Pardoe tries to hide hers. She's fond of putting on airs and graces – until she's behind bars, that is. Then she snarls like a caged tiger.'

'You said that there were *three* possible suspects.'

'Yes, Robert, but the third one has never been in custody so we've never actually seen her. Her name is Irene Adnam. All that we have to go on are the descriptions of her victims. She's not a high-class prostitute like Annie or a common criminal like Nell. This lady has some style about her. She wins people's confidence, robs them blind then vanishes for long periods. Reports of her crimes in the city are six months or more apart. But she's a Manchester girl,' said Boone, 'and I'm told she has more than a trace of a local accent.'

'That sounds promising.'

'I can put you in touch with one of her victims, if you like,' offered Boone, delving into a pile of papers. 'He can give you as exact a description of her as you're likely to get.' Pulling out a sheet of paper, he gave a smile of satisfaction. 'What did I tell you? I found it first time.' He handed it over. 'Make a note of that name and address.'

'Thank you, Zachary.'

'And if you *do* find her, hand her over to us. I'm very anxious to make the acquaintance of Irene Adnam. She's a cut above the women I normally see in here.' His voice darkened. 'She's a menace. I want her off the streets of Manchester, Robert.'

'I can understand that.'

'Do you need details of the whereabouts of Annie Pardoe and Nell Underwood?'

'I don't think it's necessary,' said Colbeck. 'Something tells me that Irene Adnam is the woman I'm after. I can feel it in my bones.'

Boone grinned. 'Is that sciatica or policeman's instinct?'

'A little of both, I fancy,' said Colbeck with a grin.

Irene had changed before she visited her father. Going to Deansgate in the smart clothing she usually wore would make her incongruous. It was the poorest part of the city, an ugly, squalid, malodorous place that was the haunt of criminals and the refuge of beggars. That her father had been reduced to living there was a source of regret and embarrassment to Irene. When she was born, her parents had owned a house in a more salubrious part of Manchester. Those days seemed a lifetime away. She now had to venture into more perilous territory. In sober apparel, and in a hat that covered much of her face, she could easily pass for a servant. That was her disguise.

Though she met with unpleasantness at every turn, Irene had no qualms for her own safety. She had learnt to look after herself and built up a protective shield. She therefore ignored the army of beggars, pushed aside the ragged children who tried to harass her and repelled any lustful men who lurched at her out of the shadows. The streets were narrow, filthy and teeming with low life. The rookeries resounded to the din of violent argument. When she got to the tenement she sought, Irene knocked hard on the door with her knuckles. It was an age before anyone answered and she had to rap on the timber another three times before her father finally appeared. He was short, scrawny and whiskered. Half-asleep and with a surly wariness, he peered at her through one eye.

'What do you want?' he demanded.

'It's me, Father,' she said. 'It's Irene.'

'You don't look like my daughter.'

'I told you that I'd come back when I could.'

As he came fully awake, he stared at her with a mixture of shame and gratitude, hurt that she should see him living in such degradation yet anticipating some financial help from her. Silas Adnam stepped back so that she could go into the ground-floor room that was his home. It was cramped, gloomy and sparsely furnished, with an abiding stench of beer that assaulted Irene's nostrils. Closing the door, her father limped in after her. His clothes were tattered and

76

his wispy hair unkempt. He stood back to appraise her properly.

'Thank God!' he said with a toothless smile. 'It *is* you.'

'I'm sorry that I couldn't come earlier.'

'It's been months and months, Irene.'

'I've been very busy, Father.'

'Are you still with the same family?'

'No,' she replied. 'I work as governess elsewhere now.'

His eyes kindled. 'Is it well paid?'

'I've saved up enough to help you.'

When she handed over the money, he let out a cry of thanks then embraced her warmly. She could smell the beer on his breath.

'Buy some better clothes,' she advised.

He shook his head. 'They won't belong here.'

It was painful to see the depths to which he'd sunk. Silas Adnam had once worked as an assistant manager in a cotton mill. He'd had status, respect and a decent income. But the untimely death of his wife had driven Adnam close to despair. He'd become distracted and unreliable. Sacked from his job and unable to find another of equivalent merit, he'd been forced to sell the house. He'd then drifted from one badly paid job to another until an injury to his foot had left him with a permanent limp. Having turned to drink for consolation, he found a number of new friends ready to help him spend his way through his meagre savings. When they disappeared, the so-called friends did so as well. As a last resort, Adnam drifted into Deansgate and made a few pennies each day as a street musician. All that he now had in life was a rented room and an outside privy that he shared with over two dozen other tenants.

Irene was shocked to see how much he'd deteriorated.

'How have you been keeping?' she asked.

'I'm not well, Irene. My chest is worse than ever.'

'What about your foot?'

'I can't stand on it for long,' he said, collapsing onto a stool by way of demonstration. 'When I play my pipe in the streets, I have to beg a chair from someone.' He looked up pleadingly. 'I live in the hope that you'll take me away from here one day.'

'That's not possible at the moment.'

'Don't you want to be with your old father?'

'Yes, of course,' she lied, 'but I have a position with a family in London. I can't leave that. They're kind to me.'

'Couldn't they find something for me to do?' he asked. 'I'm not proud. It doesn't matter how menial it is.' He sat up and put out his chest. 'I used to have an important job in a mill, you know. People looked up to me. That should count for something, shouldn't it?'

'It should,' she agreed.

'I was born for better things.'

Irene felt desperately sorry for him but her sympathies were tempered by some harsher childhood memories. While her father had worked at the mill, he'd neglected his wife badly and treated her with something akin to contempt. It was only when she died of smallpox that he discovered he'd loved her all along. Without her to support him at home and to look after Irene, he was helpless. His anguish was genuine but, in his daughter's mind, it didn't wash away the years of misery to which he'd subjected his wife. In one sense, she was horrified at the way his life had decayed around him. In another, Irene felt that it was a due reward. She would help him with money from time to time but she would never try to rescue him. Her life was elsewhere now. There was no room in it for an inebriated father.

'How long can you stay?' he wondered.

'Not for long,' she replied. 'I have to catch a train to London.'

He was nostalgic. 'I haven't been on a train for years. I used to travel to work by rail every morning in the old days. Do you remember that, Irene?'

'Yes, Father.'

She also remembered the number of times

she and her mother had sat up late, waiting for him to come home. Disregarding his wife, Adnam at least had enough interest in his daughter to pay for her education. It was the one thing she had to thank him for, though he would be scandalised if he realised to what use she'd later put that education. Irene looked around. The place was dirtier and more disordered than ever. Empty flagons of beer stood near the bed. The heel of a loaf was the only food in sight. She was glad that she had not brought Oxley with her and let him view the pitiful condition into which her father had fallen.

Adnam made a pathetic gesture towards hospitality. 'Can I get you something to drink, Irene?'

'No, thank you.'

'What time is your train?'

'It's just after two o'clock.'

'I can walk to the station with you.'

'There's no need for that,' she said, sharply.

'But I can look after you. Deansgate is a jungle. You need a father to protect you.'

Irene was about to reply that the time she needed protection was when she was much younger and when he had gone into decline. But she saw no point in dredging up the horrors of the past. Her father was a sick man. He might not survive another bad winter. She would not have long to wait. Once he'd died, she would be free to pursue her new life without any vestigial family ties. Meanwhile, she still had sufficient family loyalty to keep an occasional eye on her father. Her gift had been generous but it would not last long. It would soon be wasted on drink and a few sordid nights with some of the whores who infested the area. Irene was disgusted at the thought, yet it did not stop her giving him the money in the first place. She'd salved her conscience and that was why she came.

'Why don't you write to me anymore?' he asked.

'I never have the time, Father.'

'Well, I have plenty of time. Let me have your address and I can write to you instead.'

'I'm not allowed to have letters.'

He was indignant. 'Not even from your father? What sort of hard-hearted employers do you work for, Irene? They've no right to stop you having letters.'

'I have to go,' she said, planting a token kiss on his cheek. 'I don't want to miss my train.'

'But you've only been here a few minutes,' he complained.

'I'll stay longer next time.'

And before he could stop her, she let herself out and hurried off down the street. Crime had helped her to escape from Manchester and to give her a surface respectability. Yet a visit to her father plunged her back into the city's most notorious area of vice, lawlessness and grinding poverty. Irene did not belong there. She was destined for a better life with the man she loved. While she was still disturbed by the thought of shooting someone, she was quick to see its benefit. It had earned her Oxley's respect and love. In pulling the trigger, she had passed a kind of test. They were kindred spirits now.

The quality that most irritated Leeming about their new recruit was his willingness. Ian Peebles was like a dog, eager to do anything that might please his owner. Had the sergeant thrown a stick, he was sure that the Scotsman would fetch it for him.

'What can I do, Sergeant Leeming?' asked Peebles.

'For the moment, you can just watch and wait.'

'The superintendent explained the background to the case and I read the reports in this morning's newspapers. According to one of them, Jeremy Oxley is a will-o'-the-wisp.'

'Don't believe everything you read in the press, Constable. They are often unjustly critical of us. Above all else, don't talk to any journalists. They'll twist your words to their own advantage.'

'Och, man, I found that out when I was in uniform.'

'Where were you based?'

'In K Division at first,' said Peebles. 'That's in Barking. It's a very rough district. I was later moved to A Division.'

Leeming was impressed. 'That's Hyde Park Police Station,' he noted. 'We'd all like to have worked there. It was a kind of promotion for you. What did you do to earn it?'

'I made one or two significant arrests,' said Peebles, modestly. 'I enjoyed my time in A Division, then I was recommended for the Detective Department.'

'You were lucky,' said Leeming. 'My days in uniform were spent in the worst parts of London, the kinds of places where police are very unpopular.'

Peebles stood to attention. 'I didn't join the police in search of popularity,' he declared as if taking an oath. 'All that matters to me is that we sweep the streets clean of villainy. London is the greatest city in the world. It deserves to be purged of crime.'

'You've been listening to Superintendent Tallis.'

'I think he's an inspiration – don't you?'

'In some ways,' said Leeming, hiding his true feelings.

'But then the same could be said of you and Inspector Colbeck.'

'We do our job to the best of our ability, no more, no less.'

'The superintendent told me that you're

his best men.'

'Really?'

It was a surprise to Leeming, who got a continuous string of complaints from Tallis, often couched in unflattering language. It was the same for Colbeck. There was an underlying tension between the superintendent and him that prevented Tallis from giving anything but the most reluctant praise to the Railway Detective. Yet behind their backs, it transpired, the superintendent was lauding them. Leeming was annoyed that he was prepared to confide in a detective who was effectively on probation while saying nothing to the two people about whom he was talking. In Leeming's view, Tallis was a different breed of dog. If Peebles was a tail-wagging retriever, the superintendent was a terrier barking incessantly at their heels.

They were in Colbeck's office and Peebles was diverted by some of the posters on the walls. They listed wanted criminals and the rewards that were on offer. He peered intently at them.

'That's one of the things I admire most about you and the inspector,' he said, turning to face Leeming. 'You never rely on informers or people in search of a reward. You solve your cases by hard work and deduction.'

'It may be true up to a point,' conceded Leeming. 'I provide the hard work and the inspector supplies the deduction. But we take help from anyone we can. Inspector Colbeck is a great believer in picking up something useful wherever he can find it. He has a word for it.'

'Serendipity.'

'Yes, that's right – serendipity.'

'I think there's far more to it than that,' argued Peebles. 'I've kept a scrapbook of your cases, you see. I cut out newspaper reports of them and paste them in. It's taught me a lot about your methods.'

Leeming was uneasy. 'Has it?'

'Look at that train robbery, for instance. You were so thorough. You dealt with the railway company, the post office, the Royal Mint, a bank in Birmingham, a lock manufacturer in the Black Country and you infiltrated the Great Exhibition to make your first arrests.' He grinned with frank adoration. 'It was brilliant detective work.'

'One thing led to another,' explained Leeming.

'You got through an immense amount of work between you.'

'That's certainly true.'

'Then there was the severed head found on Crewe station.'

'You don't need to remind me of that.'

'How on earth did Inspector Colbeck know that there was a connection with the forthcoming Derby? He even sailed off to

Ireland at one point.'

'He was acting on a sixth sense. It's what he always does.'

'Well, I don't have that gift.'

'Neither do I, Constable.'

'The case that really intrigued me was the one that took you and the inspector to France. It all began when someone was killed on a train then hurled off the Sankey Viaduct. In fact–'

'Let me stop you there,' said Leeming, interrupting with both hands raised. 'This may surprise you but we never look back at old investigations. We always have our hands full with new ones.'

Peebles was astonished. 'You don't keep a scrapbook?'

'It would never cross my mind.'

'But you should have a record of your triumphs.'

'I'm not that vain, Constable.'

'I keep a list of every suspect I've questioned and every arrest I've made,' said Peebles. 'Not that I've handled the sort of complex cases that you and the inspector do, of course. I'm still a raw beginner.' He rubbed his hands. 'I can't wait to join the hunt for Oxley and his accomplice. When we catch them,' he went on, face shining and buck teeth aglow, 'we'll have wonderful press cuttings. If you don't wish to record your successes, I'll happily do so.'

Leeming groaned inwardly. While they were involved in a difficult case, the last thing they needed was a self-appointed recording angel like Ian Peebles. Their every move would be enshrined in his scrapbook. It would make them far too self-conscious to do their job properly. Leeming was so alarmed at the prospect that he made a silent wish.

'Come back soon, Inspector Colbeck – I *need* you.'

Colbeck had never been in a cotton mill before and he found the noise deafening. Ambrose Holte, the mill owner, occupied a large, almost palatial office that was insulated against the pandemonium. When Colbeck explained why he was there, Holte was more than ready to help. He was a beefy man of middle years with a pallid face and white hair that had retreated to the rear of his head like so much foam left on a beach by the receding tide. He had a strong Lancashire accent and a habit of keeping one thumb in his waistcoat pocket as he spoke.

'Yes, I remember Irene Adnam very well,' he said with rancour. 'She robbed us of items worth hundreds of pounds.'

'Female burglars are rare, thankfully.'

'She didn't break *into* the house, Inspector. She was already there, working as a governess to my youngest daughter.'

'When did you begin to suspect her?' asked Colbeck.

'We never did,' said Holte, 'that was the trouble. She wormed her way into our affections until we trusted her completely. Alicia, whom she taught, doted on her.'

'Did she come to you with good references?'

'They were excellent, Inspector. It was only after she'd left that we learnt that they were forgeries. When the police tried to find the various addresses, they discovered that none of them existed.'

'How would you describe Miss Adnam?'

Holte snorted. 'I think she's the most loathsome, duplicitous, black-hearted creature on God's earth.'

'You're saying that with the advantage of hindsight,' Colbeck reminded him. 'Try to remember how she struck you when she first came for interview. What made you choose Irene Adnam?'

'It was sheer folly!'

'You didn't think so at the time.'

'No, Inspector,' admitted Holte, jowls wobbling. 'That's correct. She seemed ideal for the position. Not to put too fine a point on it, I was beguiled by the cunning little vixen.'

Holte gave a clear and detailed description of Irene Adnam and she began to take on more definition in Colbeck's mind. Her work as a governess had been above reproach and she had stayed long enough in Holte's employ to become an auxiliary member of his family, taking her meals with them and joining them at church on Sundays. It was because he had placed such trust in her that Holte was so embittered when she turned out to be a thief.

'What exactly did she steal?' asked Colbeck.

'She emptied my wallet and took some of my wife's jewellery. But the bulk of the haul consisted of small items of silver. They'd be fairly light to carry and easy to sell to a pawnbroker.'

'Oh, I think that Miss Adnam might have higher ambitions than relying on a pawnbroker. If she's the seasoned criminal she appears,' said Colbeck, 'she'd probably deal with a fence who'd offer better terms. I don't think she'd steal anything unless she knew exactly where she could get a good price for it.'

'You could be right, Inspector. When I gave them a list of stolen items, the police visited nearly all the pawnbrokers in the city. They drew a blank. None of our property was recovered.'

'Evidently she knew exactly what to take and when to take it.'

'We were all fast asleep at the time.'

'How did she know where everything was kept – your wife's jewellery, for instance?

Surely that was in a safe?' Holte lowered his head, plainly discomfited. 'I can't believe that items of such value were not locked away.'

'They *were* locked away, Inspector.'

'Then how did she get her hands on them?'

'Someone told her the combination.'

Colbeck was surprised. 'She had an accomplice on the staff?'

'He was a member of the family,' said Holte, running his tongue over dry lips. 'Not that he realised what he was doing at the time. I'm talking about my eldest son, Lawrence. He became enamoured of Miss Adnam. I warned him against it, of course, and urged him to pay for his pleasures like a gentleman. That way they don't infect the family home.' He sucked his teeth. 'But Lawrence wouldn't listen, I fear. He fell completely under her spell. When she asked if she could leave a few valuables of her own in our safe, he duly obliged by opening it.'

'And she memorised the combination while he was doing it,' guessed Colbeck. 'She's a calculating young lady, no doubt about that. I can see why you're so anxious to see her caught.'

'You can imagine the embarrassment this has caused me,' said Holte, running a hand over his forehead. 'It's been a heavy cross to bear. The woman is a monster. She betrayed me, stole irreplaceable items of my wife's jewellery, broke Alicia's heart in two and relieved Lawrence – idiot that he was – of his virginity. I'd not only *pay* to see her executed, Inspector,' he growled, 'I'd even volunteer to act as the hangman.'

CHAPTER SIX

Caleb Andrews had lost count of the number of times he'd brought a train safely into New Street station in Birmingham. As one set of passengers departed and another set converged on the carriages, he had time to wipe the sweat from his brow with the back of his hand.

'I won't be doing this for much longer,' he announced.

'You keep saying that, Caleb,' said his fireman, 'but I don't believe you. The only way you'll quit the railway is in a coffin.'

'That's what you think, Dirk.'

'It's what we *all* think.'

'Then perhaps you should have a word with Mr Pomeroy.'

Dirk Sowerby shrugged. 'Why?'

'I handed in my resignation earlier on today. Mr Pomeroy accepted it with regret. The decision is made. I'm going to retire and put my feet up at last.'

The fireman was amazed. No driver in the LNWR had the same enthusiasm for railways as Andrews. It was at once a job and a passion for him. Spending each day hurtling up and down the track helped him to defy age. He seemed indefatigable. How the company would manage without such a dedicated servant was an open question. Sowerby would miss him, both for his companionship and for his fund of knowledge about the operation of the railway system. Firemen who'd been taught their trade by Caleb Andrews were uniformly grateful for his expertise.

'Did you talk it over with your daughter?' asked Sowerby.

'I told her what I was going to do, if that's what you mean.'

'And Maddy had no objections?'

'None whatsoever, Dirk. She's seen the early shifts and the long hours taking their toll on me.'

'When is she getting married?'

'Sooner rather than later,' said Andrews with a smile. 'It's part of the reason I decided to retire. If I'm at home all day, it will annoy her like mad and make her set a date for the wedding at last. I've been waiting an eternity for that to happen.'

'I thought that they only got engaged last year.'

'They did – but it seems much longer to

me. I don't want Maddy hanging around for ever when I retire. Not when Inspector Colbeck has a much larger house than ours. She should move in with him.'

Sowerby frowned. 'Don't you *mind* her marrying a detective?'

'She can marry anyone she likes as long as she does it fairly soon.' He cackled. 'No, that's not true,' he said, seriously. 'She's found herself a good man and I couldn't be happier with her choice.'

'But he's a policeman, Caleb.'

'I don't hold that against him.'

'Have you forgotten what happened when we steamed into this station yesterday? Two policemen were left behind us on the track. They'd been murdered,' said Sowerby, his frown deepening. 'That tells you what a dangerous job it is.'

'The inspector can take care of himself, Dirk.'

'But he's chasing the man who escaped from the policemen.'

'I know and I mean to help him catch the fellow.'

'This man who escaped – I think his name is Oxley – has no respect for the law or the people who try to uphold it. And there are far too many people just like him. I'd hate a daughter of mine to marry a policeman.'

'You don't *have* a daughter, you imbecile.'

'I know,' agreed Sowerby, 'but if I did, I'd

be afraid that she'd be a widow before too long. I hope that doesn't happen to Maddy.'

'There's little chance of that.'

'The inspector spends all his time chasing desperate criminals. It only takes one of them to fire a gun or pull a knife on him and you'll be attending the funeral of your son-in-law.'

'That's arrant nonsense!'

Andrews's vehement denial masked his deep anxiety. His fireman was only airing concerns that the driver had raised with Madeleine on a number of occasions. Loving his daughter and wanting her future happiness, he was troubled by the nagging fear that Colbeck might one day lose his life in pursuit of a suspect. Madeleine had dismissed the suggestion but it remained a source of deep unease to her father. It was why he kept urging her to set a date for their wedding. If Colbeck's career in Scotland Yard was indeed to be foreshortened by disaster, Andrews wanted his daughter to have as full a taste of married bliss as possible. After years of waiting, she deserved that.

It was late evening when she heard the footsteps on the pavement outside. They did not belong to her father and, in any case, Madeleine did not expect him back until he'd repaired to the pub he routinely frequented at the end of the day. Thinking that the pedestrian would walk past the house, she was surprised when there was a knock on the door. It made her rise from the chair and cross to the window. The moment she looked out, she emitted a cry of joy and ran to open the door. Colbeck was waiting to enfold her in his arms and kiss her.

'What a lovely surprise!' she exclaimed. 'The only time I know that it's you is when I hear a cab drawing up outside the house.'

'I made the driver stop at the end of the street this time,' he said, 'so that I could catch you unawares.' He looked over her shoulder into the house. 'Am I to be allowed in, Madeleine?'

'Of course – nobody is more welcome.'

Ushering him into the house, she closed the door behind them before surrendering to another embrace. Only when they parted did he take off his hat and set it aside. He glanced at her easel.

'Is there anything for me to see?' he asked.

'Not until it's finished, Robert.'

He pointed a finger. 'Can't I just take a peek?'

'No,' she said, administering a playful pat on his hand. 'You must behave yourself. An artist must not be hurried into displaying her work until she feels that it's ready.'

He smiled. 'I'm glad to see that you consider yourself to be an artist now. When I first urged you to be more ambitious, you claimed that you were nothing more than a painter with moderate talent.'

'My attitude changed when I first sold something.'

'I knew that it would,' he said, kissing her cheek. 'But I can't tarry, I'm afraid. This is only a flying visit on my way to Scotland Yard. I have to report to the superintendent.'

She glanced at the clock on the mantelpiece. 'Will Mr Tallis be working *this* late?'

'He's at his desk until midnight sometimes, Madeleine. Nobody can accuse him of being lazy. He'll sit there until I turn up and tell him what happened in Manchester.'

'Is that where you went looking for Jeremy Oxley?'

He raised an eyebrow. 'You *know* about the case, do you?'

'I know more than you think,' she replied. 'By coincidence, my father was driving the train when the prisoner escaped. Be warned, Robert. He thinks that entitles him to join in the investigation.'

'He always did fancy that he had the makings of a detective.'

She was firm. 'One detective is enough in any family.'

Colbeck gave her an abbreviated account of his visits to Wolverhampton, Birmingham and Manchester. He did not simply do so out of courtesy. To begin with, he knew that he could trust her to keep all the information to herself. But there was another reason why he liked to keep her abreast of his movements. Madeleine had been able to offer practical help in some of his past investigations. Had he known about the involvement of a woman, Tallis would have been apoplectic. The superintendent felt that policing was essentially a male preserve. He'd be astounded if he knew how much Colbeck had relied on Madeleine to collect evidence on his behalf.

'Now that you've told me *your* news,' she said, 'I can pass on mine. Brace yourself for a shock, Robert.'

'Is it that serious?'

'It is to me – Father is going to retire.'

He was startled. 'Does he really mean it this time?'

'He was going to hand in his resignation this morning.'

'Well, that *is* an unexpected disclosure,' said Colbeck, 'but it's a pleasing one. After all those years of sterling service, he's earned the right to retirement. A lesser man would have given up when he took that beating from the train robbers but your father fought his way back to full health and was soon back on the footplate.'

'It will bring about some changes,' she cautioned.

'Yes, you won't have to get up early every morning to make his breakfast and to send him off.'

'That's a benefit but there'll be hazards as well.' Her gesture took in the whole room. 'The main one is that I'll lose my studio. I work best when I'm alone and I'm going to have Father here.'

'There's a simple answer to that, Madeleine.'

'Is there?'

'Yes – you can use a room in my house as a studio. After all, it's only a matter of time before you move in there permanently.'

'That's what I was coming to,' she said, tentatively. 'Father has been badgering me to set a date for the wedding. I know that you don't wish to be rushed and I understand why, but it would be helpful if I had at least some idea of when it would be.'

Colbeck took her impulsively in his arms. 'If it were left to me,' he said, softly, 'I'd marry you tomorrow. But the demands of my job won't permit that, alas. Since the time we became engaged, I've had one case after another to deal with. I work from dawn to dusk seven days a week, Madeleine.'

'I accept that,' she said, pushing back a strand of hair from his forehead. 'As soon as one investigation finishes, another one starts. I can see that this latest case will eat up all your time. That's in the nature of police work. It's just that I would like to have a date to give Father so that he'll stop hounding me.' She smiled hopefully. 'Is that an unfair request?'

'No, Madeleine,' he answered. 'It's an extremely fair one. You are right about this investigation. It will need my full commitment and take precedence over everything else. I have personal reasons for wanting to catch Jeremy Oxley. It's something of an obsession, so I must ask you to bear with me. When it's all over,' he told her, 'I promise you that we'll sit down together and finally set a date for our wedding. Will that please your father?'

She laughed happily. 'It will please *me* a lot more, Robert.'

Oxley was the best lover she'd ever had. He knew how to take his time and to ensure that Irene enjoyed full satisfaction. He was the first man to whom she gave herself completely. With the others, she'd always held something back. Irene had been in her early teens when she learnt how to use her charms on a man. She would secure his interest, tighten her hold, then tease, torment and ensnare him until he'd do whatever she wanted. All of her early victims had been young men lured by a promise of surrender that was often never fulfilled. When they made the mistake of putting absolute trust in her, she chose the moment to strike then disappeared with their money or other valuables. Many were too embarrassed by their own gullibility to report the crime to the police. Those – like Lawrence Holte – who did want her arrested discovered that she was remarkably elusive.

As she lay naked in bed with Oxley that evening, she did not have to think about stealing from him or decide when to take to her heels. They were partners and their spoils were shared equally. It was inconceivable that she would ever run away from him.

'Are you happy?' he asked, lazily stroking her breast.

'I'm happier than I've ever been, Jerry.'

'Is that because of me?'

'What other cause could there be?'

'I wondered if it was to do with what happened during the rescue. When I'd killed for the first time, I felt this glow inside me for days. Even when I'd been arrested, I had this extraordinary sense of pleasure.' He tapped his chest. 'I'd taken another man's life.'

'That thought gives me no pleasure at all.'

'It's like a coming of age.'

'I see it differently,' she said, uneasily.

It was still there at the back of her mind. Irene might no longer shiver when she recalled the moment she fired the gun, nor did she flinch when she thought about the two bodies being butchered by a speeding train. Yet it would not go away. Every so often the grotesque memories would pop up uncontrollably in her brain and cause her intense regret. Only in Oxley's arms was she safe from any twinges of guilt. Alone with him, nothing else mattered.

'You could have been an actress,' he observed.

'I don't have the training for it, Jerry.'

'Training isn't necessary when you have such natural ability. You know how to play a part, Irene. Your performance fooled all three of those policemen.'

'There were only two on the train.'

'I was thinking about the one who told you what time we'd be leaving Wolverhampton – Constable Marner.'

She giggled. 'I put a pillow inside my dress and told him that I was carrying a child. He couldn't wait to help me then.' Her face clouded. 'What will happen to him?'

'Nothing at all,' he assured her. 'He'll have the sense to keep his mouth shut. Otherwise he'll be arrested for being an accessory and will end up behind bars.'

'That's what worries me. If he's caught, he'll be able to describe me. We talked for several minutes. He had a good look at me, Jerry.'

Oxley grinned. 'Not as good as the one that I'm having,' he said with a laugh, gazing at her smooth, shapely body. 'Policemen will always be tempted by a bribe. It's the same with prison warders. They're so poorly paid that five or ten pounds looks like a fortune to them. That's how I escaped when I was on remand. I bribed someone to look the other way.'

'How did you smuggle the money into prison?'

'There are always ways to conceal it when you're searched. Mind you,' he went on, 'you have to choose the right person. I picked on Marner because I sensed that he was our man.'

'Think how he must have felt when he discovered that he'd been tricked,' she said. 'Two of his friends went to their deaths because of him. That would have upset him terribly.'

'It serves him right, Irene.'

He reached for the bottle of champagne on the bedside table and emptied it into the two glasses. Handing one to Irene, he picked up the other and raised it in a toast.

'Let's drink to a prosperous future together!'

'Yes,' she said, 'I'll drink to that any time.'

'If we take a new name, change our appearance again and keep on the move, nobody will ever catch us.'

'What about Inspector Colbeck?'

'Oh, I think I have his measure, Irene. He's very clever but I can outmanoeuvre him. I was arrested in Wolverhampton and escaped on the way to Birmingham. That's where he'll begin his search. So we'll hide in the last place he'd expect to find us.'

'And where's that, Jerry?'

'In London, of course – where there are countless places to take refuge. Ours will just be two faces among millions. Don't you think it's a wonderful idea?' he said, smirking. 'It will simply never occur to Colbeck that the two people he's after are staying not far away in the same city.'

Tallis was motionless as he listened to Colbeck's report. In the light from the oil lamp on his desk, his features took on a sinister aspect. Even though it was late, he showed no hint of fatigue. His eyes were as bright and his brain as alert as ever. Colbeck was lucid and, as usual, succinct. The one thing he did not mention was his brief call on Madeleine Andrews after his arrival at Euston station. It would not only have goaded the superintendent into a rant, it would have left Colbeck open to accusations of putting his private life before his commitments as a detective. Recounting the details of his visit to Manchester, he felt sure that he had identified the name of Oxley's accomplice. Tallis was not entirely convinced. He stroked his neat moustache meditatively.

'I expected more of you,' he said at length.

'We cannot conjure instant progress out of the air, sir.'

'There must have been dozens of clues to

pick up.'

'I've listed the majority of them for you,' said Colbeck. 'The one important discovery was that a policeman had been bribed to give information about the time of the train. Constable Marner is now enduring the wrath of his colleagues.'

'He should be locked up in perpetuity,' snapped Tallis. 'If there's one thing I abhor, it's a corrupt policeman. But let's turn our attention to this accomplice you claim to have uncovered.'

'Her name is Irene Adnam, sir.'

'How certain are you of that?'

'I'm certain enough to divulge her name to the press.'

'Well, I don't share that certainty, Inspector. You know my view of journalists – they're despicable jackals who should be kept in cages and fed on scraps. We've suffered so much unjust censure from them. But,' he continued, hunching his shoulders, 'they are a necessary evil and – if used correctly – can be extremely helpful to us.'

'That's why we must give them Irene Adnam's name, sir.'

'We need more confirmation first. What if you're wrong about her, Inspector? You've made grievous errors before. If we name her in the press and she turns out to be innocent of the charge, then we are left with very red faces.'

'With respect, Superintendent,' argued Colbeck, 'the one thing you cannot say of this woman is that she is innocent. She's committed a number of offences and is being sought by the police in Manchester. Young as she may be, she already has a substantial criminal career behind her.'

'Yet she's never been arrested.'

'That's true.'

'Nor has she been questioned by the police.'

'Miss Adnam knows how to cover her tracks, sir.'

'The only description you have of her comes from one of her victims. How reliable is that?'

'I think it's very reliable, Superintendent. She lived in his house as a governess. Mr Holte saw her every day.'

'Then he should have kept a closer eye on her. No,' said Tallis, getting out of his chair, 'it's too soon to release the woman's name to the press. I concede that she does look like a possible suspect. At the same time, however, there's something about her that makes her an unlikely ally for Jeremy Oxley.'

'And what might that be, may I ask?'

'Look at what we know of her, Inspector. By all accounts, she's a practised thief with a gift for winning the confidence of her prospective victims. More to the point – and this, I submit, is crucial – Miss Adnam chooses to work alone. Now,' said Tallis, walking around the desk to him, 'why should she suddenly decide to act as someone's accomplice, and how did she make an enormous leap from being a thief to becoming a merciless killer?'

'That's a pertinent question, Superintendent.'

'Do you, by any chance, have the answer to it?'

'Not as yet,' confessed Colbeck, 'but I will.'

'And how do you propose to go about finding it?'

'I've enlisted the help of Inspector Boone, sir. He's a very able man and has wide resources to call upon. Since she was apparently born in Manchester, Irene Adnam may well have family there. I've suggested to the inspector that he might begin with the 1851 census. It will doubtless contain a number of people in the city by that name. We simply have to eliminate them one by one.'

'That could take time and lead you down a blind alley.'

'It's a risk that we have to take, sir.'

'Supposing that this young woman *is* the accomplice?'

'Believe me, sir,' asserted Colbeck, 'there's no supposition involved. Irene Adnam is the person who shot one policeman and helped to throw another to a grisly death.'

Tallis was tetchy. 'Let me finish what I was

going to say, man.'

'I beg your pardon, sir.'

'Assuming that you are right about her...'

'I am.'

'How do you know that she and Oxley are still together?'

'There's not a scintilla of doubt about it, sir.'

'Why do you say that?'

'Put yourself in Oxley's position,' suggested Colbeck.

'That's a bizarre proposition,' said Tallis, angrily. 'You know that I'd never enter into a relationship with any woman, especially one with such a record of criminality.'

'Humour me, please,' requested Colbeck. 'After a long and successful run, you are finally arrested. When you appear in court, you will not only be charged with the crime in Birmingham for which you are being held. Once the police examine your past record, they will find that it contains at least two murders – that of a London jeweller and that of Helen Millington, who witnessed you fleeing from the premises. In short, Superintendent,' he emphasized, 'you are taking a train to the gallows.'

'Yes – and quite rightly so.'

'Now then, if a daring young woman boards that train and actually rescues you from your fate, how are you going to view her?'

Tallis sniffed. 'I suppose that I'd be very grateful to her.'

'Would you be tempted to cast her aside?'

'Well, when you put it like that...'

'Oxley and she are both accomplices and lovers,' said Colbeck, forcefully. 'The murder of those policemen has bonded them at a deep level. They'll never part until they're caught. *That's* why Irene Adnam must be our target. Wherever we catch up with her, she and Jeremy Oxley will be together.'

Once again, they travelled independently so that nobody would view them as a couple. While Irene had a first-class ticket, Oxley settled for a train journey in second class. When they stopped at Wolverhampton station, Irene looked through the window with grave misgivings. It was a town she would have preferred to avoid at all costs. Oxley, on the other hand, gave the place a token wave. Its police had been efficient enough to catch him but not to hold on to him. He went through the escape once more in his mind, revelling in the detail. As the train pulled out of the station, he felt a pang of regret. Every newspaper had carried a description of him but Oxley had no fear of being recognised. Adept at changing his appearance, he had complete confidence that nobody would identify him.

They met up again at the cab rank outside

Euston and shared a vehicle. Irene nestled beside him.

'Where are we going?' she asked.

'We'll stay with a friend of mine,' he replied. 'You'll like him, Irene. He's killed more people than the two of us put together.'

Colbeck made his customary early start next morning. Arriving at his office, however, he discovered that Ian Peebles was there already, standing outside the door as if on sentry duty. Colbeck guessed that it was his new colleague and offered a friendly smile.

'You must be Constable Peebles,' he said, extending a palm. 'The superintendent told me about you last night.'

'I'm honoured to meet you, Inspector,' said Peebles, shaking his hand. 'I've followed your career with great interest.'

'I see.' He opened the door. 'Let's go on in, shall we?'

As they went into the office, Colbeck walked behind his desk and turned to take a closer look at Peebles. There was a suppressed eagerness in the other's face. Well groomed and watchful, he exuded an intelligence that was rare among policemen who patrolled London streets. Notwithstanding the constable's youthful appearance, Colbeck did not share Leeming's estimation of him. Where the sergeant saw fatal immaturity, Colbeck sensed promise. He just wished for a little less silent adulation from Peebles.

'Tell me about yourself, Constable,' he invited.

'There's really not much to tell, sir.'

'Stop hiding your light under a bushel. Superintendent Tallis holds you in high regard. There has to be a good reason for that.'

'I'll endeavour to repay his faith in me.'

Peebles spoke briefly about his time in the army and on the beat as a police constable. He was very articulate. Yet beneath the man's surface modesty, Colbeck sensed a burning ambition to rise in rank at the department. It was a laudable aim and, after studying him with care, Colbeck felt that he might well have a successful career ahead of him. Peebles was untypical of the men whom the Metropolitan Police Force attracted. Other discharged soldiers joined the force but few had the constable's qualities. Recruits came largely from the labouring classes, sturdy men whose former trades had given them the physical conditioning necessary to enforce the law. While the vast majority would spend their entire career in uniform, Peebles had been given promotion in a remarkably short time.

There was a shock in store for Colbeck.

'I have to repay my wife's faith in me as well,' said Peebles.

Colbeck was amazed. 'You're *married?*'

'I'm about to be fairly soon, Inspector. It's one of the consequences of moving to Scotland Yard. The increase in pay has made it possible for me to support a wife.'

'Does the superintendent know about this?'

'It was the first thing he asked me about.'

'Then he must value you highly,' said Colbeck. 'My advice is to say as little as possible to him about your private life. He believes that marriage is a distraction for his detectives and would prefer us all to lead lives of total abstinence.'

Peebles laughed. 'This is not a monastery.'

'The superintendent has yet to accept that. It's perfectly possible for detectives to combine marriage with fulfilment of their duties here. Sergeant Leeming is proof of that.'

As if on cue, Leeming came walking along the corridor. He turned in through the open door of Colbeck's office.

'Did I hear my name being taken in vain?' he asked.

'I was just holding you up as a golden example, Victor.'

'It's not often that anyone does that, sir.'

'I do,' said Peebles. 'I want to follow in your footsteps.'

'I need to redirect your footsteps, Constable,' said Colbeck. 'You will be travelling to Manchester this morning with the sergeant and me. In case we may have to spend

111

the night there, I suggest that you provide yourself with anything necessary.'

'Aye, sir,' said Peebles, keen to be involved. 'Does this mean that you made some progress when you were there yesterday?'

'I'll tell you everything on the train.'

'Thank you.'

After giving each of them a smile, Peebles hurried out. Leeming closed the door after him so that he could speak in private.

He was bitter. 'Does the superintendent *want* this case solved?'

'That's a strange question. You know that he does.'

'Then why has he handicapped us with Constable Peebles? The fellow has no experience at all.'

'What better way to gain it?'

'I think that he'll hamper the investigation.'

'Then I must disagree with you,' said Colbeck. 'I fancy that he could turn out to be an asset to us.'

'He'll be too busy *watching* us,' complained Leeming.

'How else can he learn what to do?'

'You don't understand, sir. Peebles has been keeping press cuttings of all our cases. He has a whole scrapbook of them. Every move we make will be noted down and preserved.'

Colbeck smiled. 'Every Doctor Johnson

needs a Boswell.'

'Does he?' Leeming was bewildered. 'I'm sorry but I don't know any detectives by those names.'

'That doesn't matter, Victor. The simple fact is that I like our new colleague and anticipate good things of him. It's always a little unnerving to be put on a pedestal but it does have an advantage. It keeps us on our toes,' said Colbeck. 'We mustn't disillusion him. If he believes that we are the pride of the department, we must offer him some justification for our status, and we can only do that by bringing this investigation to a speedy conclusion. Gird your loins,' he urged, 'and get ready for a train journey to Manchester. We have to demonstrate to Constable Peebles the difficult art of detection.'

CHAPTER SEVEN

Inspector Zachary Boone was busier than ever, listening to reports about various incidents, dispatching constables to investigate others, speculating with his superintendent on the outcome of a trial and juggling a large number of other commitments. When three visitors from London suddenly descended on him, Boone was upbraiding a luckless constable who had foolishly allowed a suspect to evade capture. Pleased to see Colbeck again, he reserved judgement on his friend's companions. In Boone's opinion, Leeming looked like a battle-scarred wrestler in stolen apparel while Peebles resembled nothing so much as an overgrown schoolboy. The inspector was surprised to learn that they were both serving officers in the Detective Department.

'You're very welcome,' said Boone, standing behind his desk, 'but if you expect to sit down in here, it will have to be on the floor. There's only room for my chair and one other.'

'We're happy to stand, Zachary,' said Colbeck.

'Did you have a good journey?'

'Yes, we did.'

'It was an express train,' explained Peebles. 'The inspector chose it specifically. We couldn't have had a better trip.'

'Speak for yourself,' said Leeming. 'Trains upset my stomach.'

'Sympathetic as we are,' said Colbeck with a consoling smile, 'we can't have our movements dictated by your queasiness.'

'I sometimes wish that locomotives had never been invented.'

'Then you'd have been out of a job,' noted Boone. 'How could you have worked with the famous Railway Detective if there'd been no railways? If you'll pardon a dreadful pun, they've been a great boon to me. Thanks to trains, my men have been able to move around much more quickly.'

'That cuts both ways,' said Colbeck. 'It also means that villains can leave the scene of the crime and be miles away in no time at all.'

'It's exactly what happened in this case,' suggested Peebles, diffidently. 'Murder was actually committed *on* the railway, so the two suspects were immediately able to put distance between themselves and their crime. They could be anywhere in the country by now.'

'Let's hope that we can find a signpost in Manchester that will point us in the right direction.'

'You haven't given us much time,' said Boone. 'Besides, we have a large number of other crimes to solve, so I haven't been able to deploy very many of my men.'

'That's why we're here, Zachary,' said Colbeck. 'We've come to do some of the legwork and to acquaint Constable Peebles with the joys of being a detective.'

'I didn't know there *were* any,' muttered Leeming.

'Let me tell you what we've already done,' volunteered Boone.

Plunging a hand into a small mountain of papers, he drew out one that contained a list of names and addresses in a looping hand. Some of them had ticks against them. He explained that they had already been discounted as a result of visits by his men. All that remained were three names and addresses. He handed the list to Colbeck.

'We were lucky, Robert,' he said. 'There were not all that many people by the name of Adnam. Thank heaven you didn't ask me to list all the O'Briens or the O'Rourkes. In some of the Irish districts, they could run into the hundreds.'

Colbeck perused the addresses. 'Where are these places?'

'Two of them are in relatively safe areas. That's to say, they'll try to stab you in the chest rather than in the back, so you're at least accorded the courtesy of a warning. The third address is in Deansgate. I'd advise anyone against going there on his own.'

'We can all stay together,' said Leeming.

'That would only waste time, Victor,' decided Colbeck, passing the list to him. 'Memorise those details, if you will. Then you and the constable can visit two of the addresses while I pay a call on Silas Adnam in Deansgate.'

'Looking like that, you'd present a tempting target,' said Boone, appraising the debonair figure of Colbeck. 'There's nobody there as refined and elegant as you, Robert. You'd stand out like a hedgehog on a billiard table. Why don't I assign one of my men to accompany you?'

'I can manage on my own, thank you. In any case, I won't be going there in a frock coat and top hat.' Colbeck patted his valise. 'I brought a change of clothing for just such a situation.' He snatched the piece of paper from Leeming's hands. 'Off you go, Sergeant. Give me the names and addresses you've just memorised.'

Leeming gulped. 'Well...'

'I know them, Inspector,' said Peebles before rattling off the information. 'I think you'll find that I'm correct.'

'I could have told you all that,' said Leeming, hurt.

'I'm sure that you could, Victor,' said Colbeck, 'but you were fortunate to have the constable to prompt you. I told you that he'd prove his worth when we got to Manchester.'

While Peebles basked in the praise, Leeming smouldered.

Madeleine had always enjoyed her regular visits to the market. It gave her an opportunity to get out of the house and to meet a succession of friends and neighbours. Since she often incorporated a call on her aunt, she was able to keep in touch with another branch of the family as well. As she set off again with a basket over her arm, she knew exactly what to buy and where to buy it.

Most of the items on the list were chosen because they were her father's preferences. A creature of habit, Caleb Andrews was very particular about his food and drink.

Two thoughts suddenly struck her, causing her to check her stride. The first was that she would not be making this pilgrimage indefinitely. What would happen to her father's larder when she was no longer there to keep it filled? Shopping in the market was largely a chore for women, and not merely because their husbands were usually at work. When it came to meat, fruit and vegetables, they were far more discerning customers and they could also haggle more effectively. On the few occasions when her father had accompanied her, he'd been ready to accept the first price given by individual stallholders. Andrews relied on his daughter to secure the best deal.

How would he cope on his own? They hired a woman to come into the house a couple of days a week to do domestic chores but she could never replace Madeleine at the market.

The second thought was consequent upon the first. When she gave up shopping for her father, would she have to do it for her husband? Because no firm date had been set for the wedding, and because it had seemed to recede every time she raised the issue with Colbeck, she'd never really considered the details of her exact role as a wife. Would she be expected to do all the things she had done for her father? Colbeck had inherited a sizeable house in John Islip Street and had two servants to look after it. Madeleine had never employed full-time servants. Could she delegate the shopping to one of them? It was a moot point.

She had a moment of slight panic when she realised how her existence would be transformed by marriage. There would be so much for her to learn. Yet Colbeck had already brought about many major changes in her life. Until he came into it, she could never have envisaged a relationship with such a highly intelligent member of the middle class. Her father had wanted her to marry another railwayman and it was from his circle of friends that her admirers necessarily came. Colbeck had altered all that. Madeleine had been able to educate herself by means of his extensive library and to improve her talent as an artist so much that her work was now in demand. She had, in more than one sense, emancipated herself from her class. As Mrs Colbeck, she would be a very different person from Miss Andrews.

Her first thought returned with greater urgency and it posed a burning question. When she left home after the marriage, who would look after her father?

Disguise was an established part of Colbeck's armoury. There were parts of London where he would never dare to venture in his usual attire because it would make him stand out. To merge with the denizens, he had to look as if he belonged. For his visit to Deansgate, therefore, he changed into the rough garb he'd brought with him, wearing a large, battered cap and a pair of old boots. When he entered the district, he even adjusted his walk. Instead of his usual measured gait, he adopted a furtive scuffle. It meant that nobody gave him a second glance.

Having located Adnam's address, he first went to the nearest pub, reasoning that anyone who lived in such a depressing place would need the support of alcohol. The Eagle and Child was a dark, evil-smelling establishment filled with shabby characters hunched around the rickety tables. For the price of a pint of beer, Colbeck bought the landlord's attention and gained some useful information about Silas Adnam. One fact was particularly significant.

'Silas was in here last night,' said the landlord, 'drinking himself into a stupor. I reckon his daughter must have been to see him again because he had money to spend.'

'Do you know the daughter's name?' asked Colbeck.

'Yes – it's Irene.'

'Have you ever seen her?'

The landlord shook his head. 'She's too good for the likes of us.'

After finishing his drink, Colbeck walked the short distance to the house and banged on the door. He had to pound it again before it was opened. The whiskery face of Silas Adnam confronted him.

'What do you want?' he snarled.

'I've come to talk about your daughter.'

'She's not here.'

'I know,' said Colbeck, 'but she has been and that means you and I must have a conversation.'

Pushing the door open, he stepped into the house and ignored the protests from the old man. When Colbeck explained who he was, Adnam's tone became defensive.

'Irene is a good girl,' he said. 'She takes care of me.'

'Then she might have found you a more comfortable place to live, Mr Adnam. She could certainly afford it.'

'What do you mean?'

'Irene has a lot of money.'

'No, she doesn't,' insisted Adnam. 'She's a governess at a big house in London. Part of her wage comes in board and lodging. It takes her some time to save up money for her father.'

'Why did she come here yesterday?'

'She wanted to see me, of course.'

'Yes,' said Colbeck, 'but why then of all days?'

Adnam shrugged. 'Does it matter?'

'As a matter of fact, it does. How long did she stay?'

'That's none of your business, Inspector.'

'It's important for me to know.'

'There's no law against seeing my daughter, is there?'

'None at all, sir,' agreed Colbeck.

'What happened between us is our affair.'

'Under any other circumstances, it might be. As it is, the timing and duration of her visit are of considerable interest to me. So – I ask you again – how long was Irene here?'

Adnam refused to answer. In a show of obstinacy, he flopped down onto his stool, folded his arms and turned away. It gave Colbeck the chance to look around the small, fetid room and to assess the value of the man's few belongings. Adnam had clearly had a far better standard of living at one time. His voice was educated and he bore himself like someone who had once held responsibility. What had caused his fall Colbeck could only guess but it had been a very long and painful one. The man's agony was etched deep into his face. Had the situation been different, Colbeck would have felt sorry for him. As it was, Adnam was obstructing a murder enquiry. He deserved no mercy.

'It's time for us to go, sir,' ordered Colbeck.

Adnam was flustered. 'I'm not going anywhere.'

'If you won't answer my questions, then I'll hand you over to Inspector Boone at the police station. He has harsher methods than me and I'm told they always achieve the desired result.' He took Adnam by the elbow. 'Come with me, sir.'

'But I've done nothing wrong!' wailed Adnam.

'You are impeding the operation of justice, sir.'

'How am I doing that?'

'Inspector Boone will explain that to you.'

He lifted Adnam from his stool but the old man shook him off and limped to the corner of the room. Evidently, Boone's name was known to him and it did not induce confidence. Adnam was like a cornered animal, searching for escape. Colbeck slipped a hand into his pocket and took out some handcuffs.

'Do I have to take you by force, Mr Adnam?' he threatened.

'No, no – please don't do that!'

'Then tell me what I want to know.'

'Irene came here, gave me some money, then she left. That's all that happened, I swear it.'

'And how long was she here – an hour, two hours?'

Adnam looked both hunted and humiliated. The kind and caring daughter about whom he'd bragged in the pub the previous night had to be revealed in her true light. He cleared his throat.

'Irene was here for five or ten minutes,' he admitted.

'Thank you, sir,' said Colbeck. 'Now we're getting somewhere.' He pointed to the stool. 'Why don't you sit down again so that you can continue this discussion in comfort?'

The visit to the home of Kingsley Adnam was unrewarding. Leeming and Peebles learnt that the man had six sons but no daughters. Nor was there anyone in his wider family answering to the name of Irene. Since the other address they sought was in an adjoining district, they decided to spurn a cab and walk there. After taking directions from a passer-by, the two detectives set off. Unlike Colbeck, they were not in disguise. Leeming was still nursing resentment against Peebles but he tried not to let it show. The Scotsman was inquisitive.

'Is it true that you're married, Sergeant?'

'Yes, I have a wife and two children.'

'Catherine and I have yet to talk about a family,' said Peebles. 'All that we can think about at the moment is the wedding itself. She saved my life, you know.'

'Did she?'

'Not that either of us realised it at the time, mark you. It was Catherine who persuaded me to leave the army. Until she and I met, I'd planned to spend my entire career serving my country.'

'That was very patriotic of you,' said Leeming, softening towards him. 'But how was your life saved?'

'Had I stayed in the army, I'd have joined my regiment in the Crimea and might well have been one of the many casualties we sustained. Sometimes, I feel rather guilty that I escaped death when several of my comrades did not but I'd given my word to Catherine.'

'Yet you've only jumped out of the frying pan and into the fire.'

'I don't follow.'

'We, too, have our share of deaths,' said Leeming. 'They may not be on the same scale as in the army but they are there. You only have to think of those two policemen from Wolverhampton.'

'It was an appalling crime. I feel for their families.'

'It could happen to any us.'

'I dispute that,' said Peebles, beaming at him. 'It could certainly never happen to you or Inspector Colbeck. You have an uncanny insight into people's characters. It's the basis of your success. Had that woman in Wolverhampton stepped into a compartment in which *you* were guarding a prisoner, you and the inspector would have known at once that she was there to aid him.'

Leeming put out his chest. 'I like to think that we would.'

'Instinct and experience will always protect you.'

'They've done so this far, Constable.'

'I've convinced Catherine of it. That's why she was able to accept my decision to join the police.' Peebles heaved a sigh. 'I'm counting the days until we get married.'

'I wish you both joy,' said Leeming.

He spoke with sincerity. The glimpse into Peebles' private life had moderated Leeming's criticism of him. He could not bring himself to like the Scotsman but he was more tolerant of him now. Moreover, the fact that Peebles was about to get married somehow put them on an even footing. Leeming no longer felt old enough to be his father.

They were strolling side by side along a narrow thoroughfare that twisted and turned with serpentine unpredictability. Leeming kept a wary eye on everything and everybody they encountered, anticipating danger whenever they came to a dark alley or saw a gang of youths loitering on a corner. Peebles, meanwhile, was distracted by thoughts of his beloved, imagining how impressed Catherine would be when he told her about his sojourn in Manchester with Inspector Colbeck. Animated by inner excitement, he was completely off guard. When the attack came, therefore, Peebles was unprepared for it.

Ironically, the incident occurred under a railway bridge. Four men who'd been lounging against the wall sprang to life and hurtled out of the shadows to confront them. Their leader had a cudgel and, to show his readiness to use it, knocked off Leeming's top hat.

'Hand over your money!' he demanded. 'Otherwise—'

He got no further. Leeming's well-aimed kick hit him in the crotch and made him double up in pain. With one of their attackers disabled, Leeming turned to a second, a burly man with a mane of red hair merging with a tufted red beard. The sergeant landed two heavy punches before the man fought back. Peebles had to deal with the other two men. One tried to grab him from behind so that the other could pummel away at him but the constable quickly frustrated their plan. As the attacker behind him took hold of his arms, Peebles stamped hard on the man's toe and jerked one elbow back into his stomach. He then smashed his fist into the face of the man in front of him and made blood cascade from his nose. Following up with a series of punches to the body, he sent him reeling then turned to grapple with the man behind him.

Leeming had already robbed his assailant of any wish to continue the fight, catching him with a relay of blows that sent him crashing back against a brick wall. When the man with the cudgel saw what was happening, he barked an order and the four of them slunk off to lick their wounds and to reflect on their folly in choosing the wrong targets. Picking up his hat, Leeming dusted it off.

'I enjoyed that,' he said with a grin. 'It was good exercise.'

'I just didn't see them coming,' admitted Peebles.

'No matter – you acquitted yourself well. You were obviously taught how to fight in the army.'

'I'll be more careful from now on.'

'I sensed there might be trouble when I saw them lurking there. Since we were outnumbered, they thought we were easy meat.'

Peebles adjusted his coat. 'You reacted so promptly, Sergeant.'

'Forewarned is forearmed,' said Leeming. 'It's something that the superintendent keeps drumming into our heads.' He looked his companion up and down. 'Did you get hurt?'

'I'll have a few bruises, that's all, but I fancy I inflicted far more damage on them. To be honest, I felt rather cheated that it was over so quickly.' He looked under the bridge. 'Is there any point in trying to pursue them?'

'None at all – they know the backstreets and we don't. They came off worse, that's the main thing. It will make them think twice about accosting people in the future.' He offered his hand. 'Well done, Constable – and welcome to Manchester!'

Grinning broadly, Peebles shook his hand. The brawl had had one positive result for him. Having fought off his attackers with vigour, he now felt accepted by Leeming. It was a step forward.

Silas Adnam was more interested in talking about himself than about his daughter but Colbeck let him ramble on. The story was a familiar one to the detective. He'd seen any number of instances where a combination of grief and alcohol had brought about a man's ruin. The wonder was that Adnam had not dragged his daughter down with him. Entering domestic service, Irene had soon shown her mettle and been rewarded with more responsibility. Her father was proud of the fact that she'd been promoted within her first household yet surprised that she'd not stayed there long. In fact, she seemed to change jobs quite often, eventually rising to the position of governess. Adnam spoke about her with an amalgam of smugness and concern, talking in fulsome terms about Irene's cleverness while worrying that he was so rarely able to see her.

Finally, Colbeck had to shatter the old man's illusions.

'Did you know that the police are searching for her?' he asked.

129

Adnam blanched. 'Why on earth should they do that?'

'Your daughter has committed a series of crimes, sir.'

'That's a damnable lie, Inspector! I brought Irene up to respect law and order. There's not a dishonest bone in her body.'

'Then I suggest that you talk to Inspector Boone. He has kept a record of her activities in Manchester and the surrounding area. She does not always use her real name, of course, but there's no doubt that she has had a succession of victims.'

'Victims?' repeated the other. 'How can a harmless, decent, young woman like Irene have victims? She's a governess with a respectable family in London.'

'Do you happen to have their name and address?'

'No, I don't.'

'That's probably because these people do not exist.'

'But they do,' said Adnam, desperately. 'How else would Irene have earned that money? I don't have their address because Irene is forbidden to have any letters sent to her.'

'Is that what she told you?'

'Yes – otherwise I'd keep in regular touch with her.'

'She's been lying to you, Mr Adnam,' said Colbeck, levelly.

'I refuse to believe that!'

Colbeck took a deep breath before recounting details of the escape of Jeremy Oxley. He explained the role played by a female accomplice. He also pointed out that the couple had recently taken part in a robbery in Birmingham. The money that Adnam assumed had been saved by his daughter during her time as a governess had instead been stolen. In short, since her father had received a number of similar payments over the years, he had been living unwittingly on the proceeds of crime.

'Do you still claim that she works in London?' asked Colbeck.

Adnam was uncertain. 'It's what she told me.'

'Did you never ask yourself some obvious questions? Why would any daughter take a train all the way to Manchester to see her father, then spend less than ten minutes with him? Why didn't Irene let you take her to the railway station? Why has she been so secretive all these years? Why does she refuse to give you the addresses of the places at which she pretends to work?' He stepped in close. 'It pains me to tell you that Irene Adnam is a thief and a killer. She is working with a man whose criminal record includes violence and murder. It's your duty to help us to find them.'

Adnam was disconsolate. Pride in what he

saw as his daughter's achievements was the one last source of pleasure in his life. It kept him afloat in the noisome swamp where he lived. Of equal importance was the fact that Irene supplied him – albeit irregularly – with money. At a stroke, the major prop in his grim existence had been cut from under him. There would be no more cash from Irene and no more opportunities to boast about her in the Eagle and Child. In fact, he would never be able to mention her name again. Adnam had refused to believe it at first but Colbeck had been authoritative. The truth was unavoidable. Why else would a Scotland Yard detective take the trouble to come to Deansgate if he did not have irrefutable proof of Irene's involvement in horrifying crimes? Adnam had fathered a monster. It was too much for him to bear. Bringing his hands up to his face, he let out a roar of pain then began to sob uncontrollably.

'Let's start again, shall we?' suggested Colbeck, gently. 'I want you to tell me once again what happened when your daughter came to see you. The most insignificant detail may turn out to be useful to us. I need you to rack your brain, Mr Adnam.'

The old man looked up. 'She's gone – Irene has gone for ever.'

'Do you want her to stay free to kill again?'

'No, no!' cried Adnam. 'Perish the thought.'

'Then help us to catch her and the man with whom she lives.'

Adnam sat up and used a filthy handkerchief to wipe away his tears. He was then in the grip of a fit of coughing that lasted for a couple of minutes. When he recovered, he turned to Colbeck.

'I've lost her, Inspector,' he said, sorrowfully.

'I fear that you lost her a long time ago, sir.'

'It's like a death. I feel bereft. Irene was all that I had between me and despair.' He stifled another sob. 'Have you ever lost a child?'

'No,' replied Colbeck, 'but I once lost someone I loved dearly. It's the reason this case has a personal dimension for me. However long it takes, I'll track down Jeremy Oxley and I fully expect to arrest your daughter at the same time.'

The cottage was in a leafy suburb of London. Built centuries earlier, it had a timber frame, small, mullioned windows, a solid oak front door, a thatched, overhanging roof and a well-tended garden at the front and the rear. Ivy covered one side of the facade while the other was ablaze with roses. There was such a sense of rural isolation that Irene could not believe they were actually in the capital city. The moment she set eyes on the house, her ambition was ignited. She wanted to live in such a quaint and captivating place, far away from the industrial centres to which she was accustomed. In addition, Irene yearned for an existence that was free from crime, the kind of quiet, uneventful life that people could expect in an area like this.

Having been told that their host had committed murder, she faced the prospect of meeting him with slight trepidation but it soon evaporated. Gordon Younger was a plump man of middle years with a reassuring smile. His bald head gleamed, his cheeks were red and his goatee beard was his only facial hair. Susanna, his wife, was even more rotund, her clothing carefully tailored to hide some of her contours. She was a poised, educated, middle-class woman who looked as if her natural milieu would have been a country vicarage. Clearly, the Youngers were not short of money. Their cottage was expensively furnished and there were gilt-framed paintings of hunting scenes on the walls.

Astonished to see Oxley after a long absence, they gave him and Irene an effusive welcome. Glad to offer accommodation to the visitors, neither Younger nor his wife asked why they had come to London. They simply accepted that their guests had a need and were happy to fulfil it. What struck Irene about the couple was the pleasure they seemed to take in each other's company.

There was an unforced togetherness about them that she envied. She wondered if she and Oxley would ever be able to achieve something similar. When she was shown up to the guest room by Susanna, she took the opportunity to probe a little.

'How long have you been here, Mrs Younger?' she asked.

'My name is Susanna as long as you're here,' said the other, with a hand on her shoulder, 'and the answer is that we've lived here for seven years. Gordon was able to retire early.'

'What did he retire from?'

'Medicine – he was a doctor.'

'It must be idyllic here.'

'We love it, Irene. Twenty years ago, this was a country village. It's starting to feel more like a city suburb now but it still has a whiff of a farming community.' She indicated the window. 'Watch that low beam when you open the window,' she warned. 'There are only two things wrong with this place – low beams and spiders in the thatch.'

'We can put up with those,' said Irene with a laugh.

She was wearing a wedding ring but she could see that Susanna was not fooled by it. Only people who'd been married could attain the kind of closeness that the Youngers had of right. Irene felt another pang of envy, hoping that Oxley had the same response.

She prayed that the cottage would not simply be a refuge for them but that it would exert a good influence and make Oxley want to emulate their hosts. Irene longed for permanence.

It was not until she and Oxley retired to bed that she was able to talk to him properly. After an excellent meal washed down by a fine wine, he was in a relaxed mood.

'This is a wonderful place,' she said. 'I've never been anywhere quite like it. What about you, Jerry?'

'It's very comfortable but a little too quiet for my liking.'

'Gordon and Susanna seem so at home here.'

'Yes, it's a big change from Bradford,' said Oxley. 'That's where I first met them.'

'Why did they leave?'

He laughed. 'Why did we leave Manchester?'

Irene was curious. 'Were they wanted by the police?'

'Gordon certainly was,' he replied, 'but he had the sense to plan his escape long before his crimes actually came to light. They are probably still searching for him in Bradford.'

'Is that where he murdered people?'

He put a finger to his lips. 'Don't ever say that in his presence. He doesn't believe that he murdered anyone. Gordon was a doctor. He took an oath to say that he'd always seek to preserve life. It's just that he felt there were certain exceptions – people whose existence was so dire and unendurable that they begged him to help them.'

'You mean that he *assisted* in their death?'

'That's one way of putting it. Gordon felt that he was performing a sacred duty. And, of course, there was a commercial aspect to it.'

'In what way?'

'It was a lot to ask of a doctor, Irene. His patients understood that. After he'd sent them painlessly to their deaths, he was rewarded by the provisions of their respective wills. That's how he came to buy this cottage,' he went on, taking in the whole building with a sweep of his hand. 'He and Susanna have retired on the proceeds of his work in Bradford, putting rich old ladies to sleep for the last time.' He pulled her close. 'Take heart from what happened to them, my love. It *is* possible to kill and to live happily ever after.'

CHAPTER EIGHT

Caleb Andrews was home earlier than usual that evening. He found his daughter reading the latest book she'd borrowed from Colbeck. Madeleine got up to give him a welcoming kiss. After hanging his cap on the peg, he went into the kitchen to wash the grime off his hands and face. When he came back in, she was putting a bookmark in place before setting her book aside.

'Who wrote that one?' he asked.

'Charles Dickens.'

'Ah, now there's a man who can make the blood race. I like his novels. When you've finished with it, I might take a look at it myself. What's it called, Maddie?'

'*American Notes,*' she answered. 'But it's not a novel. It's an account of a journey Mr Dickens made to America some years ago. It must have upset a lot of readers over there because it's very critical of the Americans.'

'So it should be,' said Andrews with acerbity. 'What did America ever do for this country except cause us a lot of trouble? I don't like Americans.'

'How can you say that, Father? You've never even met one.'

'I don't *need* to meet one.'

'It's unfair to make judgements about people like that.'

'Britain is best, Maddie, that's what I always say. I hate France, Germany, Russia and – most of all – America.'

'Yet you've never been to any of those countries.'

'Wild horses wouldn't drag me there.' He sat down opposite her. 'I spoke to Mr Pomeroy again today. He's given me an exact date. My retirement is only a matter of weeks away.'

She needed a moment for the full impact of the announcement to sink in. After all these years, it seemed unreal that her father was finally quitting a job that he loved so much. From the time when she was a small child, Madeleine remembered the way that he set off each morning with a spring in his step. Though he moaned about the long hours, inadequate pay and bad weather he had to endure, Andrews had never considered finding alternative work. Wholly committed to the railways, he was proud to serve them.

'Well,' he said, taking out his pipe and tobacco pouch, now that *I've* set a date, it's time that you and the inspector did the same.'

'Robert has promised to discuss it as soon as this case is over.'

'I'll believe that when it happens.'

Madeleine was hurt. 'He always keeps his promises.'

'Then why hasn't he taken you up the aisle before now? Each time he looks as if he's about to do so, there's a delay.' He filled the pipe with tobacco. 'Perhaps it's time for me to speak to him, man to man?'

'Don't you dare!' she warned.

'I'm only thinking of you, Maddy.'

'We just have to wait until Robert is ready.'

'That means you'll have to wait for ever,' he grumbled. 'Look how long you had to twiddle your thumbs while you waited for a proposal of marriage. It was years and years.'

'We had an understanding, Father.'

'Well, it's about time that Inspector Colbeck and I had a sort of understanding. I'm fed up with seeing my daughter moping around the house all day while the man she's supposed to marry keeps feeding her one excuse after another.'

'It's not like that,' she argued, 'and I certainly don't mope.'

'I'll want privacy when I retire, Maddy, and there's something else I'm looking forward to as well.'

'What's that?'

'Playing with my grandchildren, of course – where are they?'

She was startled. 'Father!'

'You can't leave these things too late,' he cautioned.

Even from her mother, Madeleine would have found such advice intrusive. From her father it was embarrassing. Like many young women on the verge of marriage, she was prepared to leave such decisions to Mother Nature, then react to them accordingly. She certainly did not wish to discuss the prospects of raising a family when she had yet to

140

wear a wedding ring. All that Madeleine longed for was to share her life with Colbeck. To do that, she was willing to be patient and forbearing.

For his own and for his daughter's sake, Andrews was keen to see a resolution at the altar. At the same time, however, he did not want to upset Madeleine. He lit his pipe and puffed away at it before taking up the conversation again. His tone was much softer.

'Dirk Sowerby was married only four months after the betrothal,' he said, meaningfully.

'His wife is welcome to him,' she replied. 'I'd have no desire to spend my life with a man like that.'

'What's wrong with Dirk?'

'I could never love him, Father.'

He was indignant. 'Is that because he works on the railway?'

'You know that it isn't.'

'Are you so high and mighty that you look down on us now?'

'No,' she said with vehemence, 'and you must never think that. I'm the daughter of an engine driver and I always will be.' She pointed to her easel. 'Do you think I'd spend all my time painting trains if I regarded railwaymen with contempt? It's unfair even to suggest it. Nobody could ever accuse me of looking down on you.'

'Very well,' he said, shamefacedly. 'I take

141

that back.'

'Thank you.'

'But I still worry for you, Maddy.' He pulled on his pipe. 'Do you remember what you once said to me?'

'I've said lots of things – but you take no notice of them.'

'This was about Inspector Colbeck. I felt that he was dragging his feet and keeping you waiting. You made an odd comment.'

'Did I?'

'Yes, Maddy. You said that there were times when it seemed as if his mind was elsewhere. He was distracted and rather sad. It was almost as if he was mourning someone.'

'You're right,' she recalled. 'I did say that.'

'And do you still believe it?'

'I don't think so. It was just a feeling I had at the time.'

'Suppose that there *was* someone in his past?' said Andrews, tentatively. 'He's a handsome man with good prospects. You weren't the first woman to notice that. I just wonder if he's been disappointed in love and that that's made him very cautious.' He shifted his pipe to the other side of his mouth. 'Has he said anything to you on the subject?'

She was firm. 'No, Father.'

'Are you sure?'

'Yes, I am.'

'There hasn't been anyone else, then?'

The question was like the jab of a needle and it hurt. Madeleine could not muster a reply. She had always felt slight concern about Colbeck's earlier life, especially as he seldom talked about it. Once they had become formally engaged, her anxiety about his past had vanished. Her father had now awakened it. It was as if an old wound had been reopened and it was smarting. When she tried to dismiss the whole thing from her mind, it remained stubbornly in place like a tiny stain on a carpet that she could always see out of the corner of her eye. It was worrying. Rising abruptly from her chair, she headed for the kitchen.

'I'll get your supper,' she said, briskly.

Edward Tallis was halfway through one of his pungent cigars. It was a signal that he was under stress once more. When he entered the superintendent's office, Colbeck could barely see him through the fug. He waved a hand to disperse some of the smoke.

'Do you mind if I open a window, sir?' he asked.

'Please do,' urged Tallis, stubbing out the cigar in an ashtray. 'I smoke far too many of these things.'

'That's your privilege, Superintendent.'

'They help me to relax and that's something I always need to do after an interview with the press. I've had a posse of journalists in here, hounding me for details of the investigation and demanding to know why we've made no arrests as yet.'

Colbeck opened the window and took in a lungful of clean air. A light breeze blew in, making the smoke swirl and eddy. He walked back to the front of the desk. It was evening and, after his visit to Manchester, he had come straight to Scotland Yard this time instead of calling on Madeleine beforehand.

Tallis glowered at him. 'I am in need of good news, Inspector.'

'Then you'll be pleased to know that we have identified Irene Adnam as the woman implicated in the murder of the two policemen.'

'Do you know where she is?'

'No, sir.'

'Have you any idea where she might be?'

'Not at the moment,' confessed Colbeck.

'Then how can this possibly be construed as good news?'

'It will enable us to turn the press from our enemies into our friends.' Tallis gave a mirthless laugh. 'Yes, I know that they often take a hostile attitude towards you, sir, but they are our best means of tracking down Miss Adnam. If we issue a description of her, it can be published in every national newspaper and in provincial editions in places like Birmingham, Wolverhampton and Manchester.'

'I want to be persuaded that we have the right person first.'

'I spoke with her father. He lives in Deansgate.'

'That's a very deprived part of Manchester, as I recall.'

'Mr Adnam has fallen on hard times.'

Colbeck described his meeting with the man and explained how astounded he'd been to learn that his daughter had been involved in criminal activities for a number of years. He absolved Adnam of any blame. All that he could be accused of was being too naive. Irene had been so plausible that he believed the lies she was telling him. Once he'd been confronted with the truth, he'd condemned his daughter's crime spree and readily answered all of Colbeck's questions. As a result, the inspector had a record of all the times she had visited her father and a list of the places at which she claimed to have worked.

'In other words,' said Colbeck, 'she still has sufficient care for Mr Adnam to want to relieve his distress.'

Tallis was harsh. 'That won't stop her from being hanged,' he promised. 'A few good deeds are heavily outweighed by the bad ones. Irene Adnam is evil. She and Oxley are clearly birds of a feather.'

'They'll be hiding somewhere until the

hue and cry passes. The only way to smoke them out is by using the press.'

'I'll summon the hungry jackals in the morning.'

'Send word to them now, sir,' urged Colbeck. 'The sooner we have the nation looking for this pair, the better. If we hurry, we might catch the later editions.'

'I'd prefer to make a concerted effort tomorrow, Inspector. That way we can ensure that national and provincial newspapers carry the information at the same time. The wider the coverage, the more chance we have of flushing them out of cover.' Reaching for a pencil, he moved the oil lamp closer so that it shed its glow over the pad in front of him. 'I'll need an exact description.'

'I've already written it down,' said Colbeck, taking a sheet of folded paper from his pocket. 'This combines what I was told by the woman's father and by her former employer, Mr Holte.' He handed it over. 'But it will not be as accurate as I could wish. According to Mr Adnam, she was fond of play-acting as a child and was skilled at changing her appearance.'

'The hangman will change it even more,' said Tallis, sourly. After glancing at the paper, he looked up at Colbeck. 'What about Sergeant Leeming and Constable Peebles?'

'They took part in the search and visited two addresses while I was in Deansgate. For obvious reasons, their efforts were in vain.'

'I was really asking how they got along together.'

'There was no friction between them, sir. Why should there be?'

'I sensed that the sergeant was very unhappy to be forced to work with a new recruit. Leeming was less than welcoming to him. Is that a fair assessment?'

'He might have had a few reservations about Constable Peebles, sir, but they disappeared in the line of duty. While they were on their way to a house in Manchester, they were set on by four ruffians.'

Tallis was alarmed. 'Was either of them hurt?'

'No,' replied Colbeck. 'They turned the tables on their attackers and put them to flight. Victor – Sergeant Leeming – was very complimentary about the way that the constable had fought. Any slight differences that might have existed between them have now been eradicated.'

'That's good to hear. Mutual respect is vital in this department.'

'In the case of Constable Peebles, it's rather more than respect.'

'What do you mean?'

'It transpires that he's been following the cases that we've been handling on the railways. As well as discharging his duties as a policeman in A Division, he somehow found time to compile a scrapbook of our successes. He draws inspiration from them.'

'I find no fault in that.'

'Neither do I, sir,' said Colbeck. 'My only worry is that he may let admiration blind him to our shortcomings. None of us is infallible.'

'Quite so – Homer sometimes nods.'

'Quandoque bonus dormitat Homerus.'

Tallis scowled. 'What heathen tongue is that?'

'It's the Latin you just translated. I think it was rather astute of you to pick up on my use of the word "blind" and mention Homer, the famous blind poet.'

'It just came to me,' said Tallis, relishing praise for something that was entirely coincidental. 'So we are celebrated in a scrapbook, are we? I find that heartening.'

'I think you should, Superintendent,' said Colbeck, tongue in cheek. 'After all, any triumphs we have to our credit have been secured under your aegis. Your control of our efforts has been decisive. I know that you loathe the press,' he went on, 'but they have trumpeted our successes from time to time. Your name is probably on every page of the constable's scrapbook.'

Tallis's broad grin was like the beam of a lighthouse.

It was the tranquillity that she appreciated

most. Irene had never had such a peaceful night. Even in a hotel, the hustle and bustle of city life could be heard outside the windows. Then there was the ever-present noise of trains hurtling along. That, too, had gone. In its place were gentler sounds that allowed her to sleep undisturbed. She awoke refreshed and happy. Irene at last felt safe.

'How long are we going to stay here?' she asked.

'Until they stop searching so hard for us,' replied Oxley. 'In the wake of a murder, the police will do all they can to find the suspects. The longer the hunt goes on, however, the fewer resources they can devote to it. Other crimes are being committed and they'll demand attention. We simply have to wait until we fade into the past.'

'We mustn't outstay our welcome, Jerry.'

'Don't you like it here?'

'I love it – but we can't impose on Gordon and Susanna.'

'They say that we can stay as long as we like.'

She was worried. 'Do they know what we did?'

'No, Irene,' he told her. 'They don't know and won't ask.'

'Shouldn't we tell them?'

'We've told them all they need to know by turning up here. We need a hiding place. They're intelligent enough to work out why.'

It was glorious weather. They were seated on a rustic bench in the garden, listening to the insects buzz and watching the birds hop from branch to branch among the trees. It all served to intensify Irene's ambition to live in such a place and to stop being on the move all the time.

'All we have to do is to copy what they did,' resumed Oxley. 'Gordon and Susanna showed us how it was done. When he was in danger of being exposed in Bradford, Gordon fled here to the house he'd bought in readiness. The police searched everywhere for them but to no avail. Mind you,' he added with a chuckle, 'they did take the precaution of changing their names.'

'Do you mean that they're not Dr and Mrs Younger?'

'I mean exactly that, Irene. I'll let you into a secret.' He put his lips close to her ear. 'Gordon and Susanna are false names as well.'

'What are their real names?'

'They don't exist anymore. They have new identities, a new house and a new life. Gordon is not a retired doctor anymore. Everyone here thinks that he used to be an archaeologist. His hobby is poking around in old ruins, so it's not a complete lie.'

'I can see why they've never been caught,' said Irene, admiringly. 'The police are looking for a doctor and his wife, not an archaeologist with a totally different name.' A question nudged her. 'But what about birth certificates and such like?'

'You can always get forgeries, if you have enough money.'

'I used to forge my own references.'

'There you are,' said Oxley, slipping an arm around her. 'You're a woman of many talents, Irene.'

'I had to be. I wasn't going to spend my life in domestic service. One day at the beck and call of someone else taught me that.'

They heard a rattle of cups and turned to see a servant bringing out a tray. Susanna followed and Gordon shambled after her, his pate gilded by the sun. Seated in a semicircle, the four of them were soon enjoying a cup of tea.

'Do you have any plans for today?' enquired Younger.

'None at all,' replied Oxley.

'How well do you know London?'

'I know it extremely well.'

'I don't,' said Irene. 'I'm a Manchester lass. I've never really had the chance to take a proper look at London.'

'Then we can remedy that for you,' said Younger.

'Yes,' said his wife. 'The nearest station is about a mile away. We can catch a train to Euston from there and spend the afternoon exploring. What would you like to see, Irene?'

Her reply was instant. 'Buckingham Palace,' she declared. 'I've always wanted to see that. When I was a little girl, my father promised that he'd take me there one day but he never did.' She looked from Susanna to Gordon. 'Can we go to Buckingham Palace, please?'

'We can go wherever you like,' said Younger, indulgently. 'I'd like to put in a plea for St Paul's cathedral.'

'Don't forget Trafalgar Square,' his wife reminded him. 'Irene must see Nelson's statue. What about you, Jerry?' she continued, turning to him. 'Where would you like to go?'

'Oh, there's only one place I'd choose,' he told her.

'And where's that?'

'Scotland Yard.'

Now that he'd got to know Peebles a little better, Victor Leeming no longer felt the same antipathy towards him. His dog-like willingness was still irritating but it was balanced by some excellent qualities. Peebles was brave, determined and inquisitive. Conscious of his deficiencies, he was always trying to repair them by firing an endless series of questions at his senior colleagues. He learnt quickly and was invariably grateful for advice. Leeming slowly warmed to him.

'Is this what being a detective means?' asked Peebles. 'Yesterday we charged up to

Manchester and pounded the streets in search of the father of a suspect. Today we're stuck here in Scotland Yard.'

'We have to wait until we have evidence of their whereabouts,' said Leeming. 'It's different from being a policeman on the beat. When you see a crime being committed there, you can wade in at once and arrest the culprit. You respond immediately to a given situation.'

Peebles grinned. 'Aye, I've done that often enough.'

'Things sometimes move more slowly here. We're involved in a cat-and-mouse game, so we have to be patient. As soon as the villains make a mistake – and they usually do – we spring into action. Have no fears, Constable, there'll be time to use those fists of yours again. Meanwhile, we have to rely on our brains.'

Colbeck had given the two men the use of his office and left them all the information pertaining to Jeremy Oxley and Irene Adnam that he could gather. They studied the sheets of paper and put them in chronological order. Most of the records related to Oxley but his accomplice had not been idle. Three different members of polite society in Manchester had been deceived into taking her on as a governess and each time she'd done a moonlight flit with a substantial haul. Ambrose Holte had been her first trusting employer. For each of her subsequent appointments, Irene had used other names. Thanks to Inspector Boone, who had provided the information, they had some indication of the way in which she operated. What was not clear from the collection of papers was when Oxley and Irene had started to work together.

'The problem is that Miss Adnam has never been caught,' said Leeming, 'so we have no details of an arrest. Jeremy Oxley, on the other hand, has been arrested twice but never convicted. On both occasions, he managed to escape. I think we both know how.'

'Money changed hands,' observed Peebles.

'It's one of the things that really makes me mad. Rich people are the most difficult to convict. No matter how black their crimes, they can buy their way out of trouble. Oxley must've made a small fortune over the years. He'll always be able to offer a juicy bribe.'

'That's a crime in itself, Sergeant.'

'Only to those who recognise it as such,' said Leeming. 'I'm afraid that a certain constable in Wolverhampton let his greed take precedence over his duty. The five pounds he accepted was the price of a prisoner's escape. Now that they have him locked up, they'll make him suffer and he thoroughly deserves it.'

'There is a pattern here,' noted Peebles, separating out some sheets of paper. 'These offences here all relate to Oxley. He either inveigles his way into people's confidence before robbing them, or he uses an accomplice to distract someone so that he can grab what he wants.' He clicked his tongue. 'I just wish that we had more detail in these records. We ought to know more about the people we arrest.'

'Inspector Colbeck thinks the day will come when we actually have photographs of villains. Think what a help that would be.'

'It will happen eventually,' said Peebles, 'though it may take some time yet. So far nobody has invented the sort of camera that we can use on a regular basis to photograph criminals. It's a pity. I'd dearly love to see a photograph of Irene Adnam.'

'I want to see one of Jeremy Oxley as well.'

'You'll have to wait until you meet him in the flesh.'

'He's the real criminal,' asserted Leeming. 'Women are the fairer sex. They don't usually have the urge to kill in cold blood. Most of them would be too afraid even to hold a gun, let alone fire it. *He* made her do it. Oxley dragged her down to his own level. If you look at her record, there's no hint of violence in it. It was Oxley who turned her into a murderer.'

Peebles picked up two sheets of paper and compared them.

'The wonder is that we have so much information about him,' he remarked. 'Many of the crimes didn't even take place in London. How did they come to our attention?'

'The inspector made sure that they did.'

'He's been after Oxley for a long time, hasn't he?'

'Oh, yes,' said Leeming. 'Every time the name has cropped up, Inspector Colbeck has made a note of it. Sometimes, of course, Oxley takes on a new identity as he befriends a victim before robbing him. The inspector can always spot if he is the culprit because the man works in a particular way. There's a phrase for it.'

'Modus operandi.'

'Yes – that's it.'

'When criminals find a method that works, they stick to it.'

'There's another side to that. It's a question of superstition. They do everything in exactly the same way because they're afraid to fail if they don't. We all have superstitions of one kind or another. I know that I do. My wife teases me about some of them.'

'Coming back to Oxley,' said Peebles, 'why has the inspector singled him out for special attention?'

'It's because of something that happened years ago before he even joined the Metropolitan Police Force. Oxley killed someone who was going to act as a witness against him in court. The crime has preyed on the inspector's mind ever since,' said Leeming. 'He felt that he was in some way to blame. It's what drives him on to catch Oxley. He wants to avenge the death of a young lady called Helen Millington.'

Edward Tallis loathed the gentlemen of the press with a passion that never dimmed but Colbeck took a more tolerant view of them. What irked him was that newspapers either praised him to the skies or excoriated him for his mistakes or for what they wrongly perceived as his slowness. There seemed to be no middle ground between applause and condemnation, no recognition of the fact that crimes could not be solved to satisfy the deadlines of editors and that progress was being made on a case even if it was not apparent to the jaundiced eye of reporters. To the superintendent, the handful of men he'd reluctantly invited into his office that day were unprincipled scribblers who'd been put on this earth solely in order to bait him. In Colbeck's view, by contrast, they were a vital tool in the fight against crime if they were used correctly. The problem was that neither he nor his superior had any control over what they actually wrote.

'Good morning, gentlemen,' said Tallis, looking truculently around his guests as if ready to challenge one of them to a fight. 'I know that you prefer to deal in wild sensation but I must ask you to take a less hysterical approach to an investigation for once.'

'This is a sensational crime, Superintendent,' argued one of the men. 'We have a shooting, a daring escape and two policemen sliced to pieces beneath the wheels of a train. You cannot expect us to report that as an everyday event.'

'All I ask is that you report the known facts instead of giving the impression that we are unequal to the task of finding the culprits.'

The man was blunt. 'We write what we see.'

Colbeck winced. Before the press conference was called, he'd urged Tallis to make sure that he did not antagonise them at the very start, yet that was exactly what his superior had just done. The superintendent's tone became more belligerent and insults from both sides were soon flying around the room like so many angry wasps. Colbeck tried to rise above the fray and let his mind settle on an aspect of the case that was unknown to any of the journalists.

The fate of Helen Millington continued to preoccupy him. He felt very sorry for the jeweller who'd been Oxley's first victim and had never forgotten the man's bravery in trying to pursue a thief. He'd also been deeply shocked by the recent murders of the two Wolverhampton policemen. The difference between them and Helen was that their occupation exposed them to risk and they had understood that when they put on the uniform. Not that either of them could ever have expected to suffer such a hideous end. Serious injuries were common among all constabularies but killings were thankfully rare.

Three things set Helen's untimely death apart from that of the others. First, she was a woman. The daughter of a financier, she was young, beautiful and well educated. Second, she posed no physical threat to Oxley. The jeweller had chased him with the intention of overpowering him and the two policemen had him handcuffed. Even had she wished to do so, Helen could not hurt Oxley. Nor was she in any position to defend herself against a violent attack. She was too slight, frail and vulnerable. But it was the third factor that weighed most with the inspector. In the course of the various meetings with Helen Millington, coaxing, advising and supporting her, Colbeck had fallen in love and his feelings had been requited.

'You were summoned here,' Tallis said, eyeing his visitors with disdain, 'so that we could demonstrate that we have made progress in this investigation.'

'Have you made any arrests?' demanded a voice.

'Not as yet, I fear.'

'Then no real progress has been made. For once, it seems, your much-vaunted Inspector Colbeck has come off the rails.'

The titter of amusement brought Colbeck out of his reverie.

'Actually,' he said, 'there *has* been an arrest. I must correct the superintendent on that point. During our visit to Wolverhampton, we discovered that a Constable Marner had been tricked into giving away information that led to the escape of Jeremy Oxley. He accepted a bribe of five pounds. He is now in custody and, as you may imagine, reviled by his colleagues. One of the murder victims, incidentally, was his brother-in-law.'

The reporters started to write excitedly in their notebooks. During the brief lull, Colbeck mimed a message to Tallis that he should be less aggressive and hand over the task of talking to them. With obvious reluctance, the older man agreed to the request.

'I will make way now for Inspector Colbeck,' he said, continuing the laboured metaphor, 'who – I think you'll find – has not come off the rails at all but is steaming along the track at full speed.'

Some muted jeers were hidden away in the polite laughter.

'Thank you, sir,' said Colbeck with a nod at Tallis. 'As a result of visits to Manchester, some important new facts have come to light. They relate to the female accomplice who assisted in the escape. The post-mortem on the remains of the two policemen established that one of them had been shot through the skull at close range. The person who fired that shot was a young woman by the name of Irene Adnam.'

He spelt the name for them and set the pencils off again. Colbeck praised Inspector Zachary Boone for the help given him in Manchester and explained how he had tracked down the woman's father. He told them that Irene and Oxley would be hiding somewhere together and that their newspapers could be the means of catching them. The large reward on offer would, he hoped, encourage anyone who had spotted them to come forward.

'The description of Irene Adnam that I'm about to give you,' he said with easy authority, 'is based on conversations with two people who knew her well – her father and a former employer. Her criminal career began in Manchester where, as you will hear, she left a number of victims in her wake.'

Colbeck went on to give details of her age, height, build, weight and hair colouring. He also mentioned that her voice had traces of a Manchester accent. Her father had described her as very lovely, and even the embittered Ambrose Holte had conceded that she had both physical appeal and natural charm. What had fooled the mill owner was her abiding air of innocence. As he offered them additional details of the woman, she began to take shape before him and did so in such clear outline that he was jolted. Colbeck had met her before. If he omitted the list of her crimes and her local accent, he could be talking about someone else entirely. The coincidence was so unexpected that it brought him to a sudden halt.

Age, height, build, weight and hair colouring – it was uncanny. Even the air of purity was an exact match. In every particular, he had just been describing Helen Millington.

CHAPTER NINE

Having taken a train to Euston, they hired two cabs to convey them to Trafalgar Square. It was carpeted by pigeons whose strutting boldness amazed Irene. Instead of taking to the air as she approached, they simply dodged her feet and continued to hunt for food on the paved slabs. One even perched on the knee of a beggar as he lay propped in a stupor up against a wall. Younger and his wife had visited the square too often to be overwhelmed by its scale and magnificence. Oxley, too, had seen it many times and was once again assessing the opportunities afforded to pickpockets by people gazing fixedly up at Horatio Nelson and therefore off guard. To Irene, however, the whole area was a thing of wonder and she was mesmerised by the fluted Corinthian column of Devonshire granite. She stared up at the statue of the nation's great naval hero.

'How on earth did they get it up there?' she asked.

'Very slowly, I should imagine,' said Younger.

'It's so high.'

'They built a wooden scaffold to help them erect the column, then they must have winched up the statue.' He pointed to the bronze bas-reliefs at the base of the column. 'Those were cast from cannon taken from enemy ships captured by Nelson in battle.'

'Gordon can even tell you which battles they represent,' said Susanna, fondly. 'He loves that kind of detail about the past.'

'History has always been my passion,' he agreed.

'Well, I always look to the future instead of the past,' said Oxley. 'I want to know what tomorrow holds for me and not what a one-eyed admiral did all those years ago at sea.'

'Jerry!' chided Irene. 'You should show some respect.'

'Why?'

'Nelson was one of the greatest sailors of

all time,' Younger reminded him. 'He defeated the French at Trafalgar even though his fleet was outnumbered. Unfortunately, he died during the action.' He tossed a glance upward. 'If anyone deserves to be honoured, it's Nelson.'

Oxley was no longer listening. His attention had shifted to an urchin who'd been mingling with the crowd and who was in the act of removing a wallet from an unsuspecting sightseer. Oxley had no desire to warn the victim. He sided instinctively with the criminal. He wanted to step forward and advise the boy to take more time. Sudden movement would alert the man. The urchin was too hasty. His final snatch of the wallet made his victim turn round and clap a hand to his pocket. The boy darted off into the throng. Yelling in outrage, the man went after him, but Oxley came to the lad's aid. Stepping sharply to the left, he deliberately collided with the victim to slow him down then showered him with apologies. By the time the man continued his pursuit, it was too late. The boy had vanished. Oxley smiled at what he considered to be a good deed. Irene was puzzled.

'What happened?' she asked.

'I don't know,' replied Oxley, innocently.

'Someone just robbed that man,' said Younger.

'No wonder he seemed so angry.'

'He ran straight into you.'

Irene was sympathetic. 'Were you hurt, Jerry?'

'No,' said Oxley, holding his lapels to straighten his frock coat. 'I hardly felt a thing. The truth of it is that he came off far worse than me because I'm bigger and stronger. Come on,' he added, 'let's walk down White-hall to see Scotland Yard. That's far more interesting to me than Nelson's column.'

He led the way through the crowd, wondering how long it would be before the irate man into whom he'd just bumped rea-lised that, in the process of doing so, Oxley had deftly relieved him of his gold watch.

Colbeck had been impressed by Ian Peebles. To begin with, the new recruit was unfail-ingly polite. It was not always the case with those whose formative years had been spent in the army. Edward Tallis, for instance, had no truck with politeness. It was a foreign concept to him and foreigners were, by definition, creatures to be shunned. The habit of command had deprived him of conversational niceties. He issued orders with the splenetic zeal of one who expected them to be obeyed without question. Unlike the superintendent, Peebles had not been an officer but he had risen to the rank of army sergeant and was thus used to drilling those under his authority. Beneath his youthful exterior, there was palpably a core of steel. Even in his short time in the department, he'd shown flashes of inspiration. Colbeck believed that he would turn out to be a formidable detective.

It was detection of another kind that prompted Peebles. When he found himself alone with Colbeck in the latter's office, he asked the question he'd be saving up for such a moment.

'Is it true that you're about to get married, Inspector?'

'Yes, it is.'

'Have you set a date for the wedding?'

'It's ... under discussion,' said Colbeck.

'Catherine and I have already started to make arrangements. It will be a quiet affair as neither of us has a large family. That's all to the good in my mind. I hate fuss of any kind. I simply want to be with the woman I adore.'

Colbeck thought about Madeleine. 'We have that ambition in common.'

'Where will you get married?

'The parish church in Camden. Madeleine has worshipped there since she was a small child. As in your case, we anticipate a very quiet wedding.'

'Are you going to invite the superintendent?'

'Oh, no,' said Colbeck, laughing. 'He will certainly not be invited and, even if he were, he would certainly refuse to attend. I don't wish to put him in a position where he has to turn down the invitation.'

'It's strange, isn't it?' mused Peebles. 'I'm talking about the way that your life can turn full circle as a result of a chance meeting. To be honest with you, I never thought that I'd ever get married. I had few opportunities to spend time in mixed company and fewer still to meet eligible young women. Besides,' he said with a self-effacing smile, 'I never considered that I had much to offer. I'm not the sort of person who courts the mirror or who has a large income to dangle in front of a prospective wife. I was prepared to stay married to the army instead. Then I met Catherine…'

'And she rearranged your priorities for you, I daresay.'

'It was rather frightening how quickly it all happened. I had no control whatsoever over it. Was it the same for you, Inspector?'

'Not quite,' said Colbeck, unwilling to confide too much about his own situation. 'The demands of my work tended to slow everything down. But,' he went on, changing the subject, 'we shouldn't be revelling in our own good fortune. The relationship on which we should concentrate is that between Jeremy Oxley and Irene Adnam. Though it falls well short of marriage, it's just as binding in their minds. They are conjoined by murder. That makes them especially dangerous and I speak for her as well as for him. People who kill once will have few qualms about doing so again. We must beware.'

'I faced death many times in the army.'

'Yes, Constable, but you had a weapon with which to defend yourself. The rules of engagement are different now. We have neither rifles nor any other firearm. Our weapons are intelligence, swiftness of re-action and surprise. We must deploy all three. At the moment, of course, Oxley and Adnam think themselves supremely safe. That will change dramatically.'

'Why is that, Inspector?'

'We've tried to harness the power of the press. Until today, everyone was wondering about the identity of Oxley's mysterious female accomplice. Her name will be voiced abroad tomorrow.'

'What effect do you think that will have?'

'I'm hoping that it will be twofold,' said Colbeck. 'With luck, it will prompt mem-bers of the general public to come forward with details of sightings of the couple. *Somebody* must have seen them and nothing jogs the memory as much as the promise of a large reward. The other consequence is obvious.'

'It will put the wind up the pair of them.'

Colbeck nodded. 'I think they'll panic

and, when people do that, they usually act on impulse. Oxley and Adnam will know that time is running out for them. They may well bolt from their hiding place.'

Madeleine made breakfast that morning with a sense of duty tinged with sadness. It was only a matter of weeks before her father could stay in bed for as long as he liked. Retirement would revolutionise their lives. It was an unsettling thought. Routine had been the salvation of Caleb Andrews. When his wife had died, he'd been inconsolable and his daughter had had to bear the crushing weight of his grief as well as her own sorrow. She'd rescued him from complete collapse by adhering to a strict routine, waking him for breakfast in the morning and having supper ready for him when he returned in the evening. On the occasions when he had time off, she insisted on taking him for a walk or invited friends and relatives to visit them. Madeleine never let her father be on his own for any length of time when he might surrender to his anguish. On Sundays she first went to church then visited her mother's grave with him.

Shared bereavement drew them together and deepened their love. It took a long time for Andrews to emerge from the long, dark tunnel of his misery. When he'd finished blinking in the light and could see properly again, he realised just how much he'd depended on Madeleine and how much responsibility she'd had to shoulder. He felt guilty that he'd unintentionally turned her into a cook, domestic servant and nurse. Caring for him for endless months had deprived her of any independent life. It was time that could never be clawed back. He was deeply in her debt. He liked to think that he'd repaid some of that debt when the injuries he received during a train robbery had led directly to Madeleine's friendship with Robert Colbeck.

'Are you certain that you told him, Maddy?' he asked.

'Eat your breakfast.'

'Does he know that I was driving that particular train?'

'Yes, Father,' she said, cutting a slice off the loaf of bread, 'I made a point of telling him.'

'Then why hasn't he made the effort to see me? I can recount exactly what happened.'

'I think he's following other lines of enquiry.'

'Dirk Sowerby and I were *there*.'

'So were all the passengers on the train but Robert doesn't think it worthwhile to interview any of them because nobody actually witnessed the shooting and the escape.'

'I'd still like to be involved, Maddy.'

'You need to be involved on another train,'

she warned him, 'and you'll be late if you dawdle over your breakfast.'

'I'll walk to work faster,' he said through a mouthful of food. 'And if you do see him again, tell him I ought to be consulted about this case. I've got a theory about that woman, you see.'

'Tell it to Dirk Sowerby.'

Gobbling the remainder of his breakfast, he washed it down with some tea then got ready to leave. As she gave him his farewell kiss, he pulled her close.

'I haven't forgotten what you did for me, Maddy,' he said with sudden emotion. 'But for you, I'd have died of grief. I was a heavy cross for you to bear. It was selfish of me to impose on you like that.'

She kissed him again. 'That's what daughters are for.'

'Well, I won't be a burden for much longer. When I retire from the railway, you can leave me to my own devices and start to enjoy life on your own.' Nudging her in the ribs, he gave a low cackle. 'Well, maybe not entirely on your own.'

'Off you go, Father,' she said, opening the door.

'Are you throwing me out?' he complained.

'Yes I am, and I have only one request.'

'What's that?'

'Make sure that you bring the newspaper home with you.'

'Supposing that I forget?' he teased.

'Then I'll forget to cook you supper.'

He cackled again. 'In that case, you'll have your newspaper. It's important for you to keep abreast of what's happening in the world.'

'There's only one thing that interests me at the moment,' she told him. 'I want to know how the investigation is going. Robert was unfairly criticised in yesterday's edition. I hope that they have the grace to recognise his qualities in today's paper.'

Face contorted with fury, Tallis read the article in *The Times* aloud.

'"Days have now elapsed since the discovery of two inhuman murders and the perpetrators of these unspeakable deeds are, we regret to say, still at liberty to kill again. Surely the distinguished Railway Detective can do better than this? The public has a right to expect certain standards from our police and they have fallen woefully below those standards in this instance. If Superintendent Tallis and Inspector Colbeck suffer these devils to remain at liberty, they will inflict on themselves indelible disgrace..."'

Scrunching the newspaper up, Tallis hurled it to the floor and reached for a cigar. Not daring to move, Leeming remained motionless but Colbeck retrieved the paper and smoothed it between his hands.

'They did name Irene Adnam,' he pointed out, 'and that, after all, was the object of the exercise.'

Tallis smouldered. 'They can never resist a chance to attack me,' he said. 'Newspapers are a despicable invention.'

'Our lives would be a struggle without them, sir. Set against their defects are many virtues. All that you read was one article out of many. Read the whole newspaper and you'll see the range of its coverage. It's a mine of useful information.'

'Superintendent Tallis is an incompetent idiot – is that what you call useful information?'

'You've been called worse, sir,' Leeming put in cheerily before recoiling from the superintendent's icy glare. 'There's one thing that we may be sure of, I fancy. Constable Peebles will not wish to include anything from that article in his scrapbook. It suggests that the police only recruit imbeciles.'

'The other newspapers were less trenchant,' noted Colbeck. 'Each and every one of them did what we asked and identified Irene Adnam as the person who shot Constable Wakeley. That will cause an enormous shock. Who would expect a young woman to be capable of such a heinous crime?'

'That's what Estelle said to me.'

'Sergeant Leeming,' growled Tallis.

'Yes, sir?'

'Your wife has no place in this discussion.'

'Estelle was only expressing a common opinion.'

'It's irrelevant to the investigation. I've told you before about quoting Mrs Leeming as if she has some kind of auxiliary role as a detective. She does not and never will have,' he said before biting off the end of his cigar and spitting it into the wastepaper basket. 'So please do not mention her name again. Learn from Colbeck. He never drags in the uninformed comments of the lady who is about to become *his* wife. A woman's place is in the home – leave her there.'

'If you say so, Superintendent,' replied Leeming.

'And you might pass on that advice to Constable Peebles.'

'I will, sir.'

'He's rather prone to mention the lady in *his* life.'

'That's only natural.'

'No woman will ever trespass on our work here.'

Leeming shot Colbeck a glance. He was aware that Madeleine had assisted in a number of investigations and was grateful for the help she'd been able to give. Tallis sniffed conspiracy.

'What's going on?' he demanded.

'Nothing, sir,' said Leeming, feeling his collar tighten.

'You gave the inspector a meaningful look.'

'I think you're mistaken.'

'I'm never mistaken about you,' said Tallis, lighting his cigar with some difficulty. 'I can read you like a book, Sergeant, though it is not one that I'd recommend to anyone else. The prose is dull, the plot is laboured and its main character is fatally hindered by his many limitations.'

'You're being very unjust to Sergeant Leeming,' said Colbeck, stepping in to defend him. 'If you care to look back over the years, you'll be reminded of the countless occasions when the sergeant showed immense courage in the course of his duties. During our time in France, for example, he risked his life and bore the marks to prove it. I suggest that you read the book named Victor Leeming more carefully in future, Superintendent,' he went on, indicating his friend. 'If you do that, you'll find that it has a most admirable hero.'

Leeming came close to blushing. He had never received such unstinting praise in that office before and – although it came from Colbeck rather than Tallis – it lifted his spirits. In his opinion, it was Colbeck who'd just shown true heroism. Leeming could never have spoken so forcefully to the superintendent. There was another bonus. Tallis had the grace to look abashed

and to mumble an apology. As another pre-
cedent was set, Leeming grinned from ear
to ear.

'It's good of you to apologise, sir,' said
Colbeck, holding up the newspaper. 'I trust
that the author of this article about us will
follow your example. When we make our
arrests, he'll have to admit that his criticism
of us was ill-judged.'

'First of all,' said Tallis, now half-hidden
by a cloud of cigar smoke, 'we have to find
these devils.'

'The press will do that for us.'

'A big reward always gets a good response,'
noted Leeming. 'Even those who may be
hiding the villains will be tempted by that
amount of money.'

'I'm not so much concerned about them,'
said Colbeck. 'We may get a flood of
information but much of it will be false and
misleading. The most important readers are
Oxley and Adnam. When they pick up a
newspaper today, they are in for a fright.'

'You're assuming that they can read,' said
Tallis scornfully. 'Most of the criminals in
this country are illiterate. They would only
reach for a newspaper when they wanted to
light a fire.'

'That's not the case here, Superintendent.
Irene Adnam's father went out of his way to
impress upon me that he'd paid for his
daughter to have a sound education and

176

Oxley is a man of more than average intelligence. This case has aroused a lot of publicity,' said Colbeck. 'Details of the investigation are printed every day. Oxley will make a point of reading the newspaper to see how close we're getting to him. When he sees that we've identified his accomplice, he'll realise that we're hot on his trail.'

'Could *we* have a house like this one day, Jerry?' pleaded Irene.

'No,' he replied.

Her face fell. 'Why not?'

'I'd want something much bigger.'

She rallied at once. 'That's wonderful!'

'We have to be ambitious.'

'Can we afford it?'

'I've got plenty of money hidden away and, as we've discovered, we can easily make more when we work together.'

'What about servants? I'll want a domestic staff.'

'You can have as many servants as you wish, Irene.'

It was something that had always rankled with her. During her childhood, she'd lived in a comfortable house and always had servants to tackle any mundane chores. When her father went into decline, she lost the security of a good home and – as they flitted from one meaner abode to another – she found herself doing jobs that had hitherto

177

been allocated to servants. The crowning disgrace was being forced to enter domestic service herself, a way of life she thought of as respectable slavery. It was after nursing rebellious thoughts against her employer that she turned to a life of crime.

'Can we ever lead a normal life?' she asked.

'Gordon and Susanna have managed to do it.'

'But their situation is rather different. Thanks to all the money he inherited from former patients, Gordon will never have to work again. They can just live contentedly here in anonymity.'

'We'll do the same one day,' he promised. 'The trick is to plan ahead as they did. Though he has no regrets about helping people in great pain to die peacefully, he knew that he was committing a crime. That's why he didn't report me when we first met. He accepted that, in the eyes of the law, we were fellow criminals. Our friendship developed from there.'

'My worry is that he and Susanna would feel impelled to report us if they knew what we did on that train.'

'There's no possibility of that happening, Irene.'

'They'd be shocked.'

'I'm sure they would,' said Oxley, 'but that doesn't mean they'd go to the police. I know too much about them. If they betrayed us, their life here would crumble to pieces when I betrayed *them*.'

Irene relaxed. 'I never thought of it that way.'

They heard a key being inserted in a lock, then there was a creak as the front door was opened. Their hosts had just returned from their morning walk. Younger and his wife came into the parlour.

'We're ready for a cup of tea,' said Younger, affably. 'Shall I ask Binnie to make some for you as well?'

'Yes, please,' said Irene. 'Did you have a nice walk?'

'It was very bracing,' replied Susanna. 'We went all the way to the railway station so that Gordon could buy a newspaper for you.'

'Heavens!' exclaimed Younger, taking the newspaper from under his arm. 'I'm forgetting my manners. Here you are, Jerry,' he went on, handing it over. 'As our guest, you should read it first.'

'Thank you,' said Oxley.

'Excuse me.'

'I'll need to speak to Binnie about luncheon,' said Susanna as she followed her husband out of the room. 'I'm not quite sure what we have in the larder.'

Left alone with Irene, Oxley sat back for what he hoped would be a leisurely read of *The Times*. Seconds later, he leapt up from his chair and stared in disbelief at the words in front of him. He read on with his mouth agape.

'They know who you are, Irene!' he gasped.

'How can they?'

'They've named you as my accomplice during the escape and given a full description of you. They've even listed some of the other crimes for which you're being sought.'

Irene was on her feet to look over his shoulder. 'That can't be true!' she cried. 'I rarely used my real name. How on earth did they connect me with you?'

'This is Colbeck's doing,' he said, angrily.

'Does that mean we're no longer safe?'

'Not as long as *he's* in charge of the investigation. Nobody else would have been able to identify you, Irene, but Colbeck managed it somehow. I told you that he was tenacious.'

She grabbed his arm. 'What are we going to do, Jerry?'

'There's only one way to keep the police at bay.'

'Is there?'

Oxley grinned malevolently. 'We have to kill Inspector Colbeck.'

The public response was immediate. Lured by the promise of a large reward, a handful of people arrived at Scotland Yard claiming to have information about the fugitives.

Gerald Kane was typical of them. He was a small, round, smirking individual in his thirties. Invited into Colbeck's office, he took a seat and rubbed his hands excitedly. Ian Peebles was there to watch the inspector in action. Colbeck was excessively civil to their visitor.

'We're most grateful to you for coming here, Mr Kane,' he said. 'I don't need to explain how important it is to catch these two people.'

'They're deep-dyed villains,' declared Kane, 'and I'm glad to be able to put them behind bars.' He looked around. 'Do I get the reward *before* I give my evidence or afterwards?'

'Let's not talk about the money at this stage, sir. We'd like to hear what you have to say so that we can assess its value to us.'

'But I saw them, Inspector. I served them.'

'Are you sure that it was Oxley and Adnam?'

'I'd swear that it was.' Kane took a deep breath before launching into what was patently a well-rehearsed speech. 'I'm a watchmaker by trade and work for Mr Berrow in Makepeace Street. Of necessity, I have excellent eyesight. Most of my time is spent repairing watches and clocks but, whenever Mr Berrow steps out of the shop, I take his place behind the counter. That's where I was yesterday when a gentleman entered with a female companion. Since she was carrying her gloves, I noticed that she was wearing a wedding ring, but I had the feeling that they were not married. Don't ask me to explain why. There was just something about them. Anyway,' he continued, 'the gentlemen wished to buy a watch for his so-called wife and I showed them what we had in the shop. They took several minutes examining them, so I had plenty of time to observe them closely. It's a habit of mine,' he said with a sycophantic smile. 'Our stock is extremely valuable. It therefore behoves us to take careful note of anyone who comes through the door. People – though I need hardly tell this to detectives – are not always what they seem.'

Colbeck already knew that he was lying but Peebles still believed they might be hearing crucial information. He was surprised when the inspector's tone hardened.

'Describe them, Mr Kane,' snapped Colbeck.

'Well, yes, I will,' said Kane, importantly.

He then proceeded to offer what was an exact recitation of the details given in the newspapers about Oxley and Adnam. Kane might have been reading them out line by line. When he finished, he beamed as if expecting applause. He rubbed his hands again.

'Can I take the reward now, please?'

'Oh, you'll get your reward, Mr Kane,'

said Colbeck. 'You'll be charged with telling lies to an officer of the law in pursuit of monetary gain. Constable Peebles...'

'Yes, Inspector?' said Peebles, stepping forward.

'Take this man out and arrest him.'

'Are you certain that he's deceiving us, sir?'

'The fellow is a barefaced liar.'

'That's not true!' howled Kane. 'I'd swear it on the Bible.'

'Then you'd be committing a form of perjury before God,' said Colbeck, 'and that's equally reprehensible. Get this man out of my sight, Constable.'

'Come on,' said Peebles, taking Kane by the collar and yanking him upright. 'By wasting our time here, you've delayed a murder investigation. Out you go, Mr Kane.'

The watchmaker's assistant was marched unceremoniously out.

Colbeck looked at the list on his desk. Kane's was the fifth name on it. His four predecessors had also tried to trick their way to the reward and were now regretting their attempt to mislead Colbeck. With an air of resignation born of experience, he put a cross beside the name of the latest culprit. There was a tap on the door. When it opened, Leeming entered the room.

'What happened, sir?' he asked.

'Mr Kane told us a pack of lies.'

'When did you know that?'

'The moment he asked about the reward,' said Colbeck. 'A genuine witness would simply want to see the arrests made. I know that policemen will never be popular but we do strive to keep the streets safe for people, and, when horrendous crimes of this nature take place, we do everything in our power to apprehend those who committed them. The public should be reminded of that regularly.'

'I agree,' said Leeming. 'Oh, the super-intendent told me to give you this.' He handed over a letter. 'He'd like your opinion of it.'

Opening the letter, Colbeck read it and his interest quickened.

'I believe it to be genuine,' he decided.

'The superintendent thought it was sent as a deliberate attempt to misinform us.'

'Then he and I must agree to differ,' said Colbeck. 'If someone goes to the trouble of sending a letter all this way by a courier, then she does have something of value to tell us. There's no mention of the reward here, Victor. That's very encouraging.' Folding the letter up, he slipped it into his pocket. 'I'll take the next train to Coventry.'

'Will you get permission from Mr Tallis first?'

'No, Victor. I'll leave you to do that on my behalf. Persuade him that I simply had to dash off.' He took his copy of *Bradshaw* from a drawer. 'Now that he's starting to appreciate your true value as a detective, he can hold no fears for you.'

Leeming was nonplussed. 'What am I to say to him?'

'Tell him that I've gone to see a dark lady.'

CHAPTER TEN

Tolerant by nature, Gordon Younger was nevertheless annoyed by the sudden departure of his guests. Without any explanation, Oxley and Irene had left without even drinking the tea they'd requested. What upset Younger most was the fact that they'd taken the newspaper with them. After the long walk to the station to get it, he felt that he at least had the right to read it. His wife was also distressed. She liked Oxley and had found Irene pleasant company. Having offered both of them hospitality, she'd expected gratitude. Yet during their hasty exit, there had been no whisper of thanks from their guests.

'Have they gone for good?' asked Younger.

'They didn't say.'

'Have you looked in their room?'

'No,' she replied. 'I'll do that now.'

Susanna went upstairs and opened the bedroom door to peep in. Her guests had

185

brought very little luggage with them but most of it was still there. She resisted the temptation to poke into a valise. It was private property. In any case, she and her husband had agreed never to look too closely into what Jeremy Oxley did. It was much more sensible to take him at face value. Whenever he came to them, he was invariably in trouble of some kind. Their job was simply to offer unquestioning help to a friend.

When she returned to the parlour, Gordon was on his feet.

His eyebrows arched. 'Well?'

'It looks as if they're coming back.'

'Then I'll give Jerry a piece of my mind.'

'Don't start an argument,' she said, querulously. 'He's always been well behaved with us but we know he has a temper.'

'So do I, Susanna. Nobody is going to treat us like that.'

'There's probably an innocent explanation.'

'You can't excuse bad manners,' he said, taking a stand. 'If they want to remain here any longer, then they owe us a grovelling apology and a promise to mend their ways.'

'Jerry is to blame. Irene simply does what she's told.'

'She was rude to us, Susanna, and I won't stand for it.'

He paced up and down to relieve his anger, then he remembered something and looked at the clock on the mantelpiece. Reaching a decision, he headed for the door.

'Where are you going, Gordon?'

'Across the road,' he said. 'Martin Baber gets a copy of *The Times* most days. He'll have finished with it by now.'

'Jerry may bring our copy back.'

'I can't wait until he does that.' He went out. 'I only make the effort to get a paper once or twice a week, so I'm feeling deprived of news. I won't be long.'

Susanna resumed her seat and thought about the time they'd spent with their unexpected visitors. They had been tense when they first arrived but had gradually relaxed. Irene, in particular, had loved the semi-rural location and the gardens. They had been quiet and undemanding guests, falling in with the daily routine of the Youngers. Oxley was a criminal and always at odds with the law, Susanna accepted that. It had been difficult for a person as law-abiding as herself but Gordon had pointed out that he knew the secret in their past. As a result, they had to maintain their friendship with him and make allowances for his irregular appearances on their doorstep. Oxley held the key to their continued existence under false names. They had to trust him as much as he clearly trusted them.

For that reason, she wanted to prevent any quarrel breaking out. By the time that they returned, she hoped, her husband's ire would have subsided. Susanna was still going over details of their visit when her husband came back to the house. He waved the newspaper triumphantly in the air.

'It's pristine,' he said. 'I can catch up on almost a week of news that I missed. Martin hasn't even looked at it yet. He's had to go out at short notice. Rose said that we can keep the paper until he gets back.'

'That's kind of her.'

'Such is the value of cultivating good neighbours, Susanna.'

'Rose has a heart of gold,' she said with a sigh. 'There are times when I feel so guilty about having to deceive her and Martin.'

'It's not deception,' he insisted. 'We are Gordon and Susanna Younger now. We've grown into it and cast off our other identities like snakes shedding their skins.'

She pulled a face. 'That's a horrid comparison.'

'Yet it's an accurate one.'

As he settled down to read the paper, she reached for her embroidery. It was nearing completion now and she recalled how much and how wistfully Irene had admired it. Evidently, it was the sort of accomplishment she'd never had time to master. Putting the thimble in place, she extracted the needle and began work. She was soon interrupted. With a cry of horror, Gordon shook the paper.

'This explains everything,' he said.

'What does?'

'It's a report of two policemen who were murdered in the Midlands. The police are hunting for two suspects – Jeremy Oxley and Irene Adnam.' He was aghast. 'We're harbouring killers, Susanna.'

'Irene was not involved, surely.'

'According to this, she shot one man at close range.'

'Dear God!' she exclaimed.

'No wonder he took my copy of *The Times*. He didn't want me to see this. Now we know why they charged out of here.'

'We must inform the police at once.'

'Don't be silly.'

'It's our duty, Gordon. They're both guilty of murder.'

'The same charge can be laid against me,' he warned.

'You released people from agony,' she said. 'That's not murder.'

'A jury would think otherwise. We have to be very careful, Susanna. If we start running to the police, our own secret will come out. That would be a catastrophe.'

'Yet if we don't report them, somebody else might. Martin and Rose must have seen them in the front garden.'

'Yes,' he agreed, 'but they don't know their names. There's a description of the pair of them here but it could apply to thousands of other people of their age. Martin and Rose are not suspicious. They'd never think that their neighbours were hiding two people on the run from the police.'

'Let me read the article.'

'You'd find it too disturbing.'

'Did she *really* shoot a policeman?'

'Irene also helped to throw the body of another out of a moving train. Jerry was under arrest and she planned his escape. *Those* are the people who've been sleeping under our roof as if they didn't have a care in the world.'

Susanna let out a yelp. All the time they'd been talking, she'd been carrying on unthinkingly with her embroidery. As full realisation dawned, and as the faces of Oxley and Irene were conjured into her mind, she jabbed the needle into her hand by mistake and drew blood.

The letter was addressed to Colbeck but the superintendent had no hesitation in opening it. If it was relevant to the investigation, he wanted to see it immediately. When he read it through for the first time, he felt that it might be a hoax, but a second reading made him change his mind. It contained too many details that only Jeremy Oxley could know. The missive was genuine. Intended for Colbeck, it invited him to meet with the man he was trying to catch so that they could 'discuss matters of mutual interest'. The phrase made Tallis snort. He looked up at Leeming.

'Who brought this?' he demanded.

'A young lad,' replied the other. 'He said that a gentleman had given him sixpence to deliver it.'

'Did you take the money off him?'

'No, Superintendent – he's done nothing wrong.'

'He's consorting with a wanted man.'

'The lad wasn't to know that. He was picked at random. You could hardly expect Oxley to slip it under the front door himself. That would be taking far too big a risk.'

'I don't need to be told that, Leeming.'

'It proves one thing, sir – Oxley has read today's paper. It's just as Inspector Colbeck predicted. He's been seized by panic. He's given himself away by revealing that he's actually in London.' He took a step towards the desk. 'May I have a look at it, please?'

Tallis dithered for a few moments then handed it over to him. Leeming read it through twice before passing judgement. He put the letter back on the desk.

'It's him, sir, no question about it. He's issuing a challenge.'

'Unfortunately, it's to the inspector and he's not here, is he? No, he went charging off to Coventry on a whim.'

'He felt that there was evidence to be collected there.'

'*This* is evidence,' said Tallis, snatching up the letter. 'It's evidence that Jeremy Oxley is here in the capital with that murderous doxy of his. It's evidence that he has the nerve to taunt us.'

'I'm not sure about that,' said Leeming, thoughtfully. 'I didn't get the feeling that he was taunting us. There's a note of desperation there. Look at it, Superintendent. There are blots and squiggles everywhere. That letter was dashed off in haste by a man who is *losing* his nerve.'

Tallis glanced at it again. 'You could be right,' he conceded.

'Inspector Colbeck has been after this man for many years. He knows how Oxley's mind works. He'd be able to read between the lines of that letter.'

'Well, he can't do that from Coventry,' said Tallis, waspishly. 'It's one feat beyond even his extraordinary powers. Oh, where is the man when we really need him?' he continued, banging the desk. 'And what was all that nonsense about a dark lady?'

'I daresay that he'll tell us when he returns.'

'And when will that be, pray?'

'He'll no doubt catch the fastest train from Coventry, sir.'

'Damnation!' roared Tallis, hitting the

desk again as if trying to split it asunder. 'I want Colbeck here *now!*'

Coventry was a pleasant town that had retained much of its medieval flavour. Centuries earlier, it had been one of the largest communities outside London but its thriving cloth trade had declined somewhat and it had lost its pre-eminence. It was the home of over thirty thousand souls, a number that swelled on market days when people poured in from the surrounding villages. Colbeck enjoyed his walk through twisting streets lined with half-timbered houses that dripped with character. The Sherbourne Hotel, named after the river on whose bank it was sited, was of more recent construction, a solid and symmetrical edifice that offered its guests comfort, privacy, good food and excellent views.

Gwen Darker was the owner's wife but, since he was now disabled by chronic arthritis, she had taken over the running of the hotel. She was a short woman in her fifties with a soaring bosom and surging backside that made her seem bigger. Impeccably groomed, she wore a dress of red velvet splashed with silver buttons. Coils of pearls hung around her neck. When Colbeck introduced himself, she was amazed that he'd come from London to see her immediately on receipt of her letter. Leaving her assistant to take over, she led her visitor into a private room.

'May I offer you refreshment, Inspector?' she said.

'Later, perhaps,' he replied. 'First of all, I'd like to establish that the two people I'm pursuing did actually stay here.'

'There's not a flicker of doubt about that, Inspector. They were here less than a fortnight ago. As soon as I read the report in the newspaper, I recognised them – and so did my husband.'

'Did they book in here as man and wife?'

'Yes, they called themselves Mr and Mrs Salford.'

'That's a suburb of Manchester,' noted Colbeck, 'so I can guess why it was chosen. Irene Adnam hails from Manchester.'

'She did sound as if she came from further north.'

'How long did they stay here?'

'Almost a week,' said Gwen, proudly, 'and I thought that was a compliment to us. I mean, you don't stay long at a hotel unless it treats you well. They did say that they might come back again one day but, in view of what I know about them now, they'll get no welcome at the Sherbourne.'

'What was your impression of them, Mrs Darker?'

'They seemed to be a nice, quiet, respectable couple. I usually know if people are not really married and reserve the right to turn them away if they ask for a double room. In their case, I had no qualms. They looked as if they'd grown into a true partnership, the way that only married couples do.'

'I understand.'

'We don't allow impropriety here, Inspector. We conduct our business on sound Christian values and we'd hate to get a name as a place that permitted any licence.'

'It's why the hotel obviously has such a good reputation.'

Colbeck had noticed on arrival that the lounge was full of guests, all patently happy with the facilities on offer. Prices were quite steep but they were matched by exceptional service. The place was spotlessly clean, well appointed and efficiently run. To stay there almost a week, Oxley and Adnam must have been able to foot a substantial bill. When they were not engaged in criminal activities, he concluded, they could afford to live in a degree of luxury.

'How well did you get to know them?' he wondered.

'We exchanged a few words each day,' said Gwen, 'but they were not very talkative. They liked to keep themselves to themselves. Mr Salford – or whatever his real name is – told us that he'd worked in a bank for many years.'

'That's one way of putting it,' said Colbeck,

wryly. 'What he really meant was that he was closely acquainted with the banking system. To be more exact, Mrs Darker, Oxley is linked to at least three bank robberies.'

'You'd never have guessed it by looking at him. He fooled me completely, but then, so did the young lady. I'd marked them down as a harmless couple, not as a pair of vicious killers.'

'What did they do all day?'

'They took the train to Birmingham a couple of times.'

'Did they say why?'

'They were moving on there when they left here and wanted to spy out a good hotel.'

'So when they left here, they went on to Birmingham.'

'Yes, they said they were visiting his relatives.'

'Why didn't they stay with them?'

'There was no room, apparently. The house was too small. Besides, Mrs Salford – Irene Adnam, that is – confided to me that she preferred to stay in a hotel.' She wrinkled her nose. 'That was the curious thing, Inspector.'

'Go on,' he encouraged.

'Well, she treated me with respect, of course, but she did tend to order the staff around. It was almost as if she'd never dealt with servants before and wanted to make the most of it. She could be quite sharp with them at times.'

'What else can you tell me about them, Mrs Darker?'

Gwen was an observant woman and was able to give Colbeck enough detail to make it absolutely certain of the real identity of her two guests. He was astonished to learn that they'd attended church on Sunday but less surprised to hear that Jeremy Oxley had been seen consulting a copy of *Bradshaw*. Railway timetables were as important to him as they were to Colbeck. Trains were his means of escape after a crime. He'd stayed in Coventry until the day before the robbery. Once he struck in Birmingham, he and Irene fled instantly with the takings. It was while he was in hiding in Wolverhampton that he'd been caught. Colbeck did not believe for a moment the claim that the couple were going to stay with Oxley's relatives. They did not exist. As in all his previous robberies, he had chosen the right moment to make his move then ran swiftly away from the scene of the crime. It was a time-honoured pattern.

When she came to the end of her tale, Colbeck thanked her profusely and told her that the information she'd been able to give him had more than justified his visit to Coventry. Gwen was gratified. Horrified to have given accommodation to ruthless criminals, she was desperate to help some-how in their capture.

'I'll never forget her face,' she said. 'It was truly beautiful.'

Colbeck thought about Helen Millington, the woman whom Irene Adnam resembled in every way. He recalled the delicate loveli-ness of her features, the exquisite splendour of her hair and the honeyed softness of her voice. He could see her, hear her and inhale her fragrance. He could actually feel her presence.

'Yes,' he said at length. 'She is beautiful – *very* beautiful.'

There was safety in numbers. As long as they were in a crowd, Oxley and Irene would not be recognised from the description in the newspapers. To passers-by, they looked like any other young middle-class couple, walk-ing arm in arm along the pavement. When they adjourned to a restaurant, they found that the other diners were far too preoccu-pied with eating their food to take any notice of them. Irene began to voice her concerns.

'What if the inspector doesn't turn up?' she asked.

'He'll be there,' said Oxley with confidence. 'Colbeck can't resist a challenge.'

'I thought you'd never met him.'

'I haven't. My case never came to court.'

'Then how will you recognise him?'

'He's the dandy of Scotland Yard, by all accounts. I've seen it mentioned in newspaper reports. He likes to dress a little better than other detectives. Well, his days as a peacock will soon be over.' He patted the gun concealed in his belt. 'I'm going to put a bullet into Beau Brummell.'

'I still think it's too dangerous, Jerry.'

'Leave the thinking to me.'

'So many things could go wrong.'

'Not if we hold our nerve. I thought we were already in the clear but I reckoned without Colbeck. Somehow the clever devil found out your name. All at once, I can hear his footsteps coming up behind us.'

'So can I,' she admitted. 'I'm scared.'

Oxley made her drink some wine to steady herself, then he assured her that one decisive strike would be their salvation. Once the man leading the investigation had been killed, it would lose its shape and thrust. Nobody could replace Robert Colbeck Irene was slowly convinced of the necessity of committing another murder. A second anxiety then came to the fore.

'Gordon and Susanna will be upset at the way we left so abruptly,' she said. 'I feel embarrassed about going back there.'

'I'll smooth their ruffled feathers.'

'What if they read today's newspaper?'

'They don't have it anymore,' he pointed out. 'I took it with us and we know that they very rarely buy a paper. If they did, they'd already have seen that I was wanted by the police.'

'They're bound to suspect something, Jerry.'

'They'll keep their suspicions to themselves, Irene. They know what's at stake. The law doesn't condone euthanasia. Gordon is well aware of what will happen if he's exposed as a killer. Susanna will be charged as his accessory.'

She pursed her lips. 'I can't say that I approve of what they did.'

'Well, I do,' he argued. 'When I'm old and ailing and in constant pain, I'd love some kind doctor to put me out of my misery. What about your father? Didn't you tell me that he's failing badly and coughing up blood? Euthanasia might be the answer for him as well.'

'I daren't even think about it.'

'We all have to die sometime.'

'Let's not talk about my father,' she said, reaching for her wine again. 'He's always on my conscience.'

She might have added that Constable Arthur Wakeley was on her conscience as well but she didn't want to admit it. Oxley was not only capable of shrugging off the murders he'd committed, he was calmly planning another. She wondered if she would ever acquire the same immunity to guilt.

'Coming back to Gordon and Susanna,' he said, 'there's one thing we must always remember. Gordon not only dispatched a number of wealthy old ladies to heaven, he got paid for doing so in their wills. He called it an incidental bonus. If he'd been so high-minded about what he was doing, he'd have refused the money.'

'What are you saying, Jerry?'

'For all his blather about performing a sacred duty, Gordon is really the same as us. He has clear criminal tendencies. He was quick to learn that there's money in euthanasia.'

'It's helped them to lead an entirely new life.'

'They'll do nothing to jeopardise it, Irene,' he told her. 'That's why you have no call to fret about them. They'd never report us – even if they saw me shoot Inspector Colbeck.'

Less than forty minutes after arriving at Coventry station, he was standing on the platform again. Colbeck's was a distinctive figure and, as the train steamed in on time, its driver recognised him. A hand waved excitedly from the footplate and Colbeck knew that it must belong to his future father-in-law. Not wishing to delay the departure of the train by speaking to Andrews, he stepped into a compartment and spent the journey reflecting on what he had learnt from Gwen Darker. As the train finally reached its terminus, Colbeck walked briskly along the platform to the locomotive. Overjoyed to see him, Andrews introduced his fireman.

'Don't shake hands with him,' he cautioned. 'His hands are covered in coal dust.'

Sowerby grinned inanely. 'So you're the Railway Detective,' he said in wonderment. 'Have you caught them yet?'

'We are well on the way to doing so,' said Colbeck.

'It all happened on our train, you know,' said Andrews.

'So Madeleine tells me.'

'In a sense, we're working on this case together.'

'You've certainly been of great assistance today, Mr Andrews,' said Colbeck, checking his watch. 'You've brought the train in six minutes early.'

'Caleb likes his beer at the end of the shift,' said Sowerby with a chuckle. 'That's why we made such good time.'

'I don't suppose you'd like to join us?' invited Andrews.

'I'd like to,' said Colbeck, 'but duty calls. I have two important visits to make this evening.'

After chatting with them for a couple of minutes, he took his leave and picked up a cab outside the station. What he hadn't told

Andrews was that his first port of call was a certain house in Camden. He got the usual rapturous welcome from Madeleine. Drawing him into the house, she fired a whole series of questions at him. He had to raise both hands to stem the interrogation.

'I can't answer everything at once,' he said. 'Suffice it to say that we are making headway with the case, so much so that I was able to spurn a very tempting offer of help.'

'Help from whom?' She saw the twinkle in his eye. 'Have you been talking to Father?'

'It was the other way around, Madeleine. He happened to be driving the train I caught in Coventry. I had a discussion with him when we got to Euston. Apparently, he has a theory about Irene Adnam, though it's not one that I particularly want to hear.'

'Father is always having theories about something.'

'What he did tell me is that his retirement has been finalised.'

'He'll be here permanently in a matter of weeks.'

'Then we must create a studio for you in my house,' he said, correcting himself at once with an apologetic smile. 'I should have said *our* house. It belongs to both of us now.'

'I'll only feel that when we're actually married.'

He took her in his arms again and held her close. It was only now that he realised just how he'd missed her. In pursuit of one woman – and haunted by the memory of another – he'd allowed Madeleine to slip to the back of his mind. Sweeping off his hat, he kissed away the long hours since he'd last seen her, then he flicked his eyes at the easel.

'Is your new masterpiece ready for display yet?'

'It's not a masterpiece, Robert, and it's not yet ready.'

'I do envy you your creative talent,' he said. 'There are times when I feel my work is dull and pedestrian by comparison.'

'That's nonsense!' she retaliated. 'I love art dearly but the world could manage very easily without my paintings. You, on the other hand, are indispensable. Think how many villains would still be walking the streets if you hadn't caught them.'

'It's slow, methodical work with nothing creative about it.'

She was dismayed. 'Does that mean you're losing your appetite for it?'

'Not in the slightest,' he said, quickly. 'I'm privileged to be doing a job that I enjoy above all else. There are just occasional moments when I would like to hang something on a wall that I'd painted myself, or open a book that I'd written, or hum a tune that I'd managed to compose. I'd like to do one thing that was startlingly original.'

She giggled. 'Apart from marrying me,

you mean?'

'That will be my greatest achievement.'

'And mine,' she said, hugging him tight. 'But if you really want to be an artist, I can give you a few lessons at no cost whatsoever.'

'I believe in repaying a kindness, Madeleine. If you teach *me*, I'll promise to give you some lessons of my own.' He ran a gentle finger down her nose. 'Then we can attain a degree of artistry together.'

Tallis had read the letter so often that he knew it by heart. It was a temptation he was finding hard to resist. Although it was directed at Colbeck, he felt that it should more properly have been sent to him as the senior investigating officer. Oxley wanted to make contact. The letter was quite specific about that. It was so important for him that he was even prepared to break cover and disclose his whereabouts. It was a chance too good to miss. Instead of trailing the man all over the country, Tallis was being offered the opportunity to catch him here in London. Some kind of trap would be involved. He knew that. But he was relying on his experience to be able to anticipate and thereby avoid the trap. In pursuit of glory, he was ready to accept all the hazards. Colbeck would have taken up the challenge implicit in the letter and that is what Tallis resolved to do. For once in his life, he would overshadow his illustrious colleague.

There was a tap on the door. When it opened, Peebles came in.

'You sent for me, sir?' he enquired.

'I need you to accompany me, Constable.'

'Where are we going?'

'We are going to arrest Jeremy Oxley,' said Tallis, grandly. He handed the letter to Peebles. 'You had better read this.'

The constable did so, his brow furrowing with surprise.

'Is this genuine, Superintendent?'

'I believe so.'

'By rights, Inspector Colbeck should respond to it.'

'I'd be happy for him to do so if it were not for the fact that he is gallivanting around the country on trains. An exact time has been set for the meeting. As Colbeck is not here, someone else has to go.'

"What about Sergeant Leeming?'

'I have decided to take the responsibility on myself, Constable, and I am ordering you to come with me. There will be danger, of course, but that is ever present when one wears an army uniform. As a result, I'm impervious to fear and so, I hope, are you.'

'Lead on, sir. I'll follow wherever you go.'

Peebles was thrilled to be given such a task. There were many other detectives on whom Tallis might have called. Instead, he had picked out the newest of them. It was an exciting assignment and he was already relishing the pleasure of telling his beloved about it when he and Catherine were together again. She would be so proud of him. It never crossed his mind that Tallis was deliberately ignoring Leeming and the other detectives because they would object to doing something that was exclusively the right of Robert Colbeck.

Oxley had chosen the venue with care. It was at the end of a quiet road that was as straight as an arrow. From his hiding place among the trees, he had a clear view and could easily escape to a waiting cab if he saw that his demands were not being met. Colbeck had to come alone. That was his requirement. Apart from anything else, he wanted to meet the person who'd been stalking him for so many years. The pistol was loaded and hidden from view. All that he had to do was to get his target close enough to be able to kill him.

Crouched beside him, Irene was ready to beat a retreat.

'He's not coming, Jerry.'

'Give him time.'

'It's past the hour already,' she said. 'Maybe the inspector didn't even get your message. Maybe he wasn't at Scotland Yard.'

'You saw what it said in the newspaper.

The police appealed to the public for help. Inspector Colbeck would have been waiting to sift any information that came in. He was there, believe me.'

'Then where is he now?'

'He'll come soon, Irene.'

Even as he spoke, a tall figure of a man came round the corner and walked towards them. Both stiffened and Oxley put a hand on the gun. But it was a false alarm. Instead of continuing his walk, the man suddenly turned into a doorway, took out a key and let himself into the house. Oxley relaxed but Irene's tension remained.

'What if he brings a lot of policemen with him?' she said.

'He's not stupid enough to do that. In any case, we'd see them long before they saw us. We'd have time to vanish into thin air.'

'Not if the policemen were mounted,' she argued. 'They could run us down, Jerry. We're taking too big a risk.'

'I know Colbeck – he'll come alone.'

'But you've never even seen him before.'

'That's why I'm so anxious to make his acquaintance, brief as it's destined to be. This man is the difference between freedom and arrest, Irene. I can't stress that enough. When he's been disposed of, we can breathe easily once more.'

'I can't breathe at all at the moment,' she confessed.

'All you have to do is to stay here and keep quiet.'

They stiffened again as two figures appeared at the end of the road. Oxley took a long, hard look at both of them before making his decision. One of them had to be Colbeck. He had come, after all.

Tallis and Peebles had walked in step side by side. Not long after turning the corner, however, they came to a halt so that they could survey the scene. They were looking along a tree-lined road with houses on both sides. If an ambush had been set, an attacker could be hiding in a variety of places. Yet Tallis sensed no immediate danger. It was unlikely that Oxley had access to any of the houses and, in any case, the trees would impede any shots that were fired. With a steady stride, they walked on, eyes darting from one side of the road to another. They'd gone fifty yards before Tallis spoke.

'Where the blazes is the fellow?' he asked.

'Perhaps he changed his mind, sir.'

'He nominated this place and this time. Oxley must be here somewhere yet I can see neither hide nor hair of him.'

'Neither can I, Superintendent,' said Peebles as they walked on. 'But I'm starting to get the feeling that we're being watched.'

Tallis looked around. 'From which direction?'

'I'm not sure.'

'I don't see anyone.'

'The feeling is getting stronger. He's definitely here.'

'Then why doesn't he show himself?'

'Stop there!' yelled a voice and they came to a dead halt.

'Is that you, Oxley?' shouted Tallis. 'Come out into the open.'

'Be quiet! I'll only talk to Inspector Colbeck.'

'I'm his superior.'

'I don't care. Tell the inspector to come forward.'

'He's mistaken you for Colbeck,' whispered Tallis.

'What am I to do?' asked Peebles.

'Pretend that you are. We can't miss an opportunity like this.'

'Are you coming or are you not?' taunted Oxley.

'He's coming,' returned Tallis aloud. Out of the side of his mouth, he spoke to Peebles. 'Beware of tricks, Constable.'

'Yes, sir,' said the other.

Straightening his shoulders, he walked forward towards the trees at the end of the road, scanning the houses as he did so. Oxley's voice seemed to have come from ahead of him rather than from either side but he was taking no chances. Tallis was now thirty yards behind him and in no position to offer help.

Peebles was entirely alone. Yet he showed no alarm. He did what he imagined Colbeck would do in the same circumstances. He remained alert and moved calmly on. When he got close to the end of the road, he was stopped by a command.

'That's far enough!' yelled Oxley.

'Show yourself.'

'I'll give the orders, Inspector. I've come to strike a bargain.'

'What kind of bargain?'

'I want to ensure my continued freedom.'

'That's something I can't guarantee, Mr Oxley. You *are* Jeremy Oxley, aren't you?' he went on. 'I'm beginning to have doubts about that, you see. I heard that you were a brave and daring man and not someone too scared to show his face. Come back when you pluck up more courage.'

Turning on his heel, Peebles made as if to walk away.

'Stay where you are!' bellowed Oxley, coming into view. Peebles stopped again and turned to face him. 'I'm afraid of nobody on this earth, Inspector.'

'Not even the hangman?'

Oxley laughed. 'He'll have no appointment with me. My bargain is this. Call off your dogs and I undertake to leave the country. That way you get rid of Jeremy Oxley for good.'

'That's quite unacceptable,' said Peebles,

evenly. 'The time has come for you to answer for your crimes. I'd advise you to surrender quietly while you still may.'

'I never surrender,' said Oxley, moving slowly forward. 'You should know that by now, Inspector. You've chased me long enough.'

Peebles kept his composure and waited for the moment to pounce. The army had taught him how to overpower an assailant and he had every confidence that he could subdue Oxley even if the man pulled a knife on him. He could see a hand hovering to grab something from under his coat. Peebles knew that he had to strike first. When Oxley was only five yards away, therefore, the constable suddenly came to life and flung himself at the man with his arms outstretched. Oxley was ready for him. Whipping out the pistol, he fired it at the detective's heart from close range. Peebles got hands around him but they had no strength in them now. The wound was fatal. His body shuddered, his eyes were glassy and his mouth was wide open in disbelief. Life slipping away, he slumped to the ground with his waistcoat sodden with blood. His top hat rolled into the gutter. His impersonation of Colbeck was over.

Watching from a distance, Tallis was horror-struck. Torn between rage and grief, he lumbered forward as fast as he could but he was far too slow. By the time he reached the lifeless body of Ian Peebles, he saw that there was nothing he could do. Oxley had disappeared into the trees and, as he bent over his fallen colleague, Tallis heard the distant sound of a cab being driven away. He was in an absolute torment of remorse. In taking Peebles with him, he had effectively signed the young detective's death warrant.

CHAPTER ELEVEN

The shot had reverberated along the road and many curious heads appeared at windows. Once they'd established that the danger was past, a few people came out of their houses to run towards the prostrate figure. Tallis was bent penitently over Peebles, offering up a silent prayer for the salvation of the dead man's soul. It had been a quick death but that gave the superintendent no solace. By a rash action on his part, he'd lost a brave man with a promising future ahead of him. Ian Peebles was everything he could have asked for in a recruit. Tallis felt an even sharper stab of guilt when he remembered the forthcoming marriage. It would never take place now and it would be his job to inform the prospective bride that her future husband had been murdered in broad daylight. Overwhelmed with the implications of it all, he did not realise that more and more people were coming to view the corpse. When he finally looked up, therefore, he saw that there was a ring of faces around him. Tallis got angrily to his feet.

'Stand back!' he ordered. 'This is not a peep show.'

'What happened?' asked someone.

'Isn't it obvious? He's been shot dead. Show him some respect and stop staring like that.' Taking off his coat, he used it to cover Peebles' chest and face. 'Someone call a cab.'

As a man ran off down the road, a woman stepped forward.

'It's a policeman we need to call,' she suggested.

'We *are* policemen, madam,' said Tallis with rasping authority. 'We are detectives from Scotland Yard in pursuit of a wanted man named Jeremy Oxley. It was he who just fired a gun.'

'Oh, I read about someone called Oxley in this morning's newspaper,' she said.

'He was standing right here only minutes ago.' He looked around the faces. 'Do we have any witnesses? Did anyone see the fellow lurking in the trees? I believe that he had a cab waiting for him. Did any of you happen to notice the way that it drove off?' When the faces remained blank, he became exasperated. 'Good God!' he yelled. 'Are you all blind? One of you must have seen something.'

There was a long, awkward, embarrassed silence during which they traded sheepish glances. An elderly man eventually spoke.

'I might have seen them, sir,' he said, stepping forward.

Tallis glowered at him. *'Them?'*

'I took my dog for a walk earlier. On my way back, I saw a cab pulling up over there.' He pointed a skeletal finger. 'A man in his thirties got out with a young woman. They went towards those trees. I thought nothing of it at the time and went home. Do you think that they could be connected to what happened?'

'I'm certain that they are,' said Tallis. 'I'll want you to show me the exact place where you saw the cab.'

'The woman must have been Irene Adnam,' said another man in hushed tones. 'I saw that report in the paper as well. She's the one who shot a policeman on a train. It's dreadful to think such people are on the loose. We should be protected from such villains.'

'We were *trying* to protect, sir,' snapped Tallis, rounding on the man. 'Constable Peebles was in the act of arresting Oxley when he was shot. The Metropolitan Police Force does all it can to make this city safe for its citizens. Courageous men like the constable are ready to sacrifice their lives in that noble cause. So don't you dare to criticise us.' He threw out a challenge. 'Which of you would tackle an armed man with a record of violence?'

'Did you *know* beforehand that he was armed?' asked the elderly man.

'There was every chance that he would be.'

'Then why did you let your colleague try to arrest him alone?'

'Yes,' said the woman who'd spoken earlier. 'Why didn't the two of you go after him?'

'And if you knew that he might have a gun,' continued the old man, 'why didn't you carry weapons yourselves?'

The woman was accusatory. 'Why didn't you bring more men?'

'Why didn't you surround him?'

'How many more will die before you actually catch him?'

'And catch *her*,' said the man. 'She's another killer.'

There was collective agreement that the police were to blame for allowing Oxley and Adnam to remain at liberty. So many questions were hurled at Tallis that he felt as if he were facing a verbal firing squad. There was far worse in store for him. These were simply concerned members of the public airing their opinions. The really searing questions would come from the family of Ian Peebles and from the young woman who was expecting to marry him.

Meeker was so shaken that perspiration was still pouring out of his brow as he gabbled his story. He was a portly man of middle years with a flabby, weather-beaten face. Seated in a chair in Colbeck's office, he kept glancing over his shoulder as if fearing an attack. The cab driver had arrived at Scotland Yard not long after Colbeck had returned there. Instead of being able to report to the superintendent, Colbeck found himself listening to a grim narrative.

'Let me stop you there, Mr Meeker,' he said, taking a bottle of brandy from his desk and pouring some into a glass. 'You're talking so fast that we can't hear much of what you're saying. Why don't you drink this and take a few moments to calm down?' He handed over the glass. 'There's no hurry. What you have to tell us is very important and we're grateful that you came to us. The sergeant and I want to hear every word.'

He and Leeming waited while their visitor took a first sip of brandy. It seemed to steady him. After a second, longer sip, he felt ready to continue. He spoke more slowly this time.

'It was like this, Inspector,' he said, still sweating profusely. 'I picked up a fare in the Strand. It was a man and woman. They looked very respectable. The man gave me no destination. I was to drive north up Tottenham Court Road until he told me to stop. It took well over twenty minutes but I wasn't going to complain, was I? He was paying and it was a pleasant enough evening. I kept going until we came to a road with big houses in it. He tells me to pull over and to wait. Then he and the woman went off into this clump of trees for quite a long time. You can imagine what I thought was going on,' he added, rolling his eyes. 'Well, it was none of my business. As long as they weren't trying to do it in my cab, I was ready to let them get on with it. Then, just as I was running out of patience and wondering if they'd simply gone off without paying, this shot rings out and the pair of them comes dashing back to the cab. Before they jumped in, the man – I'll never forget this as long as I live – puts a gun to my head and tells me to drive off fast. What else could I do, Inspector? He'd have killed me.'

'Where did you take them?' asked Colbeck.

'Euston station, sir.'

'What did you do then?'

'To be honest,' said Meeker, 'I just sat in my cab and cried. I'm not a weak man as a rule. I'm very strong-willed. You have to be if you drive a cab because you pick up all sorts of odd people. But I've never stared down the barrel of a gun before. I thought he was going to blow my skull apart.'

'I suppose that they didn't even pay you,' said Leeming.

'Not a brass farthing. They hopped out of the cab at Euston and went off into the crowd. The man had warned me not to follow him but I couldn't have done that even if I'd wanted to. My legs were like jelly.' He took another sip of brandy. 'Anyway, I waited until I felt a little better, then I told this policeman who was on duty there what had happened. When I described my two passengers, he said they sounded just like the ones involved in a foul murder up near Wolverhampton way. The policeman told me to come here at once and to ask for you.'

'He did the right thing,' said Colbeck. 'Where exactly were you when you heard the gunshot?'

He unfolded a map of London on his desk and Meeker stood up to study it. After much deliberation, he jabbed a finger. Colbeck knew that he was telling the truth. It would have taken him all of twenty minutes and more to get to that location from the Strand. Leeming confirmed the identity of the two passengers.

'It must have been them, sir,' he said. 'That's exactly the place that Oxley wanted you to go to. I read his letter.'

Colbeck was annoyed. 'I wish that *I'd* been allowed to do so.'

'The superintendent thought it might contain crucial evidence.'

'I'll take the matter up with him when he returns. As for you, sir,' he went on, turning to Meeker, 'you are to be congratulated. You've been through a terrible experience and had the sense to confide in a uniformed officer. Thank you for coming here.'

'I had to get it off my chest, Inspector,' said Meeker.

'I can appreciate that.'

Leeming was sympathetic. 'I hope you're feeling better now.'

'Oh, I am, Sergeant.' He held up the glass. 'This is good brandy.'

'The inspector keeps it for times like this.'

'It's exactly what I needed.'

Meeker downed the glass in one noisy gulp then put it on the desk. After thanking them both, he waddled across to the door. Before he left, he remembered something and produced a hopeful smile.

'Does this mean that I get the reward?' he asked.

'I'm afraid not,' said Colbeck. 'It goes to the person who gives us information that leads to the arrest of the two suspects. You're just another one of their victims, I'm afraid.'

The cab driver gave a resigned shrug before going out. Closing the door after him, Colbeck was able to confide his fears to Leeming.

'Are you thinking what I'm thinking, Victor?' he asked.

'That depends, sir.'

'Oxley's letter gave me a specific time and place.'

'It's exactly the spot that Mr Meeker went to.'

'But who else went there? That's my worry.' He glanced in the direction of Tallis's office. 'When was the last time the superintendent left his desk?'

'It was last year when he came up to Yorkshire and interfered with our investigation. It must be months and months ago. Since then, he's spent every day in his office.' He blinked as he understood the point of the question. 'You don't believe that Mr Tallis went in your place, do you?'

'I believe exactly that.'

'But the letter particularly asked for you and only you. Simply by looking at him, Oxley would have known that the superintendent couldn't possibly have been Inspector Colbeck.'

'Perhaps he took someone with him, someone more akin to me.'

'Who could that be, I wonder?'

'And what happened to him?' said Colbeck. 'Mr Meeker heard a gun being fired. Does that mean Oxley has shot one of our men?'

'If he did,' replied Leeming. 'I'll wager that he thinks he shot *you*.'

Outwardly, she had remained calm throughout, but Irene Adnam's stomach was churning. She had watched Oxley shooting his victim and – even though she believed that it had to be done – she was sickened. During the ride to Euston, she'd been on tenterhooks. After the short train journey to Willesden, the long walk to the home of their friends gave them time to talk over in detail what had happened. Evening shadows dappled the ground and a stiff breeze blew in their faces. Irene glanced across at his chest.

'You've got blood on your waistcoat,' she said.

'Yes, I know, it's a rather nasty stain. No call for alarm,' he said, smirking, 'it's not *my* blood, Irene. It was his.'

'I just hope that nobody spotted it on the train.'

'They were too busy looking at you. That's the advantage of travelling with a gorgeous woman. She's a perfect distraction.'

They walked on for a while before she spoke again. 'What are you going to tell Gordon and Susanna?'

'I'll think of something.'

'What happened today will be reported in the newspapers.'

'And so I should hope,' said Oxley. 'I did everyone in the criminal fraternity a big favour today. I killed Inspector Colbeck.'

'You don't *know* that it was him, Jerry.'

'Who else could it be? He came to the place I told him and was ready to talk. The only mistake he made was to bring that other man with him. I made sure that I separated them.'

'I didn't get a close look at him,' she conceded, 'but he was younger than I expected. And I wouldn't call him a dandy.'

'That was Colbeck,' he affirmed. 'I'm certain of it. I'm equally certain that they've got no hope of catching us now. Without him at the helm, the investigation will lose all direction.' He put an arm around her. 'I know that it was harrowing for you, Irene, but it had to be done. Colbeck would have been our nemesis.'

'He was a detective,' she said, worriedly, 'so every policeman in London will be looking for us. We've disturbed a hornet's nest.'

'Policemen have been looking for me for a long time but I usually manage to evade them. On the two occasions when I have been arrested, I've contrived to escape.'

Irene turned away so that he wouldn't see her wince. Mention of his escape on the train revived troubling memories for her and she knew that she'd lie awake that night agonising over the latest murder. She had the conscience for both of them. Oxley behaved as if they'd simply been for a ride in a cab. The brutal way that he'd threatened the driver had upset her. To Oxley, it was a source of amusement.

'How long will we stay here?' she asked.

'As long as I decide, Irene.'

'What if they find out?' she asked. 'Gordon and Susanna are bound to do so in the end.'

'They won't say a word.'

'But we're putting them in danger, Jerry. If we are caught there, the police will charge them as well.'

'They *won't* catch us,' he assured her. 'Why do you think I chose to hide there? We're completely off the beaten track. All that we have to do is to keep our heads down and watch the world go by.'

'There'll be a manhunt.'

'There was a manhunt in the Midlands when I escaped but they still haven't captured me, have they? Put yourself in their shoes, Irene. That fat fool of a cab driver will have told them that he took us to Euston. What are they going to deduce?'

'They'll know that we fled by train.'

'Yes,' he said, 'but they don't know *which* train. They'll assume that we wanted to get as far away from London as possible. In fact, we got off at a station that's only six miles away. They'd never dream we'd be careless enough to stay so close.'

Irene was heartened. 'I think you're right, Jerry.'

'Trust me. Everything will be fine.'

'There'll be no more shooting, will there?'

'That's all behind us now that Colbeck is dead.'

'Oh, I do hope so.' She became wistful. 'I want us to be like Gordon and Susanna one day.'

He grinned. 'Middle-aged and wrinkled, you mean?'

'No, Jerry – living as decent, ordinary people in a proper house and being accepted by our neighbours. Not having to fear a knock on the door all the time. I want us to have a normal life.'

'Then you should have chosen someone else,' he said, half-jokingly, 'because I'm neither decent nor ordinary. As for normal life, I think it would bore me to distraction.'

Tallis was too distressed even to reach for a cigar. He sat brooding in his chair while Colbeck and Leeming watched him. He'd not had to explain where he'd been or what had happened. One glance at his face had told them the awful truth. After wallowing in guilt for a long time, he glanced up, saw the two detectives and fished something out of his pocket. He offered it to Colbeck.

'You deserve to see this, Inspector,' he said.

Colbeck took it. 'The sergeant told me what it contains.'

'Read it yourself and you might understand why I took such precipitate action and
why...' As he thought about Peebles, his
voice faltered. 'Just read it, please.'

Colbeck read the letter and noted some of
the barbs aimed at him. Although it had
been written at speed, it was no wild dia-
tribe. There was calculation in it. There was
also a cruel mention of Helen Millington to
act as a spur. Had he seen it when it first
arrived, Colbeck would have been sorely
tempted to meet Oxley.

'Constable Peebles had no chance,' said
Tallis, bleakly. 'He was shot from a distance
of a few feet. When I got to him, he was
dead. The local ghouls came out to gawp at
him, so I covered his face with my coat. I
took the body to the morgue in a cab.'

'What exactly happened, sir?' asked
Colbeck.

'I'm ashamed to tell you, Inspector, but I
think that I ought to. After all, I was acting
on the contents of a letter addressed to you.'

'It was wrong of you to open it.'

Tallis sighed. 'Oh – if only I hadn't done
so!'

'I did make that point, sir,' said Leeming.

'Yes, I know, but Colbeck wasn't here and
I felt that something important might slip
through our fingers. I *had* to open it and
somehow I felt impelled to respond to its
demands.'

'I can accept that,' said Colbeck. 'You were fully entitled to take the risks implicit in your action. What I question is your right to engage Constable Peebles in the venture. I'm sure that he was willing but he was also inexperienced.'

'That's not true,' said Tallis, grasping at straws. 'He'd been on the streets in uniform for years. When he was at Barking, he received a commendation.'

'He was not being asked to walk the beat with you, sir. He was being confronted by a known criminal with a readiness to kill. Why, in the name of all that's holy, did you choose him?'

Tallis ran a hand through his hair and hunched his shoulders.

'I hoped that he might be mistaken for *you*, Inspector.'

'That was very unfair of you,' said Leeming, hotly. 'It was like painting a target on the constable's back.' He reined in his anger. 'I don't mean to be disrespectful, sir, but, in the short time I knew him, I grew to admire Constable Peebles. I feel that you let him down.'

Tallis nodded soulfully. 'I feel it myself, Leeming.'

Seething with fury, Colbeck took pains not to show it. He'd been shocked at the loss of their new recruit and blamed Tallis for the death. At the same time – and it was something he'd never expected to do – he felt sorry for the superintendent. Whatever reproaches Colbeck might make paled beside the torture to which Tallis was clearly subjecting himself. They were looking at a man in agony.

'We've spoken to the cabman who drove them away from the scene,' said Colbeck, 'so we know what happened *after* the shooting. Perhaps you'd be kind enough to tell us what happened before.'

There was a long silence and Colbeck wondered if Tallis had even heard him. Eventually, however, the superintendent roused himself and sat upright like a man facing his accusers in the dock.

'This is what occurred,' he began.

Slowly and with great precision, Tallis reconstructed the events. He offered no defence for his actions and sought no sympathy. It was a clear, unvarnished and completely honest account. When he spoke of Peebles, he did so with the kind of affection they'd never seen him exhibit before. He explained how he'd felt it was his bounden duty to break the bad news in a letter to the parents who lived in Edinburgh. But the real trial for him had been to inform and commiserate with the young woman to whom Peebles was engaged. It had been one of the most painful and difficult things he'd ever had to do, and it had obviously left him jangled.

'There you have it, gentlemen,' he said, extending his arms. 'I sit before you as a man who made an almighty blunder and who must suffer the consequences. In the short term, Inspector Colbeck will take full control of this investigation.'

'What about you, sir?' said Leeming.

'I will do the only thing I can do as a man of honour, Sergeant, and that is to tender my resignation. I wish it to take immediate effect.'

They knew. The second they entered the house, Oxley and Irene realised that their hosts had read about them in the newspaper. The Youngers knew that they'd been offering hospitality to killers steeped in the blood of two Wolverhampton policemen. Gordon and Susanna looked at them through different eyes now. While Irene quailed, Oxley flashed a smile at them.

'First of all,' he said, smoothly, 'let me apologise for our sudden departure this morning. Irene and I felt that we were imposing on you too much, so we decided to stay out of your way for a while. It was a decision we made on the spur of the moment, so it may have looked like appalling rudeness to you. We're very sorry, aren't we, Irene?'

'Yes, yes,' she said, 'we are.'

'That's no longer the point at issue,' said

Younger, bristling with ire. 'Since you took my newspaper with you, I borrowed one from a neighbour. I was horrified by what I read.'

'Calm down, Gordon,' warned his wife, seeing that he was about to lose his temper. 'We don't want this to get out of hand.'

'Be quiet, Susanna.'

'But I thought that we agreed to—'

'You heard what I said.'

The unaccustomed sharpness in his voice upset her. He'd always treated her with courtesy before. Accepting that her husband would pay no heed to her comments, she fell silent and took a few steps back. Younger stared at Oxley, then at Irene. When his eyes moved back to Oxley, they glinted with a mixture of hostility and contempt. Irene felt profoundly uncomfortable but Oxley was at ease. He ventured a smile of appeasement.

'I thought that we were friends,' he began.

'There are limits to even the closest friendship,' said Younger.

'Would you rather that we'd told you?'

'I'd rather you didn't come anywhere near us, Jerry.'

'You should have felt honoured that I'd chosen you,' said Oxley. 'At a moment of extreme danger, a man turns to the people he can rely on most and that's why I came to you.'

'You came under false pretences.'

'That's no more than you and Susanna did,' riposted the other. 'Your neighbours don't even know your real names, let alone what you did when you were a respected member of the medical profession in Bradford.'

'I knew that you'd throw that in our faces.'

'We're brothers in arms, Gordon.'

'That's not true!' cried Younger. 'We're not murderers!'

'There's no need to shout,' said Susanna in alarm. 'Look, why don't we all sit down instead of standing here like this?'

'What a good idea,' agreed Oxley, lowering himself onto a sofa and patting the place beside him. 'Come on, Irene,' he urged. 'Make yourself at home.'

She hesitated. 'I'm not sure that we should stay, Jerry.'

'They can hardly throw us out.'

The challenge was all the more effective for being made so casually. Younger knew that he was no match for Oxley. He had neither the strength nor means to eject him from the property. As a last resort, he tried to summon up moral authority.

'Susanna and I would like you to leave at once,' he said.

'That's not what we agreed,' corrected his wife. 'We said that they could stay another night.' She was hurt by the fierce look that

231

her husband shot her. 'That *was* what we agreed, Gordon. We discussed it.'

'But you didn't discuss it with *us*, did you?' said Oxley.

'This is *our* home,' declared Younger.

'It was bought in names that you invented for the purpose.'

'That was an unfortunate necessity.' He walked across to stand over Oxley. 'Please get out of here now.'

It was more of a request than a command and his voice cracked when he spoke. Susanna was apprehensive and Irene was unsettled but Oxley merely adjusted his position on the sofa. He flashed another smile. 'Why don't we talk about this in the morning?'

'Yes,' said Susanna, relaxing, 'why don't we?'

'It's because it's too dangerous,' argued Younger, abandoning assertiveness and falling back on reason. 'Listen, Jerry, what you and Irene have done is, strictly speaking, none of our business.'

'I'm glad that you realise that,' said Oxley.

'But we have to think of our own position. As long as you're here, then we are imperilled. The manhunt is being led by detectives at Scotland Yard. What happens if they trace you here?'

'How could they possibly do that?'

'Some of our neighbours read the newspapers, you know.'

'Have any of them been banging on your door?'

'Well, no ... they haven't.'

'Have any of them accosted you in the road and demanded to know why you're hiding two desperate fugitives? No, of course they haven't,' said Oxley. 'It would never occur to any of them to do so because they couldn't conceive of the idea that such pillars of the community as Gordon and Susanna Younger would entertain vile criminals. Nobody who spots us here will take any notice. We're your guests – that absolves us of any suspicion.'

'I suppose that there's some truth in that,' conceded Younger.

'If we'd thought we'd be endangering you, we'd never have come here. Would we, Irene?'

'No, no,' Irene chimed in.

'Have we been such a terrible nuisance to you?'

'Of course not,' said Susanna.

'Then where is the problem?' He looked quizzically up at Younger who'd been staring at Oxley's waistcoat. 'Well, Gordon?'

'What's that stain?'

'Oh, it's nothing to bother about.'

'It looks like blood.'

'No,' said Oxley, easily, 'it's a sauce that a butter-fingered waiter spilt over me. The restaurant has reimbursed me and we didn't have to pay for the meal. However,' he added, 'you didn't answer my question, Gordon.

Where is the problem?'

About to speak, Younger swallowed his words. His guests were going to stay and he was powerless to stop them. By way of reply, he flapped his hands.

'That's settled then,' said Oxley with satisfaction. 'It's getting late. Why don't you get out that excellent malt whisky of yours, then we can have a nightcap? We'll all feel better after that.'

Cyril Hythe was fast asleep when his landlady shook him by the shoulder. He came awake with a start. When she told him that a detective wished to speak to him, he thought at first that it was a practical joke. It took a long time to coax him out of bed. Yawning all the way, Hythe came downstairs to be met by a man who introduced himself as Sergeant Leeming. Fearing that he'd done something wrong, Hythe came fully awake. He was a small, stick-thin stooping man in his thirties who worked as a clerk in the ticket office at Euston. Asked to identify a customer, he laughed mirthlessly.

'I served hundreds of them in the course of the day,' he said. 'How can I remember one man out of a multitude?'

'This person is very singular,' explained Leeming. 'He's wanted for murder, so I'm asking you to think very carefully. I can give you a fairly precise time when you would have served him.'

'I wasn't the only clerk on duty today, Sergeant.'

'The others are being interviewed by my colleagues at this moment. That will tell you how keen we are to catch this man.'

Leeming told him about the murders on the train and about the more recent killing of Constable Peebles. He gave a full description of the two suspects. From the evidence of the cab driver, he was able to give the clerk an approximate time at which Oxley would have purchased two tickets. Shaking his head, Hythe was unable to help him until a last detail was supplied.

'When the constable was shot,' said Leeming, 'he fell against his killer. Our superintendent saw it happen. The likelihood is that blood could well have got onto Oxley's coat.'

Hythe perked up. 'It wasn't his coat, sir, it was his waistcoat.'

'You remember him?'

'I do – he had this dark-red stain on a very expensive waistcoat. I couldn't have missed that. He was with a young woman who looked much as you describe.'

'I don't suppose that you can recall what tickets they bought?'

As a matter of fact, I do,' said Hythe. 'That bloodstain made it stick in my mind. They bought two singles to Willesden.'

Gordon and Susanna talked long into the night before they fell asleep. Forced to offer shelter to Oxley and Irene, they both prayed that the pair would leave soon and dispel the dark cloud that hung over the house. They were aroused not long after dawn by the sound of two traps rumbling along the road and were surprised when the clattering hooves stopped directly outside. Gordon went to the window and saw a tall, elegant figure getting out of the first trap. Two large uniformed policemen were descending from the second.

Putting on his dressing gown, he went downstairs in great alarm and opened the door. Colbeck introduced himself then sent one of the policemen to the rear of the property. The other remained at the gate to block any attempt at a sudden departure.

'I believe that you have two guests staying with you, sir,' said Colbeck, glancing into the house.

'I'm afraid that you're mistaken, Inspector,' replied Younger, wishing that his heart would stop pounding so hard. 'There's only my wife and I here.'

'That's not what we've been led to believe, sir. According to the stationmaster at Willesden, you and Mrs Younger paid a visit to London recently with two people whom we are very anxious to apprehend. Not to beat about the bush,' said Colbeck, 'they are wanted for a series of murders.'

Younger gulped. If he and his wife were caught harbouring fugitives, they would face the full rigour of the law. What he could not understand was how the police knew where to find Oxley and Irene. Seeing his amazement, Colbeck enlightened him.

'Yesterday evening,' he said, 'Jeremy Oxley shot dead one of our detectives. We have established that he then took a train to Willesden. When I spoke to the stationmaster there a while ago, he remembered two people getting off a train and recognised them as the people he'd seen with you and Mrs Younger the previous day.'

'It's a case of mistaken identity,' blustered Younger.

'No man would mistake a woman like Irene Adnam, sir. I'm told that she's very striking. There was something striking about Oxley as well. The stationmaster said there were bloodstains on his waistcoat.' He stepped in close. 'Do you deny you went to London two days ago?'

Younger attempted some bluff. 'No, Inspector,' he said, 'I don't. I had a chat with Betson – he's the stationmaster at Willesden. And yes, there were two people with us but they're not our guests. We met them for the first time on the way to the station.'

'Yet you came back with them as well.

Betson saw you.'

'That was pure coincidence.'

'Stand aside, sir,' said Colbeck, tiring of the prevarication. 'You are deliberately interfering with a murder enquiry.'

'What's going on, Gordon?' asked Susanna, appearing at the door. 'Why is that policeman standing at our gate?'

'Your husband will explain, Mrs Younger,' said Colbeck. 'Now will you please let me in or I'll have to resort to force.'

She froze in horror. 'You can't come in here,' she bleated.

'Its hopeless,' Younger told his wife. 'They know.'

'Where are they?' demanded Colbeck.

'In the guest bedroom at the rear,' admitted Younger, 'but be careful, Inspector. He has a gun.'

'I'm well aware of that, sir. I came prepared.'

Taking out a pistol, Colbeck went into the house and took a quick inventory of the ground floor. He then crept slowly up the stairs with the weapon at the ready. When he got to the landing, he could see four separate rooms. A circular staircase led to the attic where, he surmised, any servants would sleep. Through the open door of one room, he could see rumpled bedclothes and decided it was the bedroom used by the Youngers. A second door that was ajar disclosed an empty room. He tiptoed to the door opposite, took hold of the knob, twisted it and pushed hard, only to discover that he was not in a bedroom at all. Lined with bookshelves, it had been converted into a study. Before withdrawing, he noted some of the objects on the desk.

Only one room was left. Since it was at the rear of the house, its occupants might not have heard the sound of the horses arriving. With luck, Oxley and Irene would be slumbering quietly. It was time to wake them. Finger on the trigger of the gun, Colbeck used the other hand to grasp the doorknob. On the other side of the door, he told himself, was the man who'd shot Ian Peebles and strangled Helen Millington. He deserved no quarter. If Oxley so much as reached for his weapon, Colbeck resolved to disable him with a bullet before arresting him. He was determined that the man would stay alive to pay for his crimes on the gallows.

With a sudden movement, Colbeck flung open the door and stepped into the room. He pointed his gun at the bed and got ready to shout out a command. It died in his throat. The bed was empty. There was no sign at all of Oxley and Irene.

Whenever he made a decision, Irene had learnt to obey it without argument. There would be time enough later for explanations. Though she was unhappy to slip out of the house in the middle of the night, she trusted Oxley's instincts. She was also given cause to admire his daring. They'd noticed the farm on their walk to the station. Oxley took her back there in the dark and, leaving her with their luggage, crept off towards the stables. Left alone in an isolated spot, Irene was prey to all sorts of fears but they proved ill-founded. Oxley eventually came out of the gloom, leading a horse to which he'd harnessed a small cart. It was not the most comfortable mode of transport but it served their purposes and got them to their destination. When the cart was abandoned, the horse cropped the grass outside the station.

When they were on the train, they could at last have a proper conversation. At that time of the morning, they had a compartment to themselves. Glad of the privacy and comfort, Irene nestled against the padded seat in first class.

'Why did we come all the way to Harrow station?' she asked. 'Willesden was much closer.'

'Yes,' he explained, 'but this early train doesn't stop there. To be sure of catching it, we had to go further up the line.'

'Couldn't we have caught a later one?'

'No, Irene.'

'Why not?'

'Call it what you will – I sensed danger.'

'Gordon and Susanna wouldn't have hurt us.'

'Yes, they would,' he said. 'You saw the state they were in last night. Our friendship was near breaking point. It was only a matter of time before they unwittingly gave us away. It was a mistake to stay another night. I only did so because I wasn't going to let him turf us out like that so I dug in my heels. It was a matter of principle.'

'Yesterday,' she recalled, 'you told me that we were completely safe now. What changed your mind?'

'I told you – I had this feeling.'

'But the police would never have found us there, especially without Inspector Colbeck to lead the hunt. It's very upsetting to be roused like that in the middle of the night, Jerry. I like to know what's going on.'

'We're making a precautionary move,' he told her. 'Gordon and Susanna won't report us. They'll just be relieved that we've gone.'

'They're bound to wonder.'

'Let them – I'm never going back there again.'

She clung to his arm. 'Will we ever be *really* safe?'

'We already are, Irene.'

'Sneaking off in the dark and stealing a horse and cart – that doesn't feel like safety to me. It scares me.'

He kissed her. 'You've no need to be

scared when I'm here.'

'Where exactly are we going?'

'Wait and see. Meanwhile, try to get some sleep.'

'I will,' she said, eyelids already fluttering.

Fatigue sent her quickly asleep. It was a noisy journey. The uproar of the engine and the rattle of the carriages failed to wake her and so did the opening and slamming of doors when they stopped at stations. What finally opened her eyes was the soft rustle of paper. The train was stationary. Irene blinked in the light then looked at Oxley through narrowed lids. Staring at a newspaper he'd bought from a vendor on the platform, Oxley had turned white. It was the first time that Irene had ever seen him truly afraid.

'What is it?' she asked, reaching out to touch him.

'There's a report about the shooting in London,' he said, lower lip trembling. 'It seems that the man I killed yesterday was Detective Constable Ian Peebles. I *knew* there was danger – Inspector Colbeck is still alive.'

CHAPTER TWELVE

Gordon and Susanna Younger felt utterly humiliated. Under the searching gaze of Robert Colbeck, they were perched side by side on their sofa like a pair of enormous birds. Their lies had been swiftly exposed. They were known to have offered sanctuary to fugitives from the law. Their only hope lay in pleading ignorance of the crimes committed by Oxley and Irene. If they could portray themselves as innocent victims rather than accomplices, they might yet escape imprisonment. They did have one shred of comfort. When he realised that the suspects had fled, Colbeck had sent the two policemen off in search of them. It spared the Youngers further embarrassment. As their neighbours woke to a new morning, they would not look across and see telltale uniforms outside the home of their friends. How long it would remain the Youngers' home, of course, was debatable.

Colbeck had searched the whole house before he was ready to question them. The long wait gave time for their fears to intensify. When he finally sat before them, he was in no mood for evasion.

'Let me make one thing clear before we start,' he said. 'You tried to mislead me on your doorstep. If you lie to me again, I'll arrest you at once and we'll continue this interview at Scotland Yard. Is that understood?'

'Yes, Inspector,' said Younger, guiltily.

'What about you, Mrs Younger?'

'We'll tell the truth,' promised Susanna.

'I'm glad to hear it,' said Colbeck. 'And bear in mind that I'll be talking to both of your servants in a while. If you say something that they are unable to confirm, then I'll know you deceived me.' He took out a pad and pencil to make notes. 'How long were they here?'

'A few days,' said Younger.

'Did they come by invitation?'

'No, Inspector, they turned up out of the blue.'

'And why did they do that?'

'Jerry Oxley was an old friend from the days when we lived in Yorkshire. We ... kept in touch from time to time.'

'Were you aware that he had a criminal record?'

'We were not.'

'He's reputed to dress well and live in some style. Where did you imagine that his money came from?'

'He mentioned an inheritance at one point.'

'That could be a play on words, I suppose,' said Colbeck, dryly. 'If you rob somebody, then – technically – you inherit their money. Had either of you met Irene Adnam before?' They shook their heads. 'What did you think when Oxley arrived unexpectedly?'

'It was typical of his behaviour.'

'You didn't mind?'

'One makes allowances for old friends,' said Younger.

'In this case, I fancy, you made incredible allowances. You offered shelter to two dangerous criminals, both of whom were named in the newspapers yesterday, as you must have noticed.'

'We rarely read newspapers, Inspector.'

'I certainly couldn't find any when I looked around.'

'They're always full of such dire news.'

'Today's editions will be especially dire,' said Colbeck. 'They will report the murder of my former colleague.'

'I swear that we knew nothing about that, Inspector.'

'We never *wanted* to know what Jerry did,' Susanna blurted out. 'It was none of our business. Until this time, we hadn't seen him for almost two years. He seldom wrote to us. We had no idea where he was or what he was doing.'

'That's perhaps just as well, Mrs Younger,' observed Colbeck. 'Had you known the full record of his villainy, you couldn't have tolerated him under your roof for a second.'

'I'm glad you understand that, Inspector.'

'We are law-abiding people,' said Younger, earnestly. 'Ask any of our neighbours. Or speak to the vicar – he's keen for me to take over as churchwarden next year. I'm happy to accept the position. Does that sound like the action of someone who consorts with criminals?'

'No, sir,' replied Colbeck, 'but it might interest you to know that days before they robbed a shop in Birmingham, your erstwhile guests attended church in Coventry. Even criminals are prone to religious promptings at times.' He scrutinised Younger's face. 'You appear to be living in retirement, sir.'

'That's right. I was an archaeologist for many years but my knees finally gave out. It's a noble profession but a dig does involve a lot of hard manual work. I restrict myself to writing the occasional article on the subject.'

'Yes, I noticed the books in your study. Several were about archaeology. But when I went back for a closer look, I saw that most of them were medical textbooks. That's an odd hobby. Do you have medical training, by any chance?'

There was a pause. 'No,' said Younger at length, forced back on deceit, 'but my father did. He was a doctor in Bradford and, when he died, he bequeathed the books to me.'

'What was his name?'

'Why do you ask that, Inspector?'

'Well, when people buy expensive books, they usually write their names in them, so I'd expect to find a Dr Younger. Yet when I glanced inside one tome, the name inscribed there was Dr Philip Oldfield.'

'That was the original owner,' said Younger, quickly. 'My father bought the book second hand.'

'Then he would surely have crossed out the name of the previous owner and replaced it with his own.' Colbeck leant forward. 'I'm a curious man, sir. It's an occupational hazard. The truth is that I looked inside the covers of half-a-dozen of the medical books. Every one of them had Oldfield's name inside. It seems that your father specialised in buying books from the fellow.' His voice darkened. 'Unless, of course, there's another explanation...'

Younger said nothing but his face was expressive. Susanna looked even guiltier than he did, shifting her position and clenching her fists. A nervous smile brushed her lips.

'I put it to you, sir,' said Colbeck with assurance, 'that *you* are Dr Oldfield and that, for some reason, you decided to be reborn as a younger man with a preference for archaeology. I'm intrigued to know why the counterfeit was necessary. When a man changes his name and invents a new profession for himself, he must have something to hide.' He gave Younger a shrewd look. 'What is it?'

Victor Leeming was bored. He'd been left at Willesden in case the fugitives eluded Colbeck and made their way to the station. Had they seen a uniformed policeman waiting there, they would have been alerted, whereas the sight of Leeming in plain clothes would not have forewarned them. The station was a small, featureless place with a few posters to divert him and a tiny kiosk that sold newspapers, books and other items that passengers might need. After a lengthy and unproductive wait, Leeming bought a newspaper and read the account of the murder of Ian Peebles. It had been drafted by Edward Tallis and copies had been sent to various editors. Leeming found no new details in it. As he read on, he felt a surge of grief at the death of their young fellow detective. Excessively proud to work alongside Colbeck and Leeming, Peebles had had his career terminated before it had really begun.

Another career had been brought to an end in the shooting and it was a much longer and more celebrated one. As a result of his action in exposing Peebles to danger, Tallis had resigned. It was a hugely significant act. At the very moment when the superintendent had announced his intentions, Leeming had experienced a sense of sheer joy. The man who'd terrified him for so many years was leaving Scotland Yard altogether. Two thoughts qualified his joy. The first was that Tallis would be a great loss to the police force. Fearsome as he could be, he was an efficient administrator and worked assiduously to improve the performance of those under him.

However, it was the second reservation that unnerved Leeming and made him wish that Tallis might, after all, stay in his job. If the superintendent left, the obvious candidate to replace him was Robert Colbeck. That would rob Leeming of the finest partner with whom he'd worked as well as his closest friend. Colbeck was at his best out in the field. Shackled to a desk and directing others, his talents would be wasted. The mistake that Tallis had made was to think that he could act just as decisively as Colbeck. He'd wanted to be an alternative Railway Detective and learnt that he was unfitted for the role. By the same token, Leeming felt, Colbeck would be a poor imitation of the superintendent. Each man needed the other in his present position. Reluctantly, Leeming accepted that Edward Tallis must somehow be persuaded to reconsider his decision to resign.

The approach of a trap made him get to his feet and walk to the exit. He saw one of the vehicles hired earlier and containing the two policemen. Leeming went across to them.

'Did you catch him?' he asked.

'No,' said one of the men, 'he did a moonlight flit. We searched everywhere for him. He stole a horse and cart from a nearby farm but we've no idea where he went with it.'

'What about Inspector Colbeck?'

'He's still at the house, talking to the owners.'

It was unkind and discourteous of him but for Colbeck it was a means to an end. In deliberately keeping his suspects in their dressing gowns, he deprived them of their camouflage and their nerve. Having found it in the wardrobe in the guest room, he also waved Oxley's bloodstained waistcoat in front of them. It weakened what little resolve they still had. Faced with his probing, Gordon and Susanna had soon capitulated. They not only talked honestly about their guests' brief stay with them, they divulged their real names and their reason for leaving Bradford. On searching for one set of fugitives, Colbeck had stumbled on another. He was astounded at the way Dr and Mrs Oldfield had maintained their new identities so successfully. They'd been Gordon and Susanna Younger for so long that they'd come to believe that that was who they really were. The vicar who'd approached Gordon to be churchwarden was in for a terrible shock.

Anna Oldfield, as she'd once been, said that she knew they'd be found out one day and that there was an element of relief in it. Her husband, however, took a very different stance, arguing that a doctor's first duty was to relieve pain and that, if someone found life itself intolerably painful, he was justified in releasing that person from agony. Colbeck let him state his case before reminding him how his actions would be viewed in a court of law. As an accessory, his wife also had to prepare herself for a harsh sentence.

When he'd squeezed what he wanted out of them, Colbeck let them get dressed and eat a final breakfast at the house. He joined them at the table. Over a cup of coffee, he searched for more detail.

'You say that Oxley kept on the move,' he noted.

'Yes,' replied Oldfield, 'that's how he evaded arrest. Jerry had a sybaritic streak, Inspector. He was very fond of staying at hotels where he could be waited on hand and foot.'

'Did he ever mention the names of any hotels?'

'Not that I can recall.'

'Jerry didn't,' said Anna, 'but Irene did. It was when she and I were sitting in the garden one day. She confided to me how exciting it was to be with Jerry. He'd introduced her to a different world.'

'Yes,' said Colbeck, 'one in which she'd have to kill someone.' He raised a hand. 'I'm sorry to interrupt you, Mrs Oldfield.'

She was startled. 'It's such a long time since I was called that.'

'You were going to name a hotel.'

'It was one in which they'd stayed not long ago and Irene said it was the most luxurious she'd ever known.'

'Where exactly was it?'

'Somewhere in Coventry.'

'Then you've no need to say any more,' Colbeck told her. 'I've actually visited that establishment. It's the Sherbourne Hotel.'

Irene was rocked. She'd never known Oxley make mistakes before yet he had now made three in succession. In retrospect, the move to London had been a grave error on his part. She had accepted the logic of it because Oxley had been so persuasive. It was their first mistake. The second had been his attempt to kill Inspector Colbeck. Having taken the trouble to choose an ideal location for the murder, Oxley had sent a note to Scotland Yard in the firm belief that it would draw the detective out into the open. In order to bait Colbeck, he'd included a reference to Helen Millington. In the end, however, the plan had turned into a fiasco. The wrong man had been shot and Colbeck remained alive to pursue them.

It was the third mistake that stunned Irene. Insisting that they were in no danger of being recognised from their descriptions in the newspapers, he suggested that they might recuperate at the Coventry hotel where they'd had such good service. Desperate for somewhere to rest, she'd agreed wholeheartedly. It was a fateful decision. Irene would never forget the look in Gwen Darker's eyes as they stepped across the threshold of the hotel. She knew exactly who Mr and Mrs Salford really were and, in a carrying voice, ordered one of her staff to summon a policeman. Oxley and Irene had to take to their heels.

They were now at a hotel in Crewe, a railway junction that would allow them to escape, if the need arose, in one of various directions. To avoid being seen together, they checked in separately. Oxley waited until the coast was clear then joined her in her room. There was a frantic embrace.

'I'm frightened, Jerry,' she said.

'You've no need to be.'

'You keep saying that but it's not true. Look what happened in Coventry. That manageress recognised us. She'll tell the police and they'll get into contact with Inspector Colbeck.'

'But they'll have no idea where we are.'

'I wonder.'

He pulled her closer. 'Stop worrying, will you?' he said. 'You never used to do this, Irene. We've had narrow shaves before and you found it exhilarating. Why get upset because Mrs Darker worked out who we must be?'

'If *she* can do it, Jerry, so can someone else.'

'Only if we're seen together and we'll move around separately from now on. The police are hunting for a couple, not for two single individuals. Wherever we stay, we'll have different rooms.'

'But I want to be *with* you,' she pleaded.

'You will be, Irene – all night long.'

'This is starting to get me down,' she admitted.

'I know,' he said, kissing her and starting to unbutton her dress. 'I have just the cure for that.'

'I keep thinking about Gordon and Susanna. What are they going to say when they realise that we ran away from them?'

'I hope they have the sense to say nothing but I can't guarantee that. Anyway, you can forget them. There's no chance whatever of Inspector Colbeck finding out where we stayed in London.' Undoing the last button, Oxley slipped his hand inside the dress to caress her breast. 'He'll still be chasing his tail at Scotland Yard.'

Victor Leeming was flabbergasted at the turn of events. When they followed the trail to Willesden, the last thing he envisaged was that they would arrest two people wanted by the Bradford Borough Police for a series of so-called mercy killings. On the train journey back to London with them, he thought that they were being arrested for having sheltered two killers. It was only when Philip and Anna Oldfield were in custody that he learnt of their criminal past. Leeming was staggered by the number of victims involved.

'There were over a *dozen?*' he gasped, eyes bulging. 'I'm glad that he was never my doctor.'

'The patients all seem to have been elderly women who begged him to rescue them from their misery. Oldfield still refuses to accept that he was committing a crime.'

'It was murder, pure and simple.'

'That's not how he describes it,' said Colbeck. 'He claims that he spared them horrid, lingering deaths. I must write to the police in Bradford. After all this time, they'll be grateful to get their hands on Dr and Mrs Oldfield again. It's their case, Victor, and not ours. We have other fish to fry.'

'I'd call Oxley more of a shark than a fish, sir.'

'He certainly has a shark's viciousness.'

'He kills anyone who gets in his way.'

They were in Colbeck's office at Scotland

Yard, reviewing the day's developments. Ordinarily, the inspector would have reported to Tallis as soon as he entered the building. That was no longer possible because his superior had resigned. He left behind him a feeling of emptiness. When Colbeck glanced in the direction of Tallis's office, Leeming read his mind.

'I don't think that the superintendent should leave,' he said.

'Neither do I,' said Colbeck.

'It's ridiculous, isn't it? There have been hundreds of times when I've wished him out of here, yet the moment he does go, I miss him. He did his job well even if it meant yelling at me whenever I got within earshot of him.'

'I don't think his resignation will be accepted, Victor.'

'If he wants to go, nobody can stop Mr Tallis.'

'I'm hoping to talk him out of it.'

'How can you do that?' asked Leeming. 'He was so shocked by what happened. Because they'd both been in the army, he looked on Ian Peebles with especial favour. I'm ashamed to say that I thought he'd never make the grade at first.'

'He won't get the opportunity to do so now, Victor. We just have to make sure that he didn't die in vain,' said Colbeck, 'and the way to do that is to call Jeremy Oxley to account. Unlike Dr Oldfield, he can't pass off his murders as mercy killings.'

'You're in complete control now, sir.'

'That rather unnerves me. It feels wrong somehow.'

'Will you draft in someone to replace Constable Peebles?'

'No, I think that we can manage on our own.'

'As acting superintendent, you'll have several detectives to deploy and lots of other cases to supervise.'

Colbeck was adamant. 'I'm still an inspector,' he said, 'and I intend to remain so for the foreseeable future. One thing I won't do is to relinquish my part in this investigation. I owe it to Constable Peebles to pursue our enquiries with vigour. In a sense, he died in place of me. That leaves me with a sense of obligation.'

'It's the young lady I keep thinking about,' said Leeming, sadly. 'He talked so fondly of her – Catherine, her name was. It's a tragedy. All their plans have suddenly turned to dust. He told me that the banns of marriage were being read for the first time next month.'

'That would have been a very special moment.'

'It was for me and Estelle. I was shaking with fear. When the vicar asked if anyone had just cause or impediment why we shouldn't be joined together in holy matrimony, I was terrified that someone would jump up and spoil everything.'

'They'd have had no reason to do so.'

'That didn't stop me worrying,' said Leeming. 'I suppose that the truth of it is that I never felt good enough for Estelle. I never believed that I deserved a wife as wonderful as her, so I kept waiting for someone to step in and take her away from me.'

'Your fears were groundless. Anyone who's seen the two of you together knows that you're ideally suited.'

'I still thank God every day for my good fortune. With a face like mine, I thought I'd be lucky to attract any woman, yet I finished up with a beautiful wife.' He laughed with delight. 'But I do remember sitting through the banns with my hands shaking. It was a test of nerves, I can tell you. Well,' he added, 'you'll find that out for yourself, sir. When are *your* banns being read for the first time?'

Colbeck was taken aback. The question was innocent enough yet it left him befuddled. The truth was that he hadn't given the matter any thought at all. Since the killer of Helen Millington had reappeared in his life after so many years, everything else had been pushed to the back of his mind. It was unfair on those close to him. They'd been neglected. Talk of marriage had reminded him of his engagement to Madeleine and he felt more than a twinge of guilt at the way he'd kept postponing a decision about the date of the wedding.

'That's yet to be decided,' he said, evasively.

'I think that you and Miss Andrews are a perfect match, sir.'

'Thank you, Victor. I like to think that as well.'

'Dirk Sowerby is still on about it,' moaned Andrews. 'He has this daft idea of sailing across the seven seas on a steamship.'

'What's so daft about it?' she asked.

'It will never happen, Maddy. He can't afford it on his pay.'

'Everyone is entitled to dream.'

'It's not a dream, it's sheer nonsense. It just won't happen.'

'You never know, Father. Look at me. I used to think about marrying Robert one day but I never really believed that my dream would ever come true. Yet, against all the odds, it did.'

'That's because you're very special, Maddy – Dirk is not.'

'You're being unfair on him. Last week you were telling me what a good driver he'll make.'

'It's only because I taught him all he knows.'

'Stop mocking his ambitions.'

'I like to tease him. What harm is there in that?'

Andrews had returned home that evening in a jovial mood. It was not simply because he'd been drinking with his friends. As his retirement got ever nearer, he was coming to see the benefits that it would bring. He could still visit his favourite pub of an evening but he would no longer have to get up early the next morning to begin work again. A yoke would suddenly be removed from his neck. When they finished supper, he touched on a subject he'd raised before.

'How would you feel if I was to get wed again, Maddy?'

She blinked. 'Do you have someone in mind, Father?'

'I might and I might not.'

'Well, I'm not going to object, if that's what you're asking. You're old enough to make your own decisions.'

'It would be different if you were still here,' he said. 'I wouldn't feel it was right to bring another woman into the house. But when you're gone and I have the place to myself, I may get lonely.'

'Do you *want* to be married again?'

'I do and I don't.'

'Stop going around in circles,' she chided. 'I might and I might not. I do and I don't. I can and I can't. If you start playing *that* game, we could be here all night.'

He cackled. 'I simply wanted your opinion, Maddy.'

'Then my opinion is that no woman would be misguided enough to take you on,' she said, jokingly. 'You're too set in your ways and you're too cantankerous. Why should anyone even look at you?'

'Your mother did.'

'You were a lot younger then.'

'Love is nothing to do with age, Maddy. It can happen to us whether we're seventeen or seventy. In fact, I fancy it goes deeper when you're more mature. You've learnt how to appreciate it by then.' She narrowed her eyelids. 'Why are you staring at me like that?'

'There's something you're not telling me, Father.'

'Is there?'

'I think you've met someone.'

'I have and I haven't. That's to say,' he added quickly to still her protest, 'I've seen someone who aroused my interest. It's nothing more nor less than that, I swear it. I just wanted to sound you out. When we've spoken about this before, there was a lot of bravado in what I was claiming. It's different now. I'm serious.'

'Then I'll give you a serious answer,' she said, affectionately. 'I want you to be happy. If the best way to achieve happiness is to get married again, then I'm very much in favour of it.' She smiled. 'I wondered why you started coming to church more often. It's someone in the congregation, isn't it?'

'Wait and see.'

'Don't be so coy about it.'

'I'm just being practical,' he said. 'It's pointless of me to think about *my* wedding when we still haven't had yours. It's only when you've left that the house will start to feel empty. That's when I'll need companionship, Maddy.'

'Robert and I will set the date very soon.'

'I think you should read today's paper before you say that.'

'What do you mean?'

'This case will take longer than you think. The man they're after has killed again. Yesterday evening, he shot one of the detectives helping the inspector.' She rushed into the other room and snatched up the newspaper. 'Don't worry – it's not Sergeant Leeming.'

'Then who is it?' she asked, anxiously.

'It was someone named Peebles.'

Tallis had always been a religious man. The Bible was his guide and he read a passage from it every day. In times of stress, he would always slip into church to pray for help and to get spiritual support. Head bowed low, he was on his knees now, pleading for forgiveness. Convinced that he was responsible for the death of Ian Peebles, he singled out pride as his besetting sin. It had blinded him to his shortcomings. He'd been too proud to admit that he had any failings and believed that he could emulate and even surpass Robert Colbeck. That myth had been shattered when he knelt over the corpse. Tallis now knew that he had profound limitations both as a man and as a detective. Given the facts, most of his colleagues would lay the blame squarely on him. Their silent disapproval was nothing compared to the way that he condemned himself. He was suffering.

He prayed hard until his knees began to ache. Hauling himself upright, he stepped into the aisle, inclined his head towards the altar then quietly left the church. On the walk back to his lodging, he was deep in thought. When he reached the house, therefore, he did not at first notice the figure standing outside it. Colbeck had to step right in front of him to get his attention.

'Good day to you, sir,' he said.

Tallis gave a start. "What are *you* doing here, Colbeck?'

'I came to talk to you.'

'I'm not in a talkative vein.'

'There have been some important developments.'

'They don't concern me any longer,' said Tallis, flicking a dismissive hand. 'I've resigned from my post.'

'That's not strictly true, sir. When I spoke to the commissioner, he told me that he'd refused to accept your resignation and that he'd asked you to take time off in order to think again.'

'I *have* thought again and my decision stands.'

'There may be factors you haven't taken into account.'

'I blundered, Colbeck, that's the only factor relevant.'

'I disagree, Superintendent.'

'And you can stop calling me that,' said Tallis, testily. 'It's a title that I've surrendered. I'm just an ordinary citizen now.'

'Not in my estimation,' said Colbeck. He looked around. 'Need we have this conversation in the street?'

'There's no need to have it at all.'

'Have you already discussed it with someone else, then?'

'No,' conceded Tallis. 'Apart from the commissioner, I haven't confided in anyone. There's no point in any discussion when my mind is so firmly made up.'

'I think there's every point, sir.'

It took Colbeck another ten minutes to persuade Tallis to invite him in. He'd never been there before and was interested to see where and how his superior lived. Tallis occupied the first floor of a large Georgian house in a square with a park at its centre enclosed by iron railings. As they entered the well-proportioned living room, Colbeck was surprised to see so much evidence of the older man's religious devotion. There was a crucifix on one wall, marble angels at either end of the mantelpiece and three paintings of scenes from the New Testament. A leather-bound Bible stood on the desk in the window.

The air of piety was offset by an array of military memorabilia. There was a display cabinet filled with medals and small weaponry, a collection of sabres hanging on the walls and, in a dominant position over the fireplace, a portrait of the Duke of Wellington, the soldier Tallis most revered. A tall oak bookcase contained a few books on aspects of Christianity but it was largely given over to histories of various battles and the memoirs of those who'd fought in them. War, religion and the pursuit of criminals had been enough for Tallis. He sought nothing else from life.

Though he waved his visitor to a wing chair, Tallis offered him no refreshment. It was a signal that Colbeck would not be staying long. He was there on sufferance. Tallis sat opposite him, his features set in a permanent scowl. It was as if he were daring Colbeck to begin so that he could deny his request.

'I've come of my own volition,' said Colbeck. 'I'm not here on behalf of anyone else – except Constable Peebles, that is.'

'What do you mean?'

'I think that you should bear him in mind, sir.'

Tallis was stung. 'How dare you!' he cried. 'Peebles has never been *out* of my mind. Since his death yesterday evening, I've thought about nothing else.'

'Then why are you turning your back on him?'

'I'm doing nothing of the kind, man.'

'Yes, you are,' argued Colbeck. 'If you feel culpable for his death, you should feel an impulse to avenge it. In your shoes, I know that I would. Yet you're actually walking away from the case. You are, in effect, letting his killer go free.'

'I've lost the right to run this investigation.'

'I don't believe that and neither does the commissioner.'

'It's all over, Colbeck. I'm finished as a detective.'

'You're bound to feel guilty,' said Colbeck. 'I understand that. But the way to assuage that guilt is to lead the pursuit of Jeremy Oxley and his accomplice – not to abandon it.'

'I'm accepting my punishment for failure.'

Colbeck laughed. 'In that case, everyone in the department should resign, sir. I still squirm when I recall some of my failures and the same applies to others. Detection is not a perfectible art and never will be. The most that we can hope for is a reasonable amount of success. We simply don't have the resources to solve every crime that's committed,' added Colbeck. 'We have to select priorities and you are a master at doing that, sir. It's your forte.'

'It was, perhaps. That's all past now.'

'Is that what you wish me to tell the young lady?'

'What young lady?'

'The one who was betrothed to Constable Peebles – I believe that you spoke to her. When she gets over the initial shock of his death, she'll want to know that we're making every effort to apprehend his killer.' His smile was quizzical. 'Am I to tell her that you have no desire to take part in the search?'

'That would be a gross misrepresentation.'

'It's exactly how it will appear to Catherine, sir.'

'Nobody is more anxious to see Oxley brought to book than me. He's a fiend in human shape and his accomplice is just as bad as him. They've now killed three policemen between them.'

'I make the number four.'

'There were two from Wolverhampton and one from London.'

'You're missing someone out, sir.'

He was perplexed. 'Who's that?'

'Superintendent Edward Tallis,' said Colbeck. 'To all intents and purposes, he's been killed as well. He's withdrawn from the fight. He poses no threat to Oxley and is, in effect, posthumous.'

'That's babbling idiocy.'

'I only describe the situation as I see it.'

'And I've not withdrawn from the fight,' said Tallis, vehemently. 'I simply felt that I no longer deserve to hold the authority that I did.'

Colbeck sat back in the chair. Having planted a seed of doubt in Tallis's mind, he sought to nourish it so that it would grow. He looked up at the portrait of Wellington whose stern eyes stared down either side of the famous hooked nose. Like Tallis, the Duke had never inspired great affection in those under his command but he did earn their respect. There was another similarity. Both men had a will of iron.

'It's a striking portrait,' remarked Colbeck.

'He was a striking man,' said Tallis, 'and merits the thanks of the whole nation for trouncing the French at Waterloo.'

'Did he have an unblemished record of success?'

'Nobody has that in the army, Colbeck. There are always minor setbacks and situations over which you have no control. The Duke was often hampered by scant resources but he nevertheless managed victories against superior numbers.'

'That's another parallel with you, then, sir.'

'I'm no Duke of Wellington.'

'Perhaps not, but you have some of his qualities. For example, you know how to get the best out of men under your command, especially when they are up against insuperable odds. You are a true leader, Superintendent.'

'Stop using that title!'

'Would the Duke have resigned when he met with a setback?'

'He resigned because he had incompetent rivals alongside him. It was only when they realised how great a loss he was to the army that they restored him and put him in full command.' Colbeck glanced at the portrait then stared at Tallis. 'It's presumptuous to compare me with the Duke. He was a genius. Besides, I'm no longer in the army.'

'But you run the department with military precision.'

'That's just my way.'

'Ian Peebles understood that, sir. He admired you greatly. I think he'd have expected you to atone for what you did by helping to catch his killer. Will you desert your post now of all times?'

Tallis was discomfited. His eyes went up to the portrait and he had to make an effort to turn them away. After weighing up what he'd been told, he turned away to ponder. Colbeck did not disturb his cogitations. It was minutes before Tallis broke the silence.

'You say that there have been developments.'

'Yes, sir,' replied Colbeck, 'I made two critical arrests this morning. In doing so, I solved a crime that's been troubling the Bradford Borough Police for a number of years.'

Colbeck told him about the early morning visit to Willesden and how Gordon and Susanna Younger had been unmasked. They had provided an immense amount of information about the activities of Jeremy Oxley and Irene Adnam. Though he tried to remain indifferent, Tallis was patently intrigued by the sudden progress made. He wished that he'd been there to interrogate the two prisoners. His interest in the case was reawakened so much that he even tried to shift part of the blame onto Colbeck.

'You must take some responsibility for what happened to Peebles,' he said. 'If you had not gone off on a wild goose chase to Coventry, you'd have been there to read your letter and to take the appropriate action. Constable Peebles would still be alive today.'

'I wish that were true,' said Colbeck, 'but my trip to Coventry was not a wild goose chase. Mrs Darker, who runs the Sherbourne Hotel there, was able to identify two of her guests as Jeremy Oxley and Irene Adnam. She did so for the second time today.'

'How can you possibly know that?'

'When they fled from the house, they decided to go to ground in a hotel where they'd enjoyed their stay. Accordingly, they arrived at the Sherbourne late this morning. Mrs Darker recognised them and sent for the police.'

'Were they apprehended?'

'Alas, no,' admitted Colbeck, 'but they were chased away. I had a telegraph from the local police. They're scouring the town in case the two suspects are still in the vicinity.'

'The chase is on, then,' said Tallis, excitedly. 'We have their scent in our nostrils.'

'Are you going to miss out on the hunt, sir? Or would you prefer to sit here and read about the campaigns of the Duke of Wellington?' He stood up. 'Please excuse me. I must get back. Urgent matters demand my attention. But I leave you with this thought,' he said. 'Were his ghost standing before you now, what do you think Constable Peebles would want you to do?'

Tallis pondered afresh, looked up at the portrait then rose to his feet. He walked across to the window and stared out in the direction of Scotland Yard. Colbeck opened the door to leave.

'Goodbye, sir,' he said, hovering. 'I'm very sorry to discover that you are beyond the reach of persuasion. I'll pass on the bad news to the commissioner.'

'Wait!' said Tallis, making up his mind. 'I'll come with you.'

CHAPTER THIRTEEN

A night in her lover's arms did much to re-assure Irene Adnam and to banish her fears of arrest. In spite of setbacks and scares, the fact remained that they were still at liberty and were now over a hundred and sixty miles away from London. Crewe was essentially a railway town, far more interested in its mundane daily round than in searching for dangerous criminals. The hotel was accustomed to people coming and going on a regular basis. It had no eagle-eyed manageress like Gwen Darker and no watchful staff. Oxley and Irene were not under surveillance.

At the same time, however, she nursed one justified anxiety. It was all very well for Oxley to point out that Inspector Colbeck would have no clue as to their whereabouts but that would not stop him continuing to look for them. He would never give up. Colbeck had already spent ten years in pursuit of Oxley and – from what she'd heard of him – was the kind of man prepared to spend another decade in the hunt. His persistence was legendary. It meant that the fugitives could never fully relax.

Irene came down late for breakfast. When she entered the dining room, she saw that Oxley was already occupying a table in the far corner. She sat down on the other side of the room and made a point of ignoring him. It was too early for the newspapers to have arrived from London. Eager to read an account of their escape, Oxley had told her that he'd walk to the railway station in due course. The meal was acceptable but it lacked the quality of the breakfasts they'd had at the Sherbourne. Indeed, the hotel could not compete on any terms with the one in which they'd stayed in Coventry. Its merits were that it was quiet, anonymous and close to the station. If they had to flee from the town, they could do so very quickly.

When he'd finished his meal, Oxley made a point of walking close to her so that he could let his hand gently brush her shoulder. Irene felt a delicious thrill coursing through her, heightened by the fact that nobody else in the dining room had been aware of the contact. If this was the game that they had to play for a while, she was ready to enjoy it. Passionate nights together would be balanced by times in the public rooms of hotels where the pair of them pretended to be complete strangers. It might leave her vulnerable to propositions from amorous gentlemen but Irene was used to rebuffing those. The sight of an attractive young woman travelling on her own always excited unwelcome interest. It was a fact of life to which she had long since adjusted.

Seated near a window, she was able to watch Oxley striding jauntily away from the hotel. He looked smart, imposing and urbane. He was a man of the world, at ease in every situation. At their first encounter, she had been struck by his courteousness. As he passed an elderly woman, Irene saw him touch the brim of his hat out of politeness. Oxley was every inch a gentleman. It was one of the things that she loved about him. He'd elevated her in every way. She was no longer an unfortunate girl, forced to enter domestic service. Irene Adnam was now a lady in her own right. She could book into a hotel on her own and order the staff around at will. It made her feel empowered.

She lingered at the table so that she could watch Oxley return and feast her eyes on him. It was not long before they'd be alone together in her room again, discussing what they should do next. First, however, he'd want to celebrate. Their latest escape was bound to have been reported in the London newspapers and Oxley would gloat over them. When he came back into view, however, there was no sense of gloating and still less of celebration. His head was down and his stroll had now become something of a scurry. Passing a lady who was exercising her dog, he didn't even spare her a glance. There was no time for courtesy now.

Irene's stomach lurched. Something was wrong. Leaving her tea untouched, she rose from the table and hurried out.

Leeming was impressed. 'How on earth did you manage it, sir?'

'I appealed to his sense of duty.'

'The commissioner did that but to no avail.'

'I had an ally, Victor.'

'Oh – who was that?'

'It was the Duke of Wellington,' said Colbeck.

'He's dead. The superintendent went to the funeral.'

'He's still alive in Mr Tallis's heart.'

'I didn't know that he had one,' said Leeming, sourly. He brightened immediately. 'But it's a relief to have him back. When he bawled at me earlier on, I felt almost glad.'

They were in Colbeck's office, collating a lot of information that had come in. On the wall was a large map of the British Isles. Colbeck explained how he'd convinced Tallis to return to work and how the Duke of Wellington had unknowingly lent his aid. Not for the first time, Leeming admired the inspector's diplomacy.

'It was the revelations about Dr and Mrs Oldfield that really secured his interest,' said

Colbeck. 'It was quite miraculous. A treasure trove of crime was both unearthed and solved in one long conversation. I wish that it was always so easy.'

'Yet they appeared to be highly respectable,' said Leeming as he recalled his meeting with the Youngers. 'Looking at them, I'd never have guessed what the truth was.'

'They worked hard to reinvent themselves, Victor. Had it not been for the arrival of unexpected guests, the doctor and his wife might have lived happily ever after as Gordon and Susanna Younger. He might even have made an excellent churchwarden.'

'Not anymore, sir – they're back in Bradford now, answering for their crimes. They'll get no mercy.'

Colbeck was philosophical. 'Justice has a way of catching up with people in the end. It just takes a little longer in some cases.'

'How long will it take before Oxley and Miss Adnam are caught?'

'The net is slowly closing around them. Now that we've engaged the British public in the search, we're getting real assistance.' He opened another letter and scanned it. 'Here's another example.'

'Who sent it?'

'The manager of a hotel in Stafford,' said Colbeck. 'He believes that they might have stayed there after the escape from the train. His description of Oxley doesn't tally in

every particular with the one that we've cir-
culated but it sounds as if it could be him,
Victor.'

Leeming was sceptical. 'Wait a moment,
sir,' he said. 'Stafford is close to Wolverhampton, isn't it? If you kill two policemen and
make a run for it, surely you'd want to get as
far away as possible.'

'That's what everybody would think and
it's what Oxley and his accomplice would
want us to think. After all, they came to London, didn't they? Who would have imagined
that they'd move close to Scotland Yard when
the search for them was being directed from
here? It was a cunning move on Oxley's part.'
He took a pin from a small tray on his desk
and stuck it in the map. 'I'm sure that they
did stay at Stafford.' He studied the map then
beckoned Leeming over. 'What do you notice
about their movements?'

'They never stay long in one place, sir.'

'Take a closer look.'

Leeming stared at the map and tried to
find a connection between all the pins they'd
inserted in it. Because his knowledge of geography was limited, he struggled to discern a
pattern. Since the reward had been advert-
ised in the newspapers, information had
poured in from a number of sources. Many
of the claims were obviously fraudulent and
had been tossed aside by Colbeck, but some
deserved to be taken seriously.

Leeming was baffled. 'Give me a clue, sir.'

'Think of my future father-in-law.'

'Why should I want to think about Mr Andrews?'

'He works for the LNWR,' replied Colbeck. 'Join up all of those pins and you'll see that the majority of them are stations on the route used by the LNWR. Here,' he went on, moving a finger from pin to pin. 'We have Watford, Leighton Buzzard, Rugby, Coventry, Birmingham, Wolverhampton, Stafford and so on, all the way up to Warrington and beyond. If our informants are correct, Oxley and Miss Adnam have stayed at all of those places some time over the last few months.'

'You can see why they'd choose to be close to a railway station, sir. In an emergency, they'd be able to get away by train.' He peered at the map. 'Where are they now – that's what I want to know?'

'I'd venture to suggest that they're following tradition,' said Colbeck. 'They'll be staying in a town somewhere along the same route.' He breathed in deeply. 'Which town is it, I wonder?'

When he came into her room, Oxley's face was as dark as a thundercloud. He closed the door behind him and barked an order.

'Pack your things – we're leaving here at once!'

'Why?' asked Irene in alarm. 'What's happened?'

'Just do as you're told.'

'But nobody knows that we're here, Jerry.'

'*He* knows,' sneered Oxley. 'That bastard, Inspector Colbeck, knows every damn thing.' He handed over the newspaper. 'Read that.'

Irene took it from him and saw the relevant article. She read it with mounting concern. All her fears flooded back. She was so jittery that she almost dropped the paper.

'They've arrested Gordon and Susanna.' Irene was incredulous.

'We got away just in time.'

'How could they possibly have linked us with that house?'

'I don't know,' he confessed.

'You said that they wouldn't find us there in a month of Sundays. That's why you chose the place.'

'I thought it was safe, Irene. More important, it kept us out of the public gaze for a while. In any case, I'd wanted to see Gordon and Susanna again. We're old friends.'

'Their real names are Philip and Anna Oldfield,' she noted, looking at the article. 'They were well known in Bradford at one time.'

'They'll be even more well known now that they've been caught,' he said. 'Well, that's their problem. We can't waste time feeling sorry for them. The most disturbing line in that article is the last one. It says that the police are very grateful for the cooperation given by the two prisoners. In other words,' he added with a snarl, 'they've given us away, Irene. They've betrayed us.'

She was too stunned to reply. As she read the article for the second time, she realised how close the police had come to catching them at the house. Only hours earlier, they'd been sleeping quietly in their beds. Had they not left under the cover of darkness, they'd now be languishing in separate cells. It was a frightening thought.

'This is Colbeck's doing,' he said. 'I told you that he was clever.'

'I still can't believe it.'

'The facts are there in black and white, Irene.'

'If he can find us there,' she argued, 'he can find us anywhere. It was the perfect hiding place and yet he still managed to track us down somehow. I'm terrified, Jerry. There's no escape from him.'

'Yes, there is.'

'Please don't say that you'll try to kill him again,' she begged. 'He'll be on guard against you next time.'

'I've thought of another solution, Irene.'

'What is it?'

'We leave the country altogether.'

Hope was rekindled. 'Yes,' she said, smiling, 'that's the answer. Remember that poster we saw at the station when we arrived? It said that we could take a train to Holyhead and pick up a ferry to Ireland. Inspector Colbeck would never touch us there.'

'Oh yes he would. You haven't followed his career as closely as I have, Irene. He was involved in a case that started in this very town when a severed head was found in a hatbox. Don't ask me how he did it,' he said, 'but Colbeck went all the way to Ireland in the course of his investigation. It's far too close. We need to be on another continent altogether.'

'Where do you suggest?'

'America.'

She was dumbfounded. The only thing she knew about America was that it was a great distance away. A very long voyage would be necessary with obvious dangers attendant upon it. Irene was rattled. It would be a journey into the unknown. On the other hand, it would finally guarantee them the safety they craved. In a new continent, they could forge an entirely new life.

'If you won't come with me,' he warned, 'I'll go alone.'

She grabbed his arm. 'Don't say that, Jerry!'

'It's the one sure way to shake Colbeck off our tail.'

'What sort of a place is it?'

'There's only one way to find out, Irene.

Will you come with me?'

'Of course,' she said, embracing him. 'You don't have to ask. I'll follow you anywhere. When do we leave?'

'Not for some days at least,' he said. 'There's a lot to do first. I've got to collect all the money and possessions I have squirrelled away in various places. And it will depend on when we can take ship. Then again, we'll need documents. I'll have forgeries made and that will take time. You can say goodbye to Irene Adnam,' he told her. 'From now on, we'll both have another name as man and wife.'

'And what name will it be, Jerry?'

'Who knows? Do you have any suggestions?' He suddenly burst out laughing. 'I've just thought of the ideal name for us, Irene. In the circumstances, it's the only one to choose.'

'Stop interrupting!' roared Tallis, rounding on the hapless sergeant. "When I want advice from you, I shall ask for it. Until then, refrain from making inane comments.'

'Yes, sir,' said Leeming.

'Listen and learn – that's my advice to you.'

It had not taken Tallis long to get back into his stride. Apart from delivering a tirade at some of his officers, he had waded through a mass of paperwork relating to other cases.

He'd now come into Colbeck's office to take stock of progress on the murder investigation. In directing him towards the map on the wall, Leeming had earned himself a stinging rebuke yet, strangely, it caused no pain this time. Having the superintendent back at Scotland Yard was so comforting that the sergeant felt insulated against the fury of his tongue. It was left to Colbeck to explain the significance of the pins in the map.

'It's a valid theory,' said Tallis, 'but it doesn't tell us where he is at the moment. We could never check every hotel within reach of the line operated by the London and North Western Railway.'

'I accept that, sir,' said Colbeck.

'My question is this – what will Oxley's next move be?'

'He'll go into hiding, sir,' Leeming put in.

'Any fool could work that out.'

'It needed saying nevertheless.'

'On the contrary, Sergeant,' said Tallis. 'It could be taken as read. There are certain assumptions that we can make without having to put them into words. Agreed?'

'You could be right, sir.'

'I am right, man – now please shut up.'

'Victor is quite right in one sense,' said Colbeck, 'but wrong in another. Two people on the run will always look for a place of refuge. However...'

'Go on,' said Tallis, standing beside him.

'I suspect that they won't stay there for long. Oxley will have been shaken rudely out of his complacence by the reports in this morning's papers. The fact that we arrested his two friends will come as a terrible blow to him, sir.'

'And so it should. We trailed them to their lair.'

'It was all because I spoke to that clerk from the ticket office at Euston,' said Leeming, wishing that he'd never spoken when subjected to the superintendent's basilisk stare. He retreated into a corner. 'I'm sorry, sir. I didn't mean to interrupt.'

'Pay attention to Colbeck. He has something sensible to say.'

'Yes, sir.'

'They'll feel that we're closing in,' resumed Colbeck. 'They tried to kill me and they failed. They thought they were safe with their friends yet we found them. Our pursuit will seem inexorable.'

'That's why it must continue with vigour.'

'Why did you say that I was wrong, Inspector?' asked Leeming.

'You almost invariably are,' sniped Tallis.

'They'll hide in the first instance, Victor,' said Colbeck, 'but the ground will tremble beneath them when they learn about the way that we almost caught them. They may well decide that there's only one course of action left open to them.'

'There'll be a second attempt to kill you?' asked Tallis.

'That would be far too risky, sir. No, I believe that they will seriously consider leaving the country altogether. That way – and that way only – they'd feel out of our reach.'

'It makes sense,' remarked Leeming.

Tallis was not persuaded. 'It's yet another of the inspector's famous theories,' he said with a slight edge. 'How valid this one is, I have my doubts. We are talking about a man who's contrived to evade the law for a very long time.'

'He's beginning to lose his touch, sir,' observed Colbeck. 'He was arrested in Wolverhampton. That was careless of him. And when he set out to kill me, he shot someone else in my place.'

'There's no need to harp on about that,' said Tallis, uneasily.

'I fancy that they'll consider going abroad.'

'I wouldn't,' said Leeming. 'You can't trust foreigners. I hated it when we had to go to France. They were so shifty over there.'

'Spare us your reminiscences,' said Tallis, acidly.

'They never made us feel welcome, sir.'

'You are rapidly outwearing your welcome in this very room, Leeming. Either hold your tongue or get out of here.' Leeming shrank back into his corner again. 'Where will they go, Inspector?'

'My guess is as good as yours, sir,' said Colbeck, 'but I know one thing. If they *are* to emigrate, they'll need time to arrange everything. We might catch them before they go.'

'How do you intend to do that?'

'We've seen before that Irene Adnam still has feelings for her father. I don't believe that she'd leave the country without paying him a last visit.' He picked up a pin and jabbed it into the map. 'This is where I believe we should go next, sir – Manchester.'

Even in the relatively short time since she'd last seen him, Silas Adnam's health had visibly deteriorated. Irene saw that his cheeks had hollowed, his eyes were bloodshot and his skin pallid. His cough was now almost continuous and causing him so much pain that he kept putting a hand to his chest. Adnam's voice was hoarse.

'I'm surprised to see you again, Irene,' he said.

'How are you feeling?'

'My lungs are on fire. It's getting worse.'

'You should have spent some of that money I gave you on a doctor. You need help, Father.'

'I'm past helping.' He came forward to glare at her. 'I never thought that it would come to this.'

'It was your own fault,' said Irene.

'I'm not talking about me – I'm talking about *you*.'

'I don't understand.'

'A detective came to see me. His name was Inspector Colbeck. He told me exactly what sort of a daughter I have.'

She reeled. 'The inspector came *here?*'

'Yes. It looks as if I helped to bring a monster into the world.'

'Don't believe everything you hear,' she warned.

He went on the attack. 'You don't work as a governess in London, do you?'

'No, I don't, as it happens.'

'Then why did you tell me that you did?' he said, resentfully. 'Why did you tell me lie after lie? There was I, thinking that I had a dutiful daughter, when all the time she was stealing from the people who employed her.'

'They deserved it,' she countered. 'They treated me like dirt.'

'So it's true, then?'

'I don't deny it.'

'What about the murder?' he asked, searching her face with widened eyes. 'Did you really shoot a policeman?' She was lost for words. 'Tell me, Irene. Try to be honest with your father for once in your life. Did you or did you not kill someone?'

She lowered her head. Taking her silence as a confession of guilt, he let out a gasp of horror then had a coughing fit. He flopped down on the bed and put a palm to his chest. Irene was mortified that he now knew the truth about her. The fact that Colbeck had actually been to see her father was more than unsettling. It induced instant panic. Irene could simply not understand how he'd made contact with the old man. It altered the whole situation. Having come to tell him a rehearsed story about going abroad with the family for whom she worked, she had to think again. Before, her father had been no more than a pathetic ruin. Now, however, he was a potential danger. Shocked by the ugly truth about his daughter, he might be tempted to report her visit to the police.

Irene knew exactly what Oxley would do in her position. There'd be no hesitation. Faced with the possibility of betrayal, he'd kill the old man without compunction. He'd only be shortening a life that had very little time to run. That option was not available to Irene. She had no weapon and she was held back by a vague sense of duty to the man who'd fathered her. Besides, her conscience already had far too much to accommodate. Irene decided to buy his silence.

'I'm leaving the country,' she told him.

'Good riddance!' he said.

'You'll never see me again, Father.'

'That won't trouble me. I want nothing to do with a killer.'

'I had to do what I did,' she said. 'It's no good explaining because you'd never understand. But before you start to look down on me, you should remember how much money I've given you over the years. I've kept you alive, Father. I had no need to do that.'

'If I'd known where the money came from, I'd never have touched it,' he said, rising to his feet to strike a pose. 'I don't have much to call my own but I do have moral standards. I used to think that I'd instilled them in you.'

Irene was blisteringly honest. 'What good are moral standards when your father drags you from a decent life in a proper home into a kind of hell? What use are they when you're a mere servant and your master starts to molest you? Do you know what it's like to be at the mercy of lecherous old men?' she demanded. 'Do you know what it's like to be treated like an unpaid prostitute? *That's* what you did to me. That's the sort of father you were.'

Adnam was hurt. 'I did my best for you, Irene.'

'The only person you ever thought about was yourself.'

'It was your mother,' he whimpered. 'When she died, I lost my way. One thing led to another. It wasn't my fault, Irene.'

'You turned me into someone else's slave and I'll never forgive you for that. I had two choices,' said Irene, temper colouring her cheeks. 'I could either submit or I could fight back. I could either let my employers use my body whenever they wished or I could steal what I wanted from them and run away.'

'So you turned into a thief.'

'It was the only way I could survive, Father.'

His eyes began to water and another coughing fit seized him. When the pain finally eased, he looked at her with a disgust laced heavily with curiosity.

'When will you go?' he asked.

'At the end of the week.'

'Where will you sail from?'

'Liverpool.'

'Who are you travelling with? Is it that man, Oxley?'

'It doesn't matter,' she said, irritably. 'The point is that I'm going out of your life for ever. I'd hoped we could have a proper farewell.'

'Ha!'

'You're still my father. I came here to give you some money.'

Adnam's expression slowly changed. The look of contempt in his eyes was eventually replaced by a glint of self-interest. He despised what she'd done and was glad that she was going far away from him, but he was too wretched to be able to refuse the offer of money, even from such a tainted source. After wrestling with his conscience for a while, he eventually got the better of it.

'How much money?' he asked.

Inspector Zachary Boone gave each of them a warm handshake. He had been warned by telegraph that Colbeck and Leeming would be coming to Manchester again and the message had contained a request for him. It had asked that Silas Adnam be brought to the police station for questioning. Boone had bad news for the visitors.

'He's not there, I'm afraid,' he said.

'Did your officers go to his lodging?' asked Colbeck.

'They did, Robert. They talked to everyone else in the house, to his neighbours and to the landlord of the pub where Adnam is well known. Nobody has any idea where he is. Or if they do,' added Boone, corrugating his brow, 'they're not telling us. We don't get much help from people in Deansgate. They think policemen are vermin.'

'We have people like that in London,' said Leeming. 'They'd sooner die than be seen giving assistance to the police. We're the enemy to them.'

'There's one possibility,' suggested Colbeck. 'Adnam is a very sick man. Since the time I was last here, he may even have died.'

'I considered that,' said Boone, 'so I told

my men to check on the local undertakers. None of them had been called to collect the body of Silas Adnam. He's still alive.'

'Then where is he? The fellow can't have left Manchester. He'd have no money to do so. Unless...'

'What are you thinking, Robert?'

'His daughter got to him before your men did.'

Boone's office was more cluttered than ever. Files had now been stacked on the floor and the desk was invisible beneath a blizzard of paperwork. He presided over the general anarchy with the confidence of a man who had everything supremely under command. In one deft movement, he plucked a telegraph from beneath a pile of documents.

'All that this told me,' he said, 'was that you were coming to Manchester and that you needed to speak to Adnam. Could I have some more detail, Robert?'

'How much do you already know?'

'I read the London newspapers, so I know about the death of Constable Peebles. Such a pity – I liked him on sight.' He smiled at Leeming. 'I was a little more wary of you, Sergeant.'

'I sometimes have that effect on people,' said Leeming.

'No offence intended.'

'None is taken, Inspector. My face never wins friends.'

'It does when people get to know you, Victor,' said Colbeck, patting his shoulder. 'But let me fill in the gaps in Zachary's knowledge of the case. A lot has happened in the last few days.'

Amplifying the details given in the press, Colbeck told him about the flight of Oxley and Irene, the arrest of the two suspects and the abundance of information that had come in, enabling them to place the suspects at various hotels at specific times. Boone agreed that the fugitives might well consider emigration as their only viable option.

'I think you're right, Robert,' he said. 'If she's about to shake the dust of this country off her shoes, Irene Adnam is very likely to pay a last visit to her father.'

'There's a big difference this time,' noted Colbeck.

'Is there?'

'Yes, Zachary – her father knows the truth about her. When she kept supplying him with money, he was happy to believe the fiction that she worked as a governess. After all, he could take some credit for having got her the education that qualified her to take on such a post. Teaching the sons and daughters of the wealthy would seem to be a worthy occupation to someone who'd sunk as low as he has.'

'If his daughter *did* go to see him,' said Leeming, 'how do you think Mr Adnam would react?'

'I think he'd condemn what she did. Any father would.'

'That would take her by surprise. Irene Adnam had no idea that you'd visited her father and laid the whole facts before him. She'd be expecting to be able to wear the same mask as before.'

Colbeck nodded. 'That's a good point, Victor.'

'If he started yelling at her, she'd be very upset. Her first thought would be that he might even report her to the police.'

'I don't think he'd do that somehow.'

'It's a possibility she'd have to consider, sir,' said Leeming, as he tried to imagine the confrontation between father and daughter. 'If he did threaten to turn her in, what would she do?'

'Get away from there as fast as she could,' answered Boone.

'That wouldn't solve the problem. She'd have every policeman in Manchester looking for her. I'm wondering if she acted on impulse.'

Boone sniffed. 'She'd never kill her own father, would she?'

'We know that she's capable of murder. If she was desperate, there's no telling what she might do.'

'I think it's unlikely that she'd resort to violence,' said Colbeck, mulling it over. 'In her own way, she still loves her father. Otherwise, she'd have disowned him years ago. Anyway, why else bid him farewell unless she had a parting gift for him? If he decided to report her to the police, he wouldn't get anything. That's what it may come down to in the end,' he concluded. 'What price will he put on his silence?'

Two whole days and nights apart from Oxley had left Irene in a state of agitation. They'd arranged to meet on the third day in Liverpool. She spent the intervening time buying a cabin trunk and filling it with all the items she felt that she'd need to begin a new life in America. Without Oxley beside her to offer support, she began to lose heart. Far too many things could go wrong. What if her father made contact with the police, after all? What if Colbeck caught them before they sailed? What if Oxley made another serious mistake? Even if they did get safely away, what if the ship sank in a violent storm? What if they were refused entry to America? What if they were forced to return to England? Worst of all, she kept asking herself, what if Oxley failed to turn up? Supposing that he'd already fled the country on his own?

By the time that the third day dawned, she was convinced that their escape would somehow founder. Having spent the last night in a hotel in Liverpool, she had her trunk sent down to the harbour, more in hope than in certainty. A cab took her to the designated place. It was a windy day and, as she alighted from the vehicle, she had to put a hand to her hat to keep it on. She looked around for Oxley and was horrified to see that he was not there. He'd been very specific about the time and place of their reunion yet he had not turned up. That raised the question of whether he'd ever intended to. Had he waved the possibility of emigration in front of Irene solely to get rid of her? She would not be the first discarded mistress. She was keenly aware of that. Had the others also been tricked into thinking they were starting a new life abroad with him?

The longer she waited, the more she fretted. Standing on a corner near the harbour gates, she was also bothered by a succession of men who offered to carry her valise in order to ingratiate themselves with her. One drunken sailor even tried to steal a kiss. Irene pushed him away but the man lunged at her again. He did not even touch her this time. Oxley grabbed him from behind, spun him round then felled him with a punch to the jaw. As the sailor sagged to the ground, Oxley stepped over him and took Irene in his arms.

'I'm sorry I'm late,' he said, holding her close.

She was tearful. 'I thought you weren't coming.'

'Have I ever deserted you before?'

'No, Jerry, you haven't.'

'Then stop having such silly thoughts. I'm here now.'

'When do we go aboard?' she asked.

'Fairly soon – they give us a medical examination.'

'I sent my luggage on ahead, as you told me.'

'I did the same.' Arm around her, he led Irene through the harbour gates. 'What have you been doing since I last saw you?'

'I've been pining for you most of the time.'

'That's very flattering. Did you see your father?'

'Yes, Jerry.' She winced at the memory, 'He knew.'

'I don't understand.'

'He knew what you and I had been doing. Inspector Colbeck told him so in person.'

Oxley stopped. 'Colbeck spoke to your father? How on earth did he find out where he lived?'

'I don't know,' she said, 'but, then, I don't know how he tracked us to Gordon and Susanna's house. The one thing I do know is that he's shadowing us wherever we go. We must get away from England for good, Jerry.'

'We will,' he promised, hustling her along

again. 'We'll have three thousand miles between us and Inspector Colbeck. Even he
would never try to follow us to America.'

Leeming was dismayed at having to spend
two nights in Manchester while the search for
Silas Adnam continued. He doubted whether
they'd ever find the man in such a populous
city. Colbeck insisted that they had to stay,
arguing that Irene Adnam's father might well
hold a vital clue as to her whereabouts.
Thinking about his wife and children, the
sergeant was desperate to get back to
London. Colbeck made a telling comsment.
  'Do you want to go back empty-handed,
Victor?'
  'I just want to go home.'
  'Would you like to admit that we failed?
Imagine what the superintendent will say.
Would you like to be the one to tell him?'
  Leeming shuddered. 'No, I wouldn't, sir.'
  'Then we stay until we get a result.'
  'But that could take ages.'
  'Adnam is bound to turn up sooner or
later.'
  'I think he'll be found in a dark corner
with his throat cut,' said Leeming with a
vivid gesture. 'If his daughter gave him
money, he'll start waving it around. It won't
be long before someone seizes his chance.
According to you, Adnam wouldn't be able
to defend himself.'

'He's too old and weak.'

'And no use to us when he's dead.'

'Don't be so pessimistic, Victor.'

'I hate all this waiting, Inspector.'

The sergeant's gloom was soon dispelled. He and Colbeck were sharing a room above an inn. They were on the point of leaving when a policeman came looking for them with an urgent summons from Inspector Boone. They hailed a cab and set off. When they reached the police station, they were shown straight into the inspector's office. Hoping to find Silas Adnam there, Colbeck was disappointed.

'Where is he, Zachary?'

'Sleeping off his stupor,' said Boone.

'You found him, then?'

'Yes, Robert. That was a good guess of yours. His daughter gave him a substantial amount of money and he decided to enjoy it while he still had the strength. Adnam cleaned himself up, went off to a better part of the city, bought some decent clothes for a change, then moved into a hotel and drank his way through bottle after bottle.' Boone grinned. 'I wish I had enough money to do that. Anyway,' he went on, 'Adnam caused so much disruption this morning that the hotel manager called in the police.'

'Where is he now?' asked Leeming.

'He's snoring to high heaven in one of our cells.'

'We must speak to him,' said Colbeck.

'There's no need, Robert,' said Boone. 'I discovered what you wanted to know. I caught Adnam in a lucid moment and shook the truth out of him. Oxley and his daughter are fleeing the country.'

'From which port are they embarking?'

'Liverpool.'

'On which day are they sailing?'

'He didn't know that.'

'Thank you, Zachary,' said Colbeck, shaking his hand in gratitude. 'You'll have to excuse us. We need to get to Liverpool and hope that they haven't left yet.'

After days of inertia, there was a burst of activity. The detectives made a frantic dash to the station, bought two tickets to Liverpool and spent the journey speculating on which country the fugitives had chosen as their new home. Jerked out of his pessimism, Leeming was exhilarated at the thought of finally catching up with Oxley and his accomplice. It was the tragic death of Ian Peebles that he was eager to avenge. Colbeck, too, nursed sad thoughts of the fallen detective but it was Helen Millington who remained uppermost in his mind. He was desperate to meet Irene Adnam to see just how closely she resembled the young woman to whom he'd once grown so close.

Arriving at the station, they ran to the cab

rank and ordered a driver to take them to the harbour. Crowds of people were drifting away, suggesting that a ship had not long sailed and that friends and well-wishers were now dispersing. It was a bad omen. When they got to the pier, they saw a vessel gliding off down the Mersey. They were told that it was the *Arethusa* and that it was bound for New York. They both prayed that the fugitives were not aboard. While Colbeck went off to check on other recent sailings, Leeming stood on the pier with the wind plucking at his clothing and trying to dislodge his hat. He felt cheated. Something told him that Oxley and Irene Adnam were on the ship, sailing away from justice across the Atlantic Ocean. It was unfair. Leeming kicked a stone into the water out of frustration. After all the time and energy they'd put into the investigation, it was galling to see it collapse around them.

Colbeck eventually returned with a look of grim resignation.

'What's happened?' asked Leeming.

'They sailed on the *Arethusa*.'

'Are you certain of that, sir?'

'I'm absolutely certain.'

'But they wouldn't have used their own names, surely? That would have been far too dangerous.'

'They appreciated that,' said Colbeck, staring at the receding vessel. 'They're travelling as man and wife under a false name.'

'And what name would that be, sir?'

'It's one that convinces me that it must be them, Victor.'

'Oh?'

'They are calling themselves Mr and Mrs Robert Colbeck.'

CHAPTER FOURTEEN

'This is a meagre reward for three days in Manchester,' said Tallis, gnashing his teeth in disappointment. 'All that you've brought back is the information that the suspects have fled to America.'

'I don't call that a meagre reward, sir,' said Colbeck.

'You were too late, man. They've flown the coop.'

'We only just missed catching them, sir,' Leeming pointed out. 'It was the inspector who guessed that they'd flee the country and that Miss Adnam would be sure to visit her father beforehand. His theory was proved right even though, when he first put it forward, you had doubts about it.'

'That's beside the point, Sergeant,' said Tallis.

'Our journey was not in vain. We established the facts.'

'I wanted arrests and you failed to make them.'

They'd returned to Scotland Yard to account for their absence and to inform the superintendent that the fugitives were no longer on British soil. Tallis was appalled by the news. Instead of reaching for a cigar, however, he heaped criticism on his detectives for what he described as their lack of urgency. The attack was unjust and Leeming smarted under its severity. Colbeck, however, remained unruffled. That served to inflame Tallis even more.

'I don't know how you can stay so calm, Inspector,' he said. 'At this very moment, someone is crossing the Atlantic with your name on his passport. If that fact became known to the press, we'd be held up to ridicule. The department would be pilloried in every newspaper.'

'The situation is not irretrievable, sir.'

'Don't talk such drivel.'

'We can still capture them.'

'How?' asked Leeming, goggling. 'They're out of our jurisdiction.'

'I think we can overcome that obstacle, Victor.'

Tallis descended into sarcasm. 'What did you have in mind?' he asked. 'Are you planning to swim after the vessel and catch it up?'

'I've a much better idea than that, Super-intendent.'

'May we know what it is?'

'You will have to, sir,' said Colbeck, 'be-cause you'll need to give the sergeant and I your seal of approval.'

'What sort of approval?'

'We're going on a voyage to America.'

Leeming gasped. 'I can't go sailing across an ocean. I have obligations.'

'We both have an obligation to catch felons responsible for the deaths of three policemen as well as for a multitude of other crimes. Yes, I know it's a long way,' said Colbeck, 'but the effort will be well worth it.'

'You can't be serious about this,' said Tallis.

'I was never more so, Superintendent. We may have no jurisdiction in New York but there's such a thing as extradition. If it's handled correctly, the authorities will comply with our request. Well,' he added, 'would *you* want to allow two brutal killers to walk into your country without even being challenged?'

'But think of the time involved,' said Leeming, anxiously.

Tallis was practical. 'I'm thinking of the cost involved.'

'Your budget is not at risk, sir,' said Colbeck. 'I'm so committed to the notion that I'll volunteer to pay for the tickets my-self. Victor and I will sail from Liverpool on the next available vessel.'

'What about my wife and family?' wailed Leeming.

'I'm afraid that they can't come with us.'

'They'll miss me, Inspector.'

'It's all in a good cause. Try to think of it as an adventure.'

'Where's the adventure in being away for weeks on end?'

Colbeck lowered his voice. 'Do you want the killers of Constable Peebles to get away scot-free?'

'No, sir – of course, I don't.'

'I second that,' said Tallis, wholeheartedly. 'They must pay the ultimate penalty some-how.' He reached for a cigar then changed his mind and withdrew his hand. 'It's a bold plan, Colbeck, but it has a fatal flaw in it.'

'I've yet to detect one,' said Colbeck.

'They have a head start on you. They're already on their way. Mr and Mrs Robert Colbeck will get to New York long before you.'

'That's true,' said Leeming, relieved. 'We'd never catch them. Good as it is, I'm afraid that the idea will have to be abandoned.'

Tallis nodded. 'Sadly, I have to agree.'

'Then neither of you is familiar with the shipping lines,' said Colbeck. 'I'm surprised at you, Victor. You actually saw the *Arethusa* slowly disappearing down the Mersey. Didn't you notice something about her?'

'Only that she was out of our reach,' said Leeming.

'The *Arethusa* is a sailing ship. She relies entirely on wind power. That means the crossing will take time. If we book passages on a steamship – driven by propeller *and* wind – the chances are that we'll arrive in New York at least a fortnight before them.' He was amused by their startled reaction. 'A tall ship may look more graceful as it rides the ocean waves but a steamship is more efficient. I checked the approximate crossing times for both vessels when I was in Liverpool. We can wait over a week and still get to New York ahead of the *Arethusa*. What do you say, Superintendent?'

'It's certainly worth exploring,' said Tallis. 'I'd have to speak to the commissioner, of course, but I can't see that he'd object.'

'Well, I object,' said Leeming. 'It's simply too far to go.'

'We should be prepared to go to the ends of the earth in pursuit of murderers,' asserted Colbeck. 'Think what it will do for us, Victor. If we can show that there's no escape from justice, the publicity will be priceless. Criminals will think twice about fleeing abroad.'

'Yes,' said Tallis. 'If you succeed, reporters might actually say something nice about me in their newspapers for a change. And since Leeming is so unhappy about keeping you company, Inspector, I'm tempted to do so myself.'

Colbeck was alarmed. 'No, no, sir, that won't be necessary.'

'It will help me to atone for my part in Constable Peebles' death.'

'You'll do that by sanctioning the plan.'

'Scotland Yard can manage without me for a few weeks.'

'It will be over a month, sir – perhaps more. You can't be spared from your desk for that long,' said Colbeck, baulking at the notion that he'd have to travel with Tallis. 'It would be wrong to tear away a senior officer from a job that he does so well. The sergeant will come with me, I'm sure. Victor knows where his duty lies.'

'It's with my family,' said Leeming, disconsolately.

'Don't mention that word to me,' said Tallis, treating him to a withering glare. 'When you're inside this building, you don't *have* a family. Your first duty is to obey orders.'

'Yes, sir, I know that.'

'If I tell you to sail to America, you'll do so without complaint.'

'That's what you think,' said Leeming to himself.

'In fact, all three of us can go together. Oxley is armed. He has nothing to lose, so he's bound to resist arrest. It may need three of us to overpower him.' He slapped his desk. 'The matter is decided. I shall speak to the commissioner at once.'

Jumping to his feet, he marched out of the office. Leeming was in despair at the thought of being away from his wife and family for so long. Glad that his plan had the superintendent's approval, Colbeck was sobered by the threat of having to share the voyage with Tallis. It was not an alluring prospect.

'It was your own fault, Inspector,' said Leeming. 'You should never have persuaded him to return to work. You should have left him in retirement with his portrait of the Duke of Wellington.'

Irene had never expected it to be so noisy. The bellowed commands at the point of departure, the bustle of the crew, the whistle of the wind, the flapping of the sails, the creaking of the timbers, the smack of the water against the hull and the strident cries of the gulls all combined to buffet her ears. With the deafening new sounds came a collection of new sights and sensations. Irene had never been on a ship before and its design intrigued her. When it left the mouth of the river and hit the open sea, she was staggered at the vast expanse of water ahead of them. Covered in white-capped waves, it seemed to stretch to infinity. Sailors were climbing the rigging or hauling up other sails. Passengers were standing at the bulwark to give a farewell wave to the mainland.

Like them, Irene felt the salty spray on her face, the wind on her hair and the rocking-horse rhythm of the deck beneath her feet as the *Arethusa* rose and fell through the surging tide. She was gripped by a fear that was only partly allayed by a sense of adventure. A ship so small would be no more than a splinter of wood on a huge and turbulent ocean like the Atlantic. The excitement of leaving dry land had now been replaced by the uncertainty of ever arriving at their destination. Irene had no means of control over what was happening to her. All that she could do was to pray.

She felt a comforting arm being wrapped around her shoulder.

'Welcome to America, Mrs Colbeck,' said Oxley.

'There's a long way to go yet,' she reminded him.

'Yes, but the most important part of the voyage is over. We're clear of the coast now. We've escaped from the clutches of the law.'

'They have policemen in New York, Jerry.'

'Granted – but they don't *know* us, do they? We'll be looked upon as ideal emigrants. We're young, respectable, intelligent and financially stable. That's all they'll see.'

'I'll just be grateful to get there safely.'

'The *Arethusa* has crossed the ocean dozens of times.'

'You keep telling me that but it doesn't stop me from worrying. Now we're at sea, the ship feels so small and fragile.'

He stamped hard on the deck. 'It's as solid as a rock,' he said. 'That's seasoned English oak beneath our feet, Irene. Nobody could build ships the way that we did. If you still feel nervous about sailing, remember Nelson. He won all those naval battles because he had complete faith in the shipbuilders.'

She gave a pale smile. 'I wish I could share it.'

'You'll come to trust the *Arethusa* in time.'

For his part, Oxley was in a state of quiet jubilation. After a successful criminal career in England, he'd reached the point where it was about to be terminated on the gallows. Recent events had taught him that there was nowhere safe to hide from Colbeck. The inspector's pursuit of them was unrelenting. It was only a matter of time before he finally caught up with them. There was no danger of that now. Oxley had severed his ties with England and was embarking on an adventure that, he felt sure, would yield endless opportunities for a man with his well-honed skills. He just wished that Irene could relish the same jubilation.

'Are you still thinking about your father?' he asked.

'Yes,' she confessed. 'I'm bound to, Jerry.'

'You gave him far too much money.'

'I had to bribe him into silence.'

'Twenty pounds would have done that. There was no need to give him the best part of a hundred.'

'I could afford it and I felt guilty about him.'

'He'll be dead before he has time to spend it. That money came from the robbery in Birmingham. We could have used it in America. It was wasted on him.'

'We have plenty of money, Jerry. My father has none. Giving it to him made me feel good and stopped him from going to the police.'

'You'll never see the old fool again.'

'I know that.'

'Does that trouble you?'

She pursed her lips in thought. 'No,' she said, eventually. 'I don't think it does.'

'I'm taking *you* to America and not your father.'

She kissed him. 'I couldn't be more grateful.'

'You have to let go of the past, Irene. When we get to New York, I don't ever want to hear you talking about your family.'

'You won't, I promise you.'

'How can I be certain of that?'

'I'm not Irene Adnam anymore,' she said with conviction. 'I'm Mrs Robert Colbeck and I no longer have any family in England. What's more,' she added, gazing across the undulating waves, 'I'm going to put my trust in the *Arethusa* and enjoy every second of this voyage.'

Madeleine Andrews felt as if she'd just been hit over the head. For a moment, she was too dazed even to speak. She'd been overjoyed when Colbeck turned up unexpectedly at the house. They'd kissed and held each other in silence for a long time. When he released her and told her his news, however, it made her stagger back as if from a blow. He steadied her quickly with a hand. She had to shake her head to clear her brain.

'You're going to *America?*' she cried.

'They have to be caught, Madeleine.'

'But it's so far away and the ocean is so treacherous.'

'In the interest of arresting the fugitives,' he said, stoutly, 'we're prepared to take any risks involved. At least,' he went on, 'I certainly am. Victor is less committed to the enterprise. He hates being away from his family for any length of time.'

'How long will it all take, Robert?'

'That depends on the speed of the *Arethusa*. We'll be sailing in an iron-hulled steamship that's much faster. Some of the Cunard fleet have been known to reach New York in as little as ten or eleven days. In fact, the Blue Riband is held by a vessel that went even faster.'

'What's the Blue Riband?'

'It's a notional award for the fastest crossing between Liverpool and New York. It's currently held by *Persia*, an iron ship powered by paddles, launched two years ago. It crossed the Atlantic in nine days and sixteen hours.'

'It's not the speed I care about,' she said, 'it's the lack of safety. Remember that I've been reading that copy of *American Notes* you loaned me. Charles Dickens describes the voyage he made in a steamship as a nightmare from start to finish. He feared for his life a number of times.'

'That was several years ago, Madeleine. He sailed in the steam packet, *Britannia*. Maritime engineering has made big strides since then. Steamships are faster and safer.'

'Are they?' she questioned. 'I thought the SS *Great Britain* ran aground. Father had a good laugh when that happened because it was designed by Mr Brunel and Father despises anything connected with him. Yes,' she continued, 'and other steamships have been badly damaged in storms. A few have even been lost at sea.'

'The overwhelming majority cross the Atlantic regularly without incident, Madeleine,' he said. 'There's no need for anxiety, I assure you. Cunard has a good record.'

It was not only the safety of the vessel that

concerned her. She was worried about the danger of arresting two people who had both committed murder in order to escape. Madeleine was tortured by the thought that Colbeck might be killed thousands of miles away from her. She was enveloped by a feeling of helplessness. If he went to New York, she'd forfeit his company for a long period and lose her peace of mind into the bargain. When he was leading an investigation in Britain, she rarely had qualms about his personal safety. Now that he was going abroad, however, she was assailed by a creeping terror.

Sensing her unease, he embraced her again.

'There is one way to prevent your constant anxiety,' he said.

'Is there?'

'You could come with me.'

She laughed in surprise. 'I could never go all that way, Robert.'

'Why not?'

'Father would never countenance it,' she said. 'I know that we're engaged but he's very old-fashioned in some ways. If we were already married, of course, it would be a different matter.'

'Once this is over,' he promised, experiencing a stab of guilt, 'we will marry, Madeleine. Until then, it's probably asking too much of your father to allow us to be alone together for weeks on end.'

'I'm not sure that the superintendent

would endorse it either.'

'He'd make loud protests. You know he has eccentric views about women. Unfortunately, he's talking about coming on the voyage, so there'd be no way of smuggling you aboard without his knowledge.'

'I'll have to stay at home and count the days until you return.'

He kissed her again. 'I can't wait until this case is finally over.'

She was fatalistic. 'There'll be another one to replace it.'

'No, Madeleine,' he said, 'there'll never be a case quite like this. It's unique. When I get back, I'll explain why.'

Leeming's experience of travelling by sea was limited to a short voyage to and from France but that had been more than enough to convince him that he was no sailor. His stomach had been as unruly as the wild, green water that had tossed the vessels on which he sailed hither and thither. If crossing the English Channel had such an effect on him, then the Atlantic Ocean would be a continuous ordeal. What helped to give him much needed confidence was the response of his wife. Dismayed that he'd be away for so long, Estelle encouraged him to go because she saw the fact that he was chosen for the assignment as a mark of the esteem in which he was held at Scotland Yard.

As a detective's wife, she was habituated to adapting to situations as they arose. This one required more adjustment than usual but Estelle did not blench at that. The children's opinion also weighed with Leeming. They were highly excited at the news that their father would go on a long voyage to America. It was something they could boast about to their friends and they longed to hear about his adventures when he got back. With such unanimous family support, Leeming began to lose some of his reservations about the trip.

One particular fear, however, continued to loom large and he raised the issue with Superintendent Tallis at Scotland Yard.

'I don't see that it's possible, sir,' he said. 'How can an iron ship float on water? It's in defiance of common sense. If I drop a flat iron into a bowl of water, it will sink to the bottom at once.'

'Colbeck will explain it to you.'

'I simply can't trust an iron steamship.'

'Hundreds of thousands of people have trusted them,' said Tallis, 'and they've sailed much farther afield than America. There's a regular service to Australia now.'

Leeming grimaced. 'I hope none of our fugitives ever go there. I'd hate to have to chase them all that way.'

'We're an island race, Leeming. Our power and prosperity are based on our maritime skills. By rights, we should all have salt water in our veins.'

'Well, I don't, sir. The sea scares me.'

Tallis was brisk. 'You'll soon get over that, man,' he said. 'By the time you come back, you'll be an experienced sailor and look down on landlubbers like me.'

'I thought you were coming with us, Superintendent.'

There was a long sigh of regret. 'That's what I hoped but the commissioner has refused to authorise it. He thinks I'm too important to spare.'

'Oh, you are,' said Leeming, rushing to approve the decision. 'Without you here, the whole department would start to fall apart. In fact,' he added, groping for a historical analogy, 'I'd go so far as to say that you're as important to the Metropolitan Police Force as the Duke of Wellington was to the Battle of Waterloo.'

Tallis glowed. 'That's very kind of you to say so.'

'The inspector would say the same.'

'We must never forget that the Duke led a coalition army. His genius lay in welding so many disparate elements together. That, I fancy, is where my talent lies.'

'I agree, sir.'

Yet another of Leeming's objections had just disappeared. Travelling with Colbeck would ensure that he had someone to keep up his morale on the voyage. Having the superintendent on board as well would rob the voyage of any hope of relaxation or pleasure. Leeming had likened it to being entwined in an anchor chain. Suddenly, that chain had been snapped in two. Tallis would not be going.

'What about arrest warrants, Superintendent?'

'They'll be ready for you to take with you,' said Tallis.

'Then there's the question of extradition.'

'The documents are being prepared.'

'What if they refuse to let Oxley and Miss Adnam go?'

'Don't waste time raising possibilities that will never exist. America is a young and expanding country. It needs emigrants but it will not take just anyone,' said Tallis. 'It will discriminate. Oxley and his accomplice are bloodthirsty killers. My firm belief is that America will be glad to get rid of them.'

'We'll do our best to bring them back alive.'

'Oh, yes, you must do that. I don't want them to evade the noose by dying in a gunfight or even by shooting themselves. I want to be there when the pair of them are hanged,' declared Tallis, describing the scene with his hands. 'It's the only thing that will reconcile me to the death of Constable Peebles.'

After a week at sea, Oxley and Irene had fallen into a comfortable routine. Good weather and calm conditions encouraged them to spend a lot of time on deck, promenading arm in arm. Their affability had won them a number of new friends, all of whom regarded them as a happily married couple. Oxley was already plotting.

'People are so trusting on board,' he said, as they stood at the bulwark one day. 'It will be child's play to rob them.'

'I could have stolen a dozen reticules by now, Jerry. Ladies are so careless with their possessions. They spy no danger,' said Irene. 'I've lost count of the number of times I had to control the urge to reach out and take things.'

'It's far too early, Irene.'

'I know that.'

'We must wait until we are much nearer our destination. If there's a spate of thefts now, the captain will have weeks to look into them. Bide our time and strike hard when the moment comes.'

'There's a small fortune on this ship.'

'Then it needs to go to people like us who appreciate it.' They smiled conspiratorially. 'The crucial thing is to maintain their trust. That's why I'm careful when I play cards of an evening. If I wanted to, I could win almost every hand but that would give the game away, so I allow others to have their share of the winnings.'

'I hadn't realised you were a practised cardsharp Jerry.'

'Oh, I have many strings to my bow.'

'I've discovered that. What other secrets are there in store?'

'That would be telling,' he said, archly.

They were diverted by a shout that brought all the other passengers rushing to their side of the deck. A school of whales had appeared in the middle distance, rising playfully out of the water before diving back into it. Irene was diverted by the spectacle and Oxley savoured it for a while. He then looked along the line of passengers and saw how vulnerable they all were to anyone with light fingers. Pressed against the bulwark, feeling the spray and the wind in their faces, they were so enraptured by the antics of the whales that they'd never feel wallets being removed or watches being lifted gently from their waistcoat pockets. Tempted as he was, Oxley stayed his hand. The moment of truth would eventually come.

Only when the ship had sailed past the whales did Irene turn back to him. Her eyes were bright with wonder.

'Wasn't that a wonderful sight!' she said.

'There'll be lots more before we reach New York.'

'I've read about whales in books but I

never dreamt that I'd actually see any. They were an absolute joy.'

'Shall I tell you why?' he asked. 'They were celebrating their freedom. They have the whole ocean in which to play and they were revelling in the fact. We should do the same, Irene. Because we left England, we've bought our liberty and can enjoy it as much as that school of whales.'

'They're not entirely free,' she argued. 'People hunt whales.'

'Then we have even more liberty than they do, Irene. Nobody can hunt us now. We'll never have a harpoon hurled at us.'

'What if Inspector Colbeck finds out where we've gone?'

'That will never happen,' he said with a confident laugh. 'And even if it did, there'd be nothing he could do. Colbeck belongs in our past just like your father. We'll simply forget him as a person and preserve his memory on our passports.'

'It was an inspiration to call ourselves Mr and Mrs Colbeck.'

'I regard it as theft of the highest order, Irene. We're two unconscionable villains yet we bear the name of a famous detective.' He smirked. 'There's something almost poetic about that.'

SS *Jura*, a vessel of the Allan Line, was a propeller-driven steamship capable of a speed of eleven knots. While its beam engines provided its motive power, it also had ample amounts of canvas to harness the wind. With a gross weight of 2,241 tons, it was bigger, heavier and more majestic than Leeming had ever imagined. Launched in 1854 for the Cunard Line, it had been a troop transport during the Crimean War and had given good service. It then plied Mediterranean routes before being transferred to the Atlantic where Liverpool, Cork and New York were its ports of call. When he first stepped aboard, Leeming discovered that the vessel had a pleasing solidity. Yet even though Colbeck had explained to him how an iron ship could float without sinking, he remained nervous. When it sailed off down the Mersey, therefore, he half-expected it to founder at any moment.

'We're so low in the water,' he complained.

'That's because we have maximum coal stocks aboard,' said Colbeck. 'As they get used up, you'll notice a progressive improvement.'

'The engines are so loud.'

'You'll soon get accustomed to that.'

'Can the ship really carry so many people? It's a full passenger list and there must be well over a hundred crew members.'

'I daresay she carried far more people when she was a troop ship. Soldiers, horses and equipment would have been crammed in. The *Jura* had no problem catering for such numbers. She came through the experience with flying colours.'

Leeming pulled a face. 'I'm not sure that *I* will, sir.'

'You'll find your sea legs in time.'

'I don't think I have any.' He looked up and down the deck. 'I never thought she'd be this long.'

'She's over a hundred yards from stem to stern,' said Colbeck. 'There's enough room for us all to promenade without bumping into each other.'

'What are we going to *do* all day?'

'We'll soon fall into a routine, Victor. By the way, I noticed that they have chess-boards available in the saloon.'

'But I can't play chess, Inspector.'

'It will be a pleasure to teach you.'

For the first couple of days, Leeming was unable to concentrate on anything but the queasiness of his stomach. Once he adapted to the roll of the ship, however, he was able to exercise on deck and take a full part in the social activities on board. He shared a state room with Colbeck that had been ingeniously designed to make the utmost use of the limited space. They had comfortable bunks, a table and two chairs bolted to the floor, large cupboards and a porthole through which they could watch the waves rippling past. The food was excellent and the portions generous. The stewards were universally pleasant and efficient. Every effort had been made to ensure that the passengers enjoyed the voyage.

Colbeck decided that they would not divulge the true nature of their business aboard. He confided in the captain but everyone else was told that he and Leeming were visiting friends in New York. They could hide their credentials but they couldn't curb their instincts. When a succession of thefts occurred from first-class state rooms, the detectives felt obliged to offer their help and – by setting a trap – they caught the thief red-handed. The captain was so grateful that he invited them to dine at his table.

A week after they'd set out, Leeming admitted that all his fears about the voyage had been without foundation. Over a game of chess with Colbeck, he even claimed to be relishing the experience.

'It's been an education,' he said. 'I've learnt something new every day. There are so many interesting people aboard.'

'The most interesting person I've met is the chief engineer,' Colbeck told him. 'I spent half an hour in the engine room with him this morning. It's fascinating to see the stokers at work. They're the real heroes aboard this vessel.'

'And there was me, wondering what we'd

do all day.'

'Think of all the stories you'll have to tell your children.'

'We've seen so many amazing things,' said Leeming, moving a bishop to take one of Colbeck's pawns. 'And even when the weather keeps us below deck, there's plenty to keep us occupied. Who'd have thought there'd be a library aboard?'

'That book about New York I borrowed is a revelation.'

'I'm still reading the novel you recommended – *The Adventures of Roderick Random*. I've never had time to read a whole book before.'

'This is a voyage of discovery for you, Victor,' said Colbeck, shifting his queen to capture one of Leeming's knights. 'You're doing new things every day.'

'Yes,' said Leeming, using his bishop to capture another pawn. 'Wait until I tell my children how easily I mastered chess.'

Colbeck smiled. 'You haven't quite mastered it yet.'

'But I've taken all these pawns off you.'

'I was happy to sacrifice them because it enabled me to relieve you of more important pieces. You should guard your king with more care, Victor.' Colbeck moved his queen again. 'Checkmate.'

Caleb Andrews was not the most sensitive of

men but even he could not miss the change of mood in his daughter. As a rule, Madeleine had a sunny disposition and a natural optimism. Time and again, she'd cheered her father up or eased him gently out of any descent into grief and brooding. Their roles were reversed now. It was Andrews who was buoyant and Madeleine who was jaded. When he got back from work that evening, he spotted the signs.

'What's happened, Maddy?' he asked.

'Nothing has happened.'

'Then why are you looking so miserable?'

She manufactured a smile. 'I don't *feel* miserable.'

'You've been sad and distracted all week.'

'That's not true, Father.'

'I speak as I find.'

'Then you're mistaken,' she said with false brightness. 'I've had such a good day at the easel that I probably worked too long. I'm tired, that's all. Take no notice.'

Andrews was not fooled. He waited until they were eating their supper before he broached the subject again. She looked tense and sorrowful. Her mind was clearly elsewhere.

'Dirk Sowerby was so jealous when I told him,' he began.

She was bemused. 'What's that?'

'You know how much Dirk wants to sail in a steamship. When I told him that Inspector

Colbeck was crossing the Atlantic, he was green with envy.' He drank some tea. 'He *is* coming back, Maddy.'

'Yes, I know.'

'Time will fly past.'

'It's not doing that at the moment.'

'Are you worried about him?'

'Yes,' she confessed. 'I'm very worried.'

'Steamships have a good safety record – unless they're designed by Brunel, that is. You wouldn't get me in one of his vessels.'

'Don't be so prejudiced.'

'He's our main rival, Maddy. Everyone who works for the LNWR hates the man. For a start, he's so cocky.'

'Robert hasn't sailed on one of his ships.'

'Then there's nothing to get anxious about, is there?'

'I'm not anxious.'

'And I'm not blind. You're my daughter. I know your ways.'

'Yes,' she said with a wan smile, 'of course, you do. I'm sorry if I've been a bit lacklustre. I don't mean to be.'

'You miss him.'

'I miss him a great deal.'

'And you think something terrible could happen.'

'Well, I was upset at first but only because I'd been reading *American Notes*. Charles Dickens sailed to America with his wife and they had a dreadful voyage. They were caught in a heavy swell and everything in their cabin was tossed about. Mrs Dickens thought they were going to drown.'

'Did you mention this to the inspector?'

'I did,' she replied, 'and he pointed out that Mr Dickens made the crossing in January when the weather was at its worst. It's autumn now. Also, shipbuilding has improved since he went to America. Vessels are built to withstand whatever storms batter them.'

'So you were worrying about nothing, Maddy.'

'Not exactly...'

'You mean that there's something else?'

Madeleine hesitated. It was on occasions like this that she felt the absence of her mother or of a sympathetic female to whom she could talk in confidence. There was always plenty of light-hearted banter with her father and she would freely discuss any household matters with him. Emotional issues were more problematical. She tended to conceal those from him and try to resolve them on her own. This time, however, she felt the need of support. Her father was keen to help. She wondered if it was time to tell him the truth.

'There *is* something else,' she said, quietly.

'I knew it.'

'Though I fancy I'm probably fretting unnecessarily about it.'

'Why not let me be the judge of that?'

'It's this investigation,' she explained. 'Robert has become obsessed with it. I know that he gets immersed in every case he deals with but this one is different. It's made him so single-minded.'

'Do you know why that is?'

'Frankly, I don't.'

'Then let me tell you,' said Andrews, tapping his chest, 'because I understand what's going through his mind. It's those policemen, Maddy. Two were killed on the train and the other one was shot in London. Inspector Colbeck has a bond with fellow policemen, the same way that I do with engine drivers. It's something that goes very deep. He's single-minded because he's chasing people who murdered his kin — at least, that's what they'll seem like to him.'

'That's not the whole story, Father.'

'Yes it is, so you can stop losing sleep over it.'

'It's more personal than that.'

'What could be more personal than a detective who worked alongside you on the case being shot dead?'

'This is not about Constable Peebles,' she said. 'Robert was shocked by what happened to him but he's driven by something from the distant past. He as good as said so when I last saw him.'

'Did he explain what it was?'

'No – that's why I'm upset about it. I feel that he should have told me everything there is to tell. It's so unlike Robert. He's never concealed things from me before. This case has a real significance for him but he refused to say why. I feel as if I'm deliberately being kept ignorant,' she said, shaking her head in despair, 'and it's not what I expect from the man I'm about to marry.'

A sudden squall cleared the upper deck of the *Jura* and made the vessel dip and rock on the choppy sea. While Leeming went into the saloon, Colbeck repaired to their state room to have some time alone. As he checked through the paperwork he'd brought with him, he picked out the passenger's contract ticket, issued when he'd booked the passage. It was an interesting legal document, listing the obligations placed both on the shipping line and on the passenger. Trained as a lawyer, he noted the small print on the document. Among other things, it stipulated that the victualling scale had to be printed out in the body of the ticket. Consequently, the daily quantities of water and provisions for each person were listed. If the *Jura* defaulted in any way on its obligations, it was liable to legal redress.

Studying one form of contract made him reflect on another. Marriage was the most solemn contract of all, committing two people to lifelong conditions from which they could not waver. As he went through the service of holy matrimony in his mind, he was ready to commit himself to Madeleine when the moment arose. Yet somehow he was not prepared to state exactly when that moment would be. The urge to delay and prevaricate was implanted deep within him. Even though he could see how much distress it was causing Madeleine, he could not bring himself to name the day when he would make her his wife. The invisible barrier stopped him.

He recalled the joyous openness with which Ian Peebles had talked about his forthcoming marriage, and the way that Victor Leeming always looked back on his own nuptials with such fondness. Colbeck wished that his path to the altar had been as straight and un-complicated as theirs. Before the wedding, the banns would have to be published. He remembered how nervous Leeming had been when that phrase about just cause or im-pediment had been read out before the congregation. Had his own banns been pub-lished, the phrase would have unsettled Colbeck even more because of the secret he'd nursed for so many years. Helen Millington was his impediment. Until she was laid to rest, he could never give himself wholly and exclusively to Madeleine Andrews. The only way he could finally reconcile himself to her death was by catching Jeremy Oxley.

It had been a despicable murder. Colbeck had been shaken rigid when he read the details of the post-mortem. He was a young and impressionable barrister at the time, not a hardened detective who'd learnt to look on hideous sights without flinching. The manner of Helen's death was almost as horrid as the fact of it. Such was the searing effect on him that Colbeck had abruptly changed direction in life so that he could begin the hunt for Oxley. Equally keen to arrest Irene Adnam, he was struck by the power of love to induce blindness. Irene was so entranced by Oxley that she did not apprehend his true character. Had she been aware of what he did to Helen Millington before he killed her, she would have shunned his company in disgust.

Colbeck had a contract with the shipping line, but a far more important one with Madeleine Andrews existed. It would bind him for life. He had to remove the impediment to their marriage and return to her as a free man with no ghosts to keep them apart. As he thought about Madeleine now, he felt an upsurge of love for her that flooded through his entire body and left him exhilarated. It was an elation that had to be suppressed until the proper moment for release. Helen Millington had to be his sole inspiration for the time being. Once her unquiet spirit had been appeased, there would be a blissful future with Madeleine Andrews.

CHAPTER FIFTEEN

The suddenness of their departure from England had given them no time at all to plan for their future in a new country. That had troubled Irene deeply at first. She soon came to see that there was no need for alarm. Long weeks at sea gave them plenty of opportunity to discuss what they were going to do once they reached New York. Oxley was quick to realise that, if they befriended the right passengers, there was a fund of valuable information accessible to them. The voyage therefore became an exercise in collecting facts.

'Ours is a great country,' said Herschel Finn, expansively. 'It rewards hard work and wise investment. If he has the right qualities, any man can succeed in America.'

'That's not true of England, alas,' complained Oxley. 'Family determines everything there. If you're born into the aristocracy, you can lead a life of idle luxury. If you're the child of a poor family, the chances are that you'll remain in poverty for ever.'

'It's the main reason my father emigrated – not that he was exactly poor, mark you. His family ran a grocer's shop in Leicester and, in the fullness of time, he would have inherited it. But he felt that there was more to life than serving bags of sugar and jars of pickled onions to his neighbours. So,' said Finn, proudly, 'he saved up his money and took ship to America.'

'How old was he at the time?' asked Irene.

'He was barely twenty-one.'

'That was very brave of him.'

'My father was a brave man, Irene. He knew it would take time to fulfil his ambitions and he knew there'd be lean years beforehand. So he gritted his teeth and bent his back. And when the opening finally came,' said Finn, snapping his fingers, 'he seized it and moved into the textile business.'

'It's an inspiring story, Herschel,' said Oxley.

'It's a typical *American* story.'

They'd liked Herschel Finn and his wife from the outset and it was only days before all four of them were on first-name terms. Finn was the owner of a cotton mill in Beverly, Massachusetts and of a wool carding mill in Blackstone River Valley in the same state. Wealth had given him a confidence that never even approached brashness. He was a man of medium height and average build who'd kept his hair its original colour and who carried his fifty years lightly. His wife, Libby, was a short, round, genial woman with a chubby face and dimpled cheeks. She seemed to exude benevolence. Hearing that their new friends were about to settle in America, the Finns had taken Oxley and Irene under their wing.

'When you find your feet,' offered Finn, beaming hospitably, 'you must come and stay with us.'

'Yes,' added Libby, squeezing Irene's arm, 'we'd be delighted to have you folks as our guests.'

'That's very kind of you,' said Irene.

'We may well take you up on that invitation,' warned Oxley.

Finn chuckled. 'We'll insist on it, Robert.'

The four of them were in the saloon, relaxing in upholstered chairs and enjoying each others' company. The Finns had visited England so that Herschel could make contact with his surviving relatives and so that he could visit a number of textile factories to see if there were any technical improvements that he could adapt for use in his own mills. At both an emotional and business level, the visit had been highly successful but it had reminded Finn why he could not possibly live in the country that his father had left behind.

'To begin with,' he said, 'we speak a different language.'

Oxley shrugged. 'The words sound the same to me.'

'But they don't *mean* the same, Robert. In England, people seem to hide behind words. They're too reserved and afraid to speak out. Where we come from, everything is much more open. We say exactly what we mean and mean exactly what we say.'

'You and Libby are perfect examples of that. Here we are, chatting happily away on the strength of a very short acquaintance. You've both been so wonderfully open. To reach this degree of familiarity with any English passengers,' said Oxley, glancing around the saloon, 'would take years. Isn't that so, Irene?'

'I'd have said decades,' she put in.

Their collective laughter was interrupted by the arrival of a steward. When they'd ordered refreshments, he went off with a tray under his arm. Conversation was resumed. Irene had marvelled at the way that Oxley had selected the Finns out of all the other passengers and made sure that he got to know them early on. In fact, however, it was Irene who helped to consolidate the friendship. Hearing that Finn owned textile mills, she immediately promoted her father to the board of directors of the Manchester mill from which he'd actually been sacked. Unknown to Silas Adnam, he was rescued from the abiding squalor of Deansgate to occupy an elevated position in British textile manufacture. Irene was even able to talk about visits she'd made to the mill when she was a child.

'So,' said Finn, becoming practical, 'what are you folks going to do the moment you arrive in New York?'

'From what you've been telling us about it,' replied Oxley, 'I think we'll just stand around open-mouthed in awe. We'll be the country cousins visiting the big city.'

'You'll need somewhere to stay.'

'Can you recommend anywhere?'

'Sure I can, Robert.'

'Thank you – we'd be very grateful.'

'What about that hotel where we stay, Herschel?' said Libby.

'That's one possibility,' agreed her husband, 'but there are plenty of others. Robert and Irene can take their pick.'

'Money is no problem,' said Oxley, easily.

'Then that makes the choice much easier. New York is a city of neighbourhoods. Some are safe, others are dangerous and others again are nothing but urban jungles with gangs roaming through them. For instance, you don't want to go anywhere near Five Points. That's completely lawless. Like London, I guess, there are places where crime just thrives.'

'It's the same in Manchester,' said Irene,

thinking of her father's lodging. 'There are some districts where a woman would never dare venture out alone.'

'That's shameful,' opined Libby.

'It's the fault of our police,' said Oxley, righteously. 'There simply aren't enough of them to keep major centres of population under control. We have far too many places where there's no respect at all for law and order.'

'That's the basis of a civilised society,' asserted Finn.

'I couldn't agree with you more, Herschel.'

'Work hard, live within the law and attend church regularly. Those are the three guiding stars in my life.'

'You always told me *I* was your guiding star,' teased Libby.

Finn patted her hand. 'You are, honey.'

'Now find these good folks a hotel where they can stay.'

'Yes,' said Oxley, taking out a pad and pencil. 'I can't tell you how grateful Irene and I are to make such dear friends. You've turned this voyage into a joy. Now where would you advise us to stay?'

'Before I tell you that,' said Finn, responding to a nudge from his wife, 'there's something I must ask you. It will settle a wager I have with Libby. I hope the question won't embarrass you.'

'Not at all,' said Irene.

'Ask whatever you wish,' added Oxley.

Finn leant forward. 'Are you newly married?'

Oxley held Irene's hand and she pretended to look coy. They exchanged an affectionate glance then nodded in unison.

'There you are, Libby,' said Finn, triumphantly. 'I was right.'

'I concede defeat, Herschel.' Libby turned to the others. 'My husband is never wrong about people. The moment he saw you, he said that you were on honeymoon. I do hope we're not monopolising your time but we find you such delightful company.'

'The feeling is mutual,' said Oxley with his most charming smile. 'We can't tell you how much we look forward to seeing you every day.'

Herschel and Libby Finn chortled. They were hooked.

The voyage was not without its setbacks. Two days away from her destination, the *Jura* was caught in a violent storm that lashed her with rain, battered her with gale-force winds and turned the sea into an apparently endless switchback ride. The noise was ear-splitting. Leeming felt that Mother Nature was trying to deafen him before drowning him in the depths of the ocean. He could not believe that the vessel would ever survive such a tempest. Nor could he understand why Colbeck showed no anxiety as the ship rose high, plunged low and twisted at all manner of different angles. The ferocious rain was like a continuous firing squad aiming at the porthole in their state room. Any moment, Leeming expected it to shatter the glass and allow the sea to engulf them.

'Why did you make me come on this voyage?' he yelled.

'I thought that you were enjoying it, Victor.'

'How can anyone enjoy a storm like this?'

'It will blow itself out before too long. Would you like a game of chess to take your mind off it?'

'The pieces would never stay on the board.'

'That's nothing new,' said Colbeck with a wicked grin. 'Your pieces never stay long on the board when you play me. They seem to have made a suicide pact.'

As the ship listed again, Leeming clung to his chair. 'I think that's what *we* made when we agreed to sail to America. It was an act of suicide.'

'It was a necessary response to the given situation. Wherever Oxley and Adnam go, we'll set off in pursuit. They're sailing on the *Arethusa*, remember. When they're caught in a storm like this, they will fare even worse.'

'Nothing could possibly be worse, sir.'

'Yes, it could,' said Colbeck. 'The superintendent could be with us.' Leeming's laugh was a forlorn croak. 'The *Jura* will not let us down, Victor. Try to ignore the discomfort.'

'That's like telling a drowning man to ignore the water.'

'I find that very amusing.'

'I find it terrifying!' howled Leeming.

The rain eventually eased off and the wind relented. It took longer for the sea to stop slapping the vessel like a giant hand but there was noticeably less turbulence. From that point on, the voyage was blessed with good weather. Passengers were able to bask on deck again and put their fears behind them. Leeming felt as if he'd been reborn. He marked the occasion by beating Colbeck at chess for the first time. Unaware that he'd been given a certain amount of help by his opponent, he boasted about it for hours.

When they finally reached it, New York harbour was positively buzzing with activity. Crowds thronged the piers, wooden and iron vessels were safely moored and cranes were helping to unload luggage and freight. The pilot boat came out to guide the *Jura* to its berth. Ropes were tossed ashore and made secure. The gangplank was lowered and the passengers began to disembark. Once they'd been through customs, Colbeck and Leeming reclaimed their luggage and found a cab to take them to police headquarters. Captain Matt Riley was fascinated to learn the purpose of their visit.

'*Both* of them are killers?' he said in surprise.

'Both of them are killers of policemen,' stressed Colbeck.

'We don't have too many female killers here, Inspector. Oh, we have our share of domestic violence, of course, and, from time to time, a wife might hit a husband a bit too hard during a fight, but that's not what I'd call cold-blooded murder. Tell me about Miss Irene Adnam.'

Matt Riley was a mountain of a man who seemed on the point of bursting out of his uniform. His craggy face bore the marks of several brawls and his thinning hair revealed some ugly scars on his head. When he grinned, it was possible to count the number of teeth on the fingers of one hand. His first impression of Colbeck had not been a flattering one. There was the whiff of a peacock about him that Riley instinctively disliked. Five minutes of conversation with him, however, had removed all his reservations about Colbeck. The inspector was patently an efficient and dedicated man with an intelligence not often found among policemen of any nation.

They were in Riley's office which smelt in equal parts of pipe tobacco, damp, and stale beer. It was tolerably tidy and had a series of posters pinned to the walls. Riley sat at his roll-top desk and listened to Colbeck's account of the career of Irene Adnam. He was struck by the amount of information they'd gathered about her in such a short time. Though he was sickened by the litany of their crimes, Riley could not suppress a grin when told of the name under which they were sailing.

'So,' he said, exposing his surviving teeth, 'Inspector Colbeck has come to arrest Mr and Mrs Colbeck. It's a real family affair.'

'The joke was their undoing,' Colbeck pointed out. 'Had they called themselves something else, I might never have picked them out of the passenger list on the *Arethusa*.'

'I suppose it's a kind of compliment to you, Inspector.'

'Well, they'll get no compliments in return,' said Leeming, sharply. 'They'll travel back to England under their real names.'

'What about you, Sergeant?'

'I'll go with them,' said Leeming.

Riley grinned again. 'Does that mean I can't poach you to join the New York Police Department?' he asked. 'I can always pick out a tough man when I see one. You'd be an asset to us.'

'He's not for sale,' said Colbeck, politely. 'Victor has a wife and family back in England.'

'That's not unusual. When I first came

here, I had a wife and family back in Ireland. Talking of which,' Riley went on, 'did you stop at Cork on your way?'

'Yes, we did. We picked up several passengers.'

'It's my hometown. I emigrated here when I was in my twenties. It was three years before I could afford to bring Kathleen and the boys over here. We've never looked back since.' He felt Leeming's biceps. 'You've got strength in those arms. We could use it.'

Leeming declined the offer with a gesture. 'I'm needed back in London.'

'You know where I am, if you change your mind.'

Having established how the extradition procedure worked, Colbeck asked for advice about accommodation. Riley not only suggested a hotel, he offered to provide transport to get to it. He also pressed them to ask for any more help they might need.

'You'll have time on your hands,' he argued. 'How would you like to spend it?'

'I promised to show Victor the sights of New York,' said Colbeck.

'Come on patrol with my men and you'll see some *real* sights. When he sees what policing is like on this side of the Atlantic, the sergeant might think twice about going back home.'

'I don't know about that, Captain Riley,' said Leeming.

'We've always got room for an experienced detective.'

'So have we,' said Colbeck, firmly.

Riley laughed and massaged Colbeck's shoulder. He took them out into the court-yard and beckoned to a cab driver. As their luggage was loaded onto the vehicle, the visitors thanked Riley for his help and told him that they would need his assistance when the *Arethusa* docked. Having no juris-diction there, they had no right to arrest and hold the fugitives on American soil. They would have to wait until the extradition had been authorised before Oxley and Irene became solely their prisoners. Riley was happy to oblige.

'I can guarantee our full cooperation,' he said, chirpily. 'It's not often we have two killers trying to sneak into this country in order to evade justice in England. If it was left to me now, I'd execute the pair of them right here and save you the cost of their passages home.'

'There are legal reasons why that can't happen,' said Colbeck.

'That's a great pity, so it is.'

'We'll just get them extradited and slip quietly away.'

Riley guffawed. 'Oh, you will, will you?'

'What's so funny?' asked Leeming.

'You'll soon find out, my friend.'

'I don't understand, Captain.'

Riley slapped him on the back. 'Welcome to America!'

The first thing that Edward Tallis did when he arrived for work early that morning was to cross another day off the calendar on his wall. He estimated that his detectives would have arrived in New York by now but that it would take much longer for the *Arethusa* to complete its voyage. Counting the days to their arrest helped Tallis to bring retribution ever closer in his mind. He still regretted that he'd been unable to accompany Colbeck and Leeming but accepted that his place was directing operations at Scotland Yard.

In fact, he had deserted his desk for two days when he took a train to Edinburgh for the funeral of Ian Peebles. There'd been a dignified sadness about the whole event. While suffering pangs of remorse during the actual ceremony, Tallis had found that the most trying moment was when he had to face the constable's parents and explain to them the exact circumstances of their son's death. On the journey back to London, he'd sat in a hurt silence and relived the horror of the shooting. It had been his blunder. Peebles' parents had been too well mannered to say so but they knew the truth.

Back in his office, the first thing he did was to open his cigar box. Before he could take one out, however, his guilt stirred. He snapped the lid back down and vowed that he would never smoke again until the killers were caught and brought back to England. Denial of his favourite pleasure would be a form of expiation. As he counted the days he'd ticked off, he saw how long it had been since he'd last enjoyed the solace of a cigar. Temptation flickered. With an effort, Tallis resisted it. Until the appropriate time, he pledged, he would no more lift the lid of the cigar box than he would open the drawer that contained his bottle of brandy. Both were a means of escape and he was entitled to neither. He had to wait for Colbeck and Leeming to release him from his vow.

They timed it to perfection. On the last evening before their arrival in New York, they robbed the people they had carefully selected as their victims. Working independently, Oxley and Irene slipped into vacant cabins, picked unguarded pockets, stole unwitting reticules and generally helped themselves to items that were too much to resist. They returned to their own cabin to compare notes and to count their spoils. It had been a most satisfying haul.

'The beauty of it is,' said Oxley, holding up a gold watch, 'that most of the people won't realise things have gone until it's too late.'

'I'm glad that we spared Herschel and Libby.'

'They're our friends.'

'Yes,' said Irene, 'but they're also very wealthy.'

'I never even considered them. They've been too helpful to us. Who knows? We might accept that invitation to visit them one day.'

'Will we still be calling ourselves Mr and Mrs Colbeck?'

'I've grown to like the name. It has a pleasing resonance.'

Having sorted out the money and the items they'd stolen, they hid them cleverly in their respective valises. It was all part of the capital that would set them up in their new country.

'Well,' he said, 'it's been a long voyage but an interesting one.'

'Yes – apart from the storm that lasted two days.'

'Even that had its benefits, Irene. It gave us the chance to get to know Herschel and Libby much better.' He smirked. 'I don't set as high a value on Herschel's powers of observation as his wife does. According to Libby, he was sure that we'd just got married.'

'That just proves how good a performance we gave.'

'It doesn't *have* to be a performance.'

Her face lit up. 'You mean that we *will* get married?'

'Anything can happen in America.'

'Oh, Jerry, what a wonderful idea!' she exclaimed.

'I had a feeling you might like it.'

'Nothing could make me happier.'

'Let's get ourselves settled in first,' he said, looking at the gold watch. 'It's time to dress for dinner.'

'Herschel and Libby insisted that we sit with them.'

'Then let's not disappoint them, Irene.'

After stowing the valises away, he crossed to the cupboard, pausing in thought when he'd opened the door. She looked up.

'What's the matter?'

'I'm wondering if I should do it before or after the meal.'

'Do what, Jerry?'

'Complain to the captain that we've been robbed,' he said. 'There's no better way to shift suspicion than to portray ourselves as victims.' He made a decision. 'Let's leave it until afterwards,' he went on. 'Why spoil dinner by whingeing over a lost wallet? It would only upset Herschel and Libby. Yes, my mind is made up. I'll tackle the captain later on.'

It had not taken them long to realise why Matt Riley had burst out laughing at their expense. Colbeck's wish to catch the fugitives and take them quietly back home was an impossible one. On the day when they booked into their hotel, the first of many reporters came to hassle them. Word had travelled fast, leaked to the press by a policeman in return for a bribe. The arrival of two killers on a British vessel was an unusual event and it aroused an immense amount of interest. The detectives were soon weary of repeating the details to a succession of reporters. When the *Arethusa* finally docked, it would do so in the glare of publicity. Colbeck and Leeming had been disturbed at the thought but there was nothing that they could do about the situation. Their presence in the city was helping to sell newspapers. Unsought celebrity had been foisted onto them.

They had not wasted their time in New York. There was much to see and they had toured Manhattan in a cab. Leeming was amazed at the colourful prettiness of the houses and the comparative cleanliness of the streets. Areas of London that he'd patrolled in uniform had been filthy and noxious. There were doubtless run-down neighbourhoods in New York but they never visited any of them. What they saw were the wide avenues and bright, paved streets. Broadway had been a glorious sight, a winding thoroughfare down which coaches, cabs, carts, gigs, traps, phaetons and private carriages rumbled in abundance. Leeming had never seen so many liveried black coachmen. There was wealth in America and a desire to put it on display.

Captain Riley had been as good as his word, letting them see the work of the police department at first hand. At Colbeck's request, he also arranged for them to visit The Tombs, the city's notorious prison. In the course of their work, they'd been inside all of London's prisons and several in the provinces. Conditions there had been harsh but none could match the regime at The Tombs for severity. There was a pervading stink of despair on its four galleries. Leeming was glad to get out into the fresh air again but Colbeck had been intrigued.

'I wanted to see if his description was accurate,' he said.

'Whose description would that be, sir?'

'Charles Dickens came here once. He wrote about it.'

'I could write about it in one word,' said Leeming, 'but it's not a word that I'd repeat in mixed company.'

Sightseeing and time spent with the police were only preludes to the main purpose of their visit. The day eventually came when the *Arethusa* reached its destination and sailed up the Hudson River with its passengers crowding the deck for their first glimpse of New York. The pilot boat was rowed out to shepherd the vessel to its berth. Colbeck and Leeming were part of the massed ranks on the pier. Captain Riley was with them but so was a much larger complement of uniformed policemen than the detectives had requested. Their visible presence caused Colbeck some disquiet.

'We won't want to warn them in advance,' he said.

'I'm not giving them any chance to escape,' asserted Riley. 'I've got some of my best men on duty today.'

'It might be better if the sergeant and I go aboard first.'

'Why is that, Inspector?'

'They don't know what we look like,' explained Colbeck. 'We can take them by surprise. Police uniforms would give the game away.'

Riley was obstinate. 'We'll do it my way.'

'They're *our* prisoners,' Leeming pointed out.

'They're your prisoners in *our* country.'

The declaration was unanswerable. They were powerless. They had control neither over the police nor over the bevies of newspaper reporters who'd arrived early to secure vantage points on the pier. Having often rehearsed the boarding of the vessel in his mind, Colbeck accepted that it would simply not happen that way. Captain Riley would take the lead. Colbeck and Leeming would have to follow in his wake. As they watched the vessel gliding ever nearer the pier, they hoped that the two fugitives were not watching from the deck.

As soon as they entered the mouth of the river, Oxley and Irene had joined the rest of the passengers on deck. Now that they were at last in the harbour, they were standing with Herschel and Libby Finn, waving to the cheering hordes below and enjoying their reception. There had been moments when Irene had wondered if they'd ever arrive but those anxieties had all vanished now. Here was the country in which she would spend the rest of her life with a man who would become her husband. She was overwhelmed with relief and wonder.

Oxley shared her euphoria but it was short-lived. He, too, had been carried away at first by the sight of the welcoming multitude below. His eyesight was much keener than Irene's, however. When he scanned the pier, he noticed the plethora of police uniforms. They were gathered around the point to which the ship was slowly moving. As the vessel got closer, he was able to see the faces of those below more clearly. They did not all belong to friends and well-wishers. Some of those waiting were not cheering at all. They were tense and watchful. Among them was a tall, striking, exquisitely tailored figure standing beside a police captain. Letting out a yelp, Oxley reacted as if he'd just seen a ghost.

'We must go below,' he said, grabbing Irene.

'What's the matter, Jerry?' she asked.

'You can't miss all the fun,' said Finn. 'Stay and enjoy it.'

'There's something we left in our cabin,' said Oxley, dragging Irene away. 'You'll have to excuse us for a moment.'

Their friends were baffled by their sudden disappearance but it was Irene who'd been most surprised. As they picked a way through the people on deck, she kept asking him what had happened. He waited until they were below deck and out of earshot.

'It's him, Irene,' he said.

'Who are you talking about?'

'It's Inspector Colbeck. He's down there on the pier.'

'You must be imagining things, Jerry,' she said with a laugh. 'How could you recognise him when you don't even know what he looks like? More to the point, how could he possibly be in New York when we left him behind in England?'

'It's him, I tell you,' he said, irritably. 'I just sense it, Irene, and you know how acute my senses are. If he came by means of a steamship, he could have overtaken the *Arethusa* with ease. It's just the kind of thing Colbeck would do. Instead of giving up the chase, as I'd hoped, he's come after us.'

His panic was contagious. 'What are we going to do?'

'Let me think for a moment,' he said, hand to his head. 'I could be wrong. I pray to God that I am. If that's the case, we have nothing to worry about. You must leave the ship with Herschel and Libby.'

'What about you?'

'I'll take ... other measures,' he said.

'Why can't we leave together?'

'We have more chance of eluding him if we're apart. Don't worry,' he said, enfolding her in his arms. 'If anything happens to you, I'll come to your rescue.'

'How?' she asked, feverishly.

'I don't know but I'll find a way somehow. I swear it.'

She was perspiring now. 'Are you sure that it's Colbeck?'

'Yes, I am. Go back on deck and find the others.'

'What shall I tell Herschel and Libby?'

'Tell them that I'm searching for something that's gone astray. Tell them I'll be back directly. Go on, Irene,' he urged, pushing her away. 'They'll be wondering where we've got to.'

'I don't like leaving you on your own.'

'You have to. Now find Herschel and Libby. Being with them is the best chance you have of dodging Colbeck.'

She swallowed hard. 'If you say so, Jerry.'

With grave misgivings, she went back to the staircase that led to the upper deck. She could hear the sound of many feet shuffling across the deck. When she looked behind her, Oxley had vanished.

The *Arethusa* was determined not to be rushed. After ploughing her way through the waves under full canvas for three thousand miles, she was bent on a leisurely arrival. She seemed to drift in slow motion towards the pier, unsure whether to stop there or to float gently back downriver. As her hull made contact with the pier, there was a resounding thud. It was followed by the sound of ropes crashing onto the stone. They were quickly tied in place to steady the vessel. Members of the crew lowered the gangplank and it was fixed in place. Before anyone could descend it, Captain Riley led the way up the gangplank and ordered everyone to stand aside so that he could step onto the deck. Colbeck and Leeming were at his heels with four uniformed policemen in attendance. Riley first spoke to the captain who was poised at the top of the gangplank to shake the hands of the departing passengers. There was a brief discussion. After listening to Riley's explanation of why he and the detectives were there, the captain gave him permission to come aboard.

Riley's stentorian voice quelled the heavy murmur on deck.

'Ladies and gentlemen,' he shouted, 'I'm sorry to delay you after a long voyage but there are two people with whom we need to speak as a matter of urgency.' He stood on his toes to survey the assembled passengers. 'We wish to speak to Mr and Mrs Colbeck. Could they please step forward?'

'That's you,' said Libby, turning in amazement to Irene.

'Keep your voice down,' begged Irene.

'Why?'

'What's going on?' asked Finn.

'He's asking for Robert and Irene.'

'What do the police want with them?'

'It's probably something to do with the theft from our cabin last night,' said Irene, quivering in fear. 'It's nothing to worry about.'

'How would the police onshore even know about that?'

But Finn's question hung unheard in the air because Irene had already lost her nerve and squirmed off through the melee. Her American friends were at once shocked and bewildered. They'd never seen Irene act so impulsively and kept asking each other what had prompted her abrupt retreat. It was only when Riley barked out his request a second time that they found their voices.

'Mrs Colbeck is over here,' called Finn, raising a hand.

'She's just run away,' added Libby.

'We know her and her husband well.'

There was a commotion as Riley barged his way uncaringly through the passengers. Colbeck and Leeming followed him. When they reached the Finns, Riley asked them to identify themselves and they did so readily. Finn explained that he and Libby had befriended the Colbecks on the voyage and found them a charming couple.

'You were grossly misled, sir,' said Colbeck, stepping forward. 'Since you know what they both look like, we'll need your help to find this putative charming couple.'

'Nobody is to leave the ship without producing their passports!' bellowed Riley. 'Every document will be checked at the gangplank by my men. Please disembark in an orderly fashion.'

Police reinforcements had now come on board to cluster around the entrance to the gangplank. The passengers were mystified but at least they could now begin to make their way off the ship. As the first trickle went down the gangplank, the search began in earnest behind them. Riley stayed close to Herschel Finn while Colbeck and Leeming kept Libby in tow. Unaware of what their shipboard friends had done, the Americans were nevertheless more than ready to help

the police find them. In spite of their repeated questions, the captain and the two
detectives refused to say why they were so
anxious to find the missing passengers. The
search was thorough. They could move about
freely. Now that everyone was vacating the
vessel, all the doors had been left unlocked.
Apart from a few members of the crew, the
areas below deck were empty. Feet clattering
on the timber, the search party seemed to be
walking through a hollow.

They opened cabin doors, looked under
bunks and searched inside cupboards. Leeming soon wearied of the chase.

'This is worse than hide-and-seek,' he
moaned.

'They're here somewhere,' said Colbeck,
looking in every corner. 'They can't possibly
have left the vessel.'

'Then where are they, Inspector?'

By way of an answer, a woman's shrill
scream was heard at the other end of a pas-
sageway. The detectives hurried along it
with Libby waddling behind them. They
discovered that Irene had been found hiding
in the cupboard of what had been their
cabin. Finn identified her. With a surge of
energy, she tried to break away from Riley's
grasp but it was like iron.

'Take your hands off me!' she shouted. 'I've
done nothing wrong. Mr and Mrs Finn will
vouch for me. My name is Irene Colbeck and

I demand to be treated with respect.'

'Oh, we'll treat you with the greatest respect,' said Colbeck, doffing his hat as he entered the cabin. 'Allow me to introduce myself. I'm Inspector Robert Colbeck of Scotland Yard and I'd like to discuss the misappropriation of my name.'

Irene was transfixed. *'You're* Inspector Colbeck?'

'Yes, Miss Adnam, and this is Sergeant Leeming.' He stood back so that Leeming could step forward. 'We were friends and colleagues of Constable Peebles. Need I say more?' Irene began to gibber. 'Now tell us where Oxley is and we can put an end to this whole business.'

'I don't know,' she cried. 'I don't know where Jerry is.'

'Then we'll search until we find him.

'Is he armed?' asked Leeming.

'Yes,' replied Irene. 'He has a gun.'

'So have I, Miss Adnam,' said Colbeck, tapping the weapon beneath his coat, 'but I sincerely hope that there'll be no need to use it. We've had enough killing as it is.'

'I wish someone would tell us what's going on,' said Finn.

'Yes,' said Libby, 'it's all so confusing.'

'You're helping us to find two dangerous criminals, sir,' said Colbeck with gratitude. 'One is now in custody. Since the other is armed, it might be safer if you and your wife 'stay here with Captain Riley.'

'Will you be able to recognise the rogue on your own?' asked Riley, slipping a pair of handcuffs onto Irene's wrist.

'Oh, I think so. I've never actually seen him but I'm sure I'll know him straight away when I clap eyes on him.'

'Be careful, Inspector!' warned Libby.

She was horrified to hear that the amiable man she'd known as Robert Colbeck possessed a gun. Finn, however, was driven by curiosity as much as bravado and offered to accompany Colbeck and Leeming.

'That won't be necessary, Mr Finn,' said Colbeck.

'Leave this to us, sir,' advised Leeming. 'We came three thousand miles for the pleasure of capturing Jeremy Oxley.'

'Oxley?' Finn blinked. 'I thought his name was Robert Colbeck.'

'Not anymore, it isn't,' said Colbeck with asperity.

'What will happen to Irene?' wondered Libby.

'She'll remain in police custody until her partner in crime is arrested,' said Riley. 'Then the pair of them will go back to England to face the death sentence.'

Irene fainted. Riley was just in time to catch her. He put her gently down on one of the bunks. Hovering uncertainly, Finn and Libby did not know whether to pity or condemn her. They were shaken by the thought that they'd been taken in so easily by Irene and her supposed husband. Libby was the first to speak.

'I *knew* that there was something odd about them,' she claimed.

'So did I,' said Finn.

'That's not true, Herschel. You thought they were such nice people. They fooled you completely.'

'Hey, now that's not fair, Libby.'

Colbeck and Leeming did not stop to hear the marital dispute. They were already making a systematic search of the places they'd not yet visited. It was tiring work. The *Arethusa* was a large and capacious three-masted vessel, though lacking the refinements of the *Jura*. The problem was that there were far too many hiding places and there was always the danger that Oxley was moving from one to another as they closed in on him. Leeming began to lose patience but Colbeck was convinced they'd find their man in the end. He kept one hand on the weapon holstered at his side. When they'd exhausted almost every other possibility, they went down into the very bowels of the ship to the quarters occupied by the crew.

With a low ceiling of oak beams and only rudimentary facilities, the quarters stretched across the width of the ship. Since they were below the waterline, there was no natural light. The detectives were compelled to remove their top hats before they could move forward. Colbeck grabbed a lantern that dangled from a hook and held it up. As it pierced the gloom, it revealed an array of bunks and hammocks in close proximity. Leeming was disappointed.

'Another dead end,' he groaned.

Colbeck raised a hand to silence him, then he lifted the lantern higher and went off to take a closer look at the quarters. As his eyes adjusted to the half-dark, he could see the privations that the crew endured while the passengers travelled in relative comfort. Colbeck stopped in his tracks. Somebody was there. He could neither see nor hear anybody but he was certain that he was not alone. Slipping a hand under his coat, he removed the pistol from its holster and held it in readiness. When he inched forward, he did so with slow, quiet, deliberate footsteps. He did not get far. His toe suddenly stubbed against something and he looked down to see the dead body of a man splayed out on the floor. The corpse was almost naked and smeared with blood.

'Over here!' he called.

'What have you found, sir?' asked Leeming, coming forward until he saw the body. 'Is that Oxley?'

'No,' said Colbeck. 'It's a member of the crew.'

He held the lantern low so they could see that the man's skull had been smashed to a pulp. Behind the body was a pile of discarded clothing of a kind that looked incongruous in the crew's quarters. There was a well-cut frock coat, fashionable trousers, a silk waistcoat, a cravat and a pair of patent leather shoes. An abandoned top hat completed the outfit. Colbeck assessed the situation at once.

'Oxley has disguised himself as a member of the crew,' he said in exasperation. 'He's probably left the ship already.'

CHAPTER SIXTEEN

Retirement day had left Caleb Andrews with mixed feelings. As he celebrated with other railwaymen that evening at the pub near Euston they'd made their own, he was simultaneously buoyed up with delight and afflicted with remorse. Physically, he was ready to leave a job that made such heavy demands on his time and energy. His old bones, he told them, were crying out for a rest. Emotionally, however, his ties with the footplate were too strong to be easily broken. He could simply not imagine a life without the challenge, responsibility and sheer excitement of driving a locomotive. His departure from the LNWR was thus a confused jumble of gains and losses and it was far too early to weigh them against each other.

Over a week later, there was a more formal gathering of friends with whom he'd worked over the years. Held on a Sunday afternoon at his home, it had been organised by Madeleine who provided the refreshments. Only those who were not on duty that day were able to attend, but there were over a dozen guests crammed into the house in Camden. Men who habitually came home from work with the day's grime on their hands, face and clothing were now in their best suits. Their faces gleamed and their hair was neatly combed. Over a drink and an unlimited supply of food, they exchanged anecdotes about Andrews and the room was filled with laughter.

Madeleine was pleased to see how much respect they had for her father. She knew most of those present. They included Gideon Little, her most ardent admirer at one time. Promoted to the rank of driver, Little was now married and had two small children. There was no longer any embarrassment between Madeleine and him. He obviously nursed no resentment against her because she had once rejected his advances. There was a mood of general hilarity in the house. She made sure that glasses were regularly filled and more food offered as soon as anyone's plate was empty.

Dirk Sowerby joined her in the kitchen, his big, muscular body looking out of place in a smart suit. He accepted a cake from her.

'You've done wonders with the food, Madeleine,' he said.

'I wanted to be part of the celebration,' she told him, and to see what his friends really think of Father.'

'He's the best driver in the LNWR.'

She smiled. 'That's what he keeps telling me. Father has never been one for hiding his light under a bushel.'

'We've had some rare old arguments, Caleb and me, but it's always a pleasure to work alongside him. But let's forget your father for a moment,' he said, moving closer and lowering his voice. 'Is it true that Inspector Colbeck sailed to America on a steamship?'

'Yes, it is.'

'That's always been one of my ambitions.'

'Father mentioned that to me.'

'To be honest, I'd wanted to run off to sea and join the navy but somehow I finished up on the railway. It's not the same. On the other hand,' he said with a vacuous grin, 'it's probably a bit safer.'

'Lots of accidents happen on the railways, Mr Sowerby.'

'That's true but they're not usually fatal. If

a ship goes down in the middle of the ocean, then the chances are that everyone on board will drown. Not that that would have put me off, I hasten to say,' he added. 'Steamships, in particular, are less likely to founder. They're not at the mercy of the wind and the waves in the way that a wooden sailing ship might be.' His eye kindled. 'How long will the inspector be away, do you think?'

'I've no idea. It's been well past a month so far.'

'Then he could be on the way home already.'

'I doubt it,' said Madeleine. 'He had to wait until another vessel reached New York and that was a sailing ship.'

'When he does come back,' said Sowerby, biting a piece off the cake, 'could you ask him what it was like, please? I mean, I'd love to know in detail what sailing on a steamship is like. You could pass on the information to Caleb.'

Andrews came into the kitchen. 'What's that you're saying about me behind my back, Dirk?'

'I want to learn about steamships.'

'I'll find out all I can,' promised Madeleine.

'Thank you.'

Popping the remains of the cake into his mouth, Sowerby went back to the others. Andrews, meanwhile, helped himself to another cucumber sandwich. He nibbled at it before nodding with satisfaction.

'You've done me proud, Maddy,' he said.

'You deserve it.'

'If this is what it's like, I'll retire more often.'

'I can't promise to do this *every* Sunday,' she said, laughing.

'Everybody is saying how wonderful you look.'

'It's always nice to have compliments.'

'I hope that it means you're feeling better,' he said, probing. 'You've been very subdued this past month or so. We both know why.'

'I'm fine now,' she said, blithely.

He put a hand under her chin. 'Are you happy?'

'I'm very happy, Father.'

'Then let's make sure we keep it that way.'

Grabbing two more sandwiches from the table, he put them on his plate and went off to rejoin his friends. A roar of laughter greeted a comical remark he made as he entered the room. Left alone in the kitchen, Madeleine could now abandon the pretence of being happy. Having to maintain a permanent smile for their guests had taken a great effort. Behind the mask, she was worried and dispirited. She kept taunting herself with memories of disasters that had taken place at sea and feared for Colbeck's life. What irked her was that there was no way to verify his safe arrival in New York or to confirm that he'd managed to capture the two fugitives without being injured.

She spared a thought for Estelle Leeming, having to cope alone with two children while her husband was out of the country, but at least the Leemings had married and started a family. She and Colbeck had taken neither of those life-changing steps. If anything happened to him, all that she would have to remember him by were a series of pleasant reminiscences. Madeleine yearned for something more. But the main cause of her discontent was the comment he'd made before they parted. Colbeck vowed to explain everything once the case was closed. Until then, he was devoting all of his attention to it and she was the loser as a result. What was it about the investigation that made it so important to him? Why had he not confided in her?

Madeleine kept repeating the questions until a head peeped around the door of the kitchen. Gideon Little gave a hopeful smile.

'Is there any chance of another slice of that cake, please?'

The haul was astounding. Oxley may have escaped but he'd left his luggage behind him. In a room at police headquarters, Colbeck and Leeming had been assisted by Matt Riley as they went through the respective cabin trunks and valises belonging to Oxley and Irene. Booty of all types came to light. They laid it out on a table.

'I'll wager that some of this belonged to other passengers on the *Arethusa*,' said Colbeck, dangling a gold watch. 'This is the sixth one I've found. Nobody needs that many watches unless they're planning to sell them to a pawnbroker.'

'Look at this,' said Leeming, extracting some jewellery from the lining of a trunk. 'What a clever hiding place!'

'Some of this property can be returned to its rightful owners,' announced Riley. 'I'll have an advertisement put in the newspapers. If people can prove that it's theirs, they deserve it back.'

'You have to be careful, Captain. Whenever we advertise lost property, we always get lots of false claimants.'

'It's the same here, Sergeant. We once recovered six pairs of expensive dancing pumps. The first man through the door swore blind that they were his and begged us to hand them over.'

'And did you?'

'Oh, no,' replied Riley, chortling. 'We figured he might be lying when we noticed he only had one leg.'

When everything was arranged on the table, Colbeck did a quick estimate of its value and realised that, if this reflected their lifestyle, Oxley and Irene had a sizeable amount of capital at their disposal. It was no wonder that they could afford the luxuries of life. Irene was in a police cell at the other end of the corridor but Oxley remained at liberty. News of his escape had been carried in all the newspapers. A manhunt was taking place in New York. Riley was confident that his men would find the fugitive but Leeming was less optimistic.

'He's like a will-o'-the-wisp,' he said.

'We'll catch him,' insisted Riley.

'He could be in another city now, if not in another state.'

'No, Victor,' said Colbeck after consideration, 'I'm certain that Oxley is still in New York.'

'What makes you say that, sir?'

'I don't think he'd desert his accomplice. After all, Irene Adnam was the person who rescued him from that train. He owes her a great deal. Even someone as ruthless as Oxley wouldn't be able to walk away from that kind of obligation. He'll be determined to free her.'

'There's no hope in hell of that while she's here,' said Riley. 'At all times, there'll be at least twenty men between him and the cell she's being held in. Oxley is helpless against the New York Police Department.'

'Then we have to make it easier for him, Captain.'

'What do you mean?'

'We need to bait a trap. We'll never catch him otherwise. He's far too slippery. Since we can't get to him,' said Colbeck, stroking his chin meditatively, 'we have to devise a way to bring him to us.'

'You have an idea,' said Leeming, approvingly. 'I know that tone of voice, Inspector.'

'It might work and it might not.'

'What's the plan?' asked Riley.

'You're going to get your wish, after all,' said Colbeck, an arm around Leeming. 'You were eager to recruit Victor so I'm going to let you have him.'

'I don't want to join the police here!' protested Leeming.

Colbeck smiled enigmatically. 'Wait until you hear the conditions of service,' he said, 'and you may change your mind.'

Oxley had escaped from the *Arethusa* without any difficulty. In his stolen clothing, he'd merged with the other crew members and helped to carry the luggage down the gangplank. It was placed on the pier so that porters could load it on to handcarts. Oxley had simply mingled with the crowd and, as it drifted away, he went with it. Posing as one of the porters, he got through customs without even being challenged. Once clear of the harbour, he hailed a cab and headed for one of the hotels recommended by

Herschel Finn. Since he could hardly book in to such a respectable establishment looking like a sailor on low pay, he first found a menswear shop and transformed his appearance. When he stepped into the street, he looked like a gentleman again.

Forced to leave his luggage behind, he still had three assets. He had an appreciable amount of money and he possessed a gun. His greatest asset, however, was his acute sense of danger. Having lived off his wits all his life, he felt able to cope with anything. Since the hotel would be suspicious if he arrived with no luggage, he bought himself a valise and filled it with the items he might need during his stay. Then he took a room and stayed in it for the best part of a day. To keep track of the search for him that was taking place, he had a copy of the newspaper sent up to his room. The description of him contained details of clothing that he'd now discarded. The police were looking for a sailor from a British ship and not the beau he'd now become.

Having got free himself, his only concern now was to rescue Irene. The newspaper reported that she was in police custody but he had no chance of reaching her there. He had to be patient. Frustrating as it was, there was no alternative. On the third day, he felt the first flicker of an opportunity. There was a report in the newspaper that Irene Adnam was to appear at the courthouse the following day to face extradition proceedings. Oxley was reassured. It looked as if they'd given up hope of capturing him and were intending to return to England with their prisoner. It was unlike Colbeck to abandon a hunt but even he would have to accept the impossibility of finding a fugitive in a country as vast as America. The inspector was a realist. He would not spend time indefinitely chasing moonbeams.

Oxley's chance had come. Planning could begin.

'Your father was very proud of you, Miss Adnam,' said Colbeck.

'I'd rather not talk about him,' she snapped. 'He means nothing to me now.'

'He must have meant something or you wouldn't have given him so much money. You wouldn't even have told him that you were leaving the country. Against all the odds, you have a conscience.'

'Father belongs in my past.'

'He was proud of you until he discovered the truth. It's amazing what knowing the full facts about a person can do,' said Colbeck. 'It helps you to see them in the round.'

Seated opposite each other at a table, they were alone in a small, locked room adjacent to the cells at police headquarters. It was the first time that Colbeck had been able to question her on his own. After the crisis of her arrest, Irene had regained her composure. Now that he was so close to her, he could see that she did not resemble Helen Millington to any degree. Colbeck was grateful for that. She had similar features but their arrangement was quite different. Above all, she lacked Helen's bloom and innocence. Irene had a doll-like beauty that caught the eye. Helen's beauty could reach into a man's soul.

'Do you know why I asked to speak to you?' he enquired.

'You just want to gloat, Inspector.'

'Why should I want to do that?'

'It's because you finally caught me,' she said, 'though exactly how you did it, I still don't know. You can do as you wish with me,' she went on with an attempt at defiance. 'Jerry escaped. That's a great consolation. You'll never get anywhere near Jerry.'

'That's palpably untrue, Miss Adnam. We got very close to him on the *Arethusa*. By the way, do you know *how* he managed to elude us on the ship?'

'No, I don't.'

'He killed one of the crew and stole his clothing.'

'You're making that up.'

'I'm not, I promise you. The man's name was Nathan Holly. It turns out that he has a wife and family back in Liverpool. They'll be awaiting his return. What they don't yet know,' said Colbeck, 'is that his head was cracked open by a blunt instrument. I suspect that it might have been the butt of Oxley's gun.' He looked into her eyes. 'Are you happy to be the accomplice of a man for whom human life is so cheap?'

'Jerry only did what he had to do.'

'Are you saying that murder can be justified, then?'

'In this case – yes, it can.'

'What about the murder of those two policemen?'

'That, too, was necessary.'

'I don't believe that it was, Miss Adnam. You had a weapon. You could have held it on the policemen and ordered them to release Oxley. You could have handcuffed them so that they couldn't pursue you,' he said. 'In fact, there are all sorts of things you could have done other than shooting one man dead then hurling the two of them under an oncoming train.'

'That wasn't my idea!' she shouted, hands to her temples.

'Did you raise an objection?'

'No – it all happened so quickly. I had no time.'

'But you do have time now, Miss Adnam,' Colbeck told her. 'You have plenty of time to reflect on the crimes you helped to commit while you and Oxley were together.

In retrospect, I think you'll find, they were neither necessary nor justifiable.'

Colbeck paused to allow time for his words to sink in. Irene had a surface hardness that he believed he could penetrate. She was not as cold and heartless as Oxley. In talking about the escape from the train, he'd already put one small wedge between them. If his plan was to succeed, he needed to insert a much larger one.

'How well do you know Jeremy Oxley?' he asked.

'I know him extremely well. He's a wonderful man.'

'Then you have a warped idea of wonder, Miss Adnam. Had you seen the way that Nathan Holly's skull had caved in, I doubt that you'd have hailed his attacker as a wonderful man. I leave it to your imagination,' said Colbeck, 'how two human beings look when a train passes over them at high speed. The remains had to be gathered up in a couple of sacks.'

She began to retch and pulled a handkerchief from her sleeve to hold against her mouth. He gave her another respite. Her defences were weakening. Irene was starting to look like a cornered animal. At length, Colbeck resumed the interrogation.

'Did he ever mention that he'd killed a young woman?'

'Yes, he did.'

'Were you shocked?'

She lowered her head. 'I must confess that I was.'

'Did it make you fear for your own safety?'

'Not in the least.'

'I think you're lying, Miss Adnam.'

'Jerry would never have hurt me!' she cried.

'Do you know *how* he murdered that young woman?' There was a long pause. She refused to look at him. 'I think that you do. I think that he told you that he strangled her.'

Her head came up. 'He also told me that you and this woman were close friends,' she taunted, 'and that you were the one who persuaded her to give evidence in court against Jerry. That's why you've been chasing him so hard all these years, isn't it? You were in love with her.'

Caught off guard by her attack, Colbeck felt as if he'd been slapped across the face. It was a sobering moment. He needed a while to control the intense feelings that had suddenly welled up inside him. He inhaled deeply through his nose.

'Her name was Helen Millington,' he said, solemnly, 'and what you say about her is, to some extent, correct. I make no apology for my friendship with her. She was a remarkable young woman. I just hope that you will make no apology for someone for whom *you* care, Miss Adnam. Hear the whole story and you will see that he doesn't deserve it. As I said earlier, it's only when you know the full facts about someone that you see them in the round and can arrive at a proper judgement.'

'You'll say anything to blacken Jerry's name,' she sneered.

'I would have thought that it was black enough as it is. You don't have to believe me, of course. That's your privilege. But you must ask yourself why I should trouble to confide details that are excruciatingly painful to me.'

Irene could see the sincerity in his eyes. She was apprehensive. He was about to tell her something she had no wish to hear. She flapped a hand and turned away.

'He strangled her,' she said. 'What more is there to say?'

'He obviously didn't tell you what he did to her beforehand.'

'That's irrelevant.'

'Not in my book,' said Colbeck, forcefully. 'Every detail is highly relevant because it tells me exactly the kind of man that Oxley is.'

'You'll never change my view of him, Inspector.'

'I don't need to – Helen Millington will do that for me. She was about the same age as you, as it happens, and equally as beautiful. She'd led a blameless life. It was her ill luck to witness a man being shot outside a jeweller's shop but she had the presence of mind to take a close look at the killer. It was Oxley.'

'I know all this.'

'Then you'll know why he took his revenge on her.'

'Jerry has a temper,' she conceded. 'He can act rashly.'

'I'm glad you've found a defect in this paragon,' said Colbeck, 'because I'm going to identify a few more. It was not enough for him to kill Miss Millington, you see, he had to make her suffer for her bravery in coming forward. When he discovered where she lived, he abducted her and spirited her away to a place where nobody would interrupt them. He stripped her naked and tied her up with wire that cut deep into her wrists. The first thing he did – and I choose a polite phrase to cover a brutal act – was to relieve her of her virginity. Jeremy Oxley then began to torture her.'

As he related the details, Colbeck's voice became hoarse with disgust and his head began to pound. Seeing that he'd finally got her attention, however, he forced himself to go on and talk about things that had haunted him for years. Irene tried not to listen but the words kept hammering away at her ears. She was revolted. Much as she wanted to dis-believe it all, she knew that his account had the ring of truth. Oxley did not simply diminish in her esteem. He slowly turned into a ravening beast. There had been hints. Since the time they'd been together, there'd been several hints of darker passions in him, moments when she prayed that she would never be close to him if he lost control of his temper. That was what he'd done with Helen Millington. In a fit of anger, he'd abused her, tortured her and mutilated her so badly that neither her parents – nor Colbeck – had been able to identify her from her face.

When it was all over, Colbeck was as moved as Irene had been.

'I'm sorry I had to tell you all that,' he said, quietly. 'I just wanted you to understand why I've dedicated myself to the capture of Jeremy Oxley. He has no place in a civilised world.'

Preparation was everything. Oxley had learnt that long ago. If he failed to make adequate preparation for a crime, then the chances of a successful outcome were lessened. Time was on his side. He had a whole day in which to appraise the building and to observe the normal procedure at the courthouse. First of all, he strolled past and took a close look at the front. Then he walked around the block so that he could examine the building from the rear. Returning to the front, he crossed the road and went into the bookshop opposite. Pretending to study a book, he kept one eye on the window. From his vantage point, he could see police vehicles arrive at the courthouse. Each followed the same pattern. They would turn into the yard at the side of the building. The driver would then unlock the door at the back of the van and the prisoner would be brought out, handcuffed to a second policeman. All three of them went into the courthouse.

It was a simple, unvarying routine. Having watched it three times, Oxley knew it off by heart. His next step was to get inside the building so that he could learn its geography. It involved dodging various court officials but he was adept at that. He eventually worked his way around to the entrance where the prisoners were admitted and made a note of the rooms through which they'd have to pass. At that point, he was disturbed by a janitor.

'Can I help you, sir?' asked the man.

'I was looking for a...'

A smile and a gesture replaced the word. The janitor led him to the lavatory at the side of the building, explaining pointedly that it was not generally accessible to members of the public. Oxley had already taken the trouble to change some of his money into the local currency. He responded to the broad hint from the janitor by pressing some coins into the man's hand. It was a sound investment. Thanks to the janitor, Oxley had stumbled on another vantage point. Through the small, rectangular window in the lavatory, he had a good view of the yard into which Irene would be driven next day.

Oxley was pleased with his preparations. All he had to do now was to familiarise himself with the rest of the interior so that he could plan an escape through a rear exit. When he was challenged by one of the court ushers, he pretended that he was unwell and in need of fresh air. The man kindly showed him the quickest way to the exit at the back of the building. There was a cab rank thirty yards away. If he could smuggle Irene out of the courthouse, they could be lost in traffic within a minute. Only one thing remained. Walking around the block to the front of the courthouse, he entered the public gallery in order to watch part of a trial. As he perched on the hard bench and looked down at the wretch standing in the dock, Oxley permitted himself a complacent smile. He'd found the perfect refuge. No matter how intense the manhunt for him, the one place they'd never dream of looking for him was in a court of law.

Habits of a long working life could not easily be changed. Though he had talked about staying in bed until late morning, Caleb Andrews was downstairs at his usual time. Madeleine was awakened by the sound of her father walking around the uncarpeted kitchen. Unable to sleep, she too resumed the early breakfasts. The problem was that he was almost always there. She encouraged him to go out but Andrews preferred to stay in the house, chatting to her when she wanted to be alone, standing behind her and clicking his tongue in disapproval as she tried to paint. It was more than irritating. In taking his retirement, Andrews had effectively stopped her from working as well. Her patience began to fray.

The situation became so bad that she decided to take up the offer made by Colbeck. His house was in John Islip Street and he'd urged her to make use of it. Madeleine paid a preparatory visit. The servants knew her well and treated her with the respect befitting a future mistress of the house. They were happy to let her roam around at will. She was familiar with the downstairs rooms, particularly the library. It was the source of her education and had provided her with an endless succession of books. As she entered it once more now, she was impressed afresh by the ornate bookshelves around three walls, by the nest of occasional tables and by the elaborate desk. Colbeck's father had been a successful cabinetmaker and the library was a striking example of his handiwork.

Madeleine realised with a start that it was

the first time she had ever been in the house without Colbeck. Her immediate response was that she was trespassing, intruding on his privacy. Then she reminded herself that she would one day live there and have to shed any feelings of humility. Wandering around the downstairs rooms, she was bound to compare Colbeck's situation with her own. He'd inherited a comfortable home and enough money to permit an existence of relative idleness. It was to his credit that he chose instead to pursue a career in the Metropolitan Police Force. Coming from a very different background, Madeleine had more modest expectations. In the event of her father's death, she would inherit the house and what little of his savings he left behind him. In moving to John Islip Street, she would be climbing several rungs up the social ladder. It was a forbidding yet curiously inspiring prospect. Luxuriating in the home she would share with Colbeck, she was determined to prove herself worthy of him.

As she looked to the future, however, doubts began to cloud her mind. Would he survive the voyage to and from America? After all that time apart, would his feelings for her remain unchanged? Why had there been an element of mystery about the investigation? Was he still thinking about her? When would he return? All her fears ultimately rolled into one crucial question.

Where *was* he?

'It's too tight,' said Leeming as he did up the buttons. 'And the hat is far too big for me.'

'This is not a fashion parade, Victor,' said Colbeck, amused. 'Stop complaining. You look fine to me.'

'And to me,' agreed Riley, appraising them both. 'The uniforms might have been made for you.'

It was not true. Reduced to the ranks, Colbeck was wearing a constable's uniform that was baggy on him. At least it gave him freedom of movement. Leeming felt he was being pinched under the armpits. He had to wear the hat at a rakish angle to stop it from falling too low over his forehead. They were in Riley's office, going through the last details of their plan.

'What if Oxley doesn't turn up?' asked Riley.

'Then I can get out of this uniform and breathe properly again,' said Leeming with a grimace.

'He'll turn up,' insisted Colbeck. 'It's too good a chance to miss. Oxley will know that there may not be another one. Will your men be in position, Captain?'

'Have no worries about them,' said Riley. 'They'll be placed in strategic positions around the courthouse. I took your advice. We don't want to spook him with the sight of too many uniforms. All my men will be in plain clothes.'

'I wish that *I* was,' grumbled Leeming.

'It's not like you to miss an opportunity to arrest a killer,' said Colbeck, 'especially one who murdered a colleague of ours.'

'That's what worries me,' admitted Riley. 'This man is armed. We know he doesn't hesitate to kill. All it takes is a warning from the prisoner and one of you will be shot dead.'

'Miss Adnam won't raise the alarm, Captain Riley.'

'You can't be sure of that.'

'Oh yes I can.'

'She's in love with this man,' said Riley. 'If she sees that he's in danger, she's bound to yell out.'

'That's a good point,' said Leeming. 'We're taking a big risk.'

'And there's something else to bear in mind, Inspector. Didn't you tell me that he's tried to shoot you before? When he sees you right in front of him, he won't be able to resist the temptation.'

'He won't recognise me,' explained Colbeck. 'It was because of mistaken identity that Constable Peebles was shot in my place. And he's never set eyes on the sergeant either. He'll assume that we are what we look like – two New York policemen.' When he saw Leeming desperately trying to adjust his uniform, he laughed. 'It's only for one morning, Victor,' he said. 'Once he's in custody, you can change back into your own clothing.'

Oxley arrived at the courthouse early so that he could rehearse the escape. The police would bring Irene through the side door, then go through an anteroom and into a corridor that led to the courtroom. By going down the corridor in the opposite direction, it was possible to reach the rear exit. Oxley made the short journey a few times to see how long it would take them. Once in the street, they could run to a waiting cab and be driven away at speed. It was now only a question of waiting. The newspaper had talked of proceedings beginning at a specific time. Fifteen minutes beforehand, Oxley was hiding in the lavatory, watching the yard through the window he'd left slightly ajar.

He heard the clatter of hooves and the rumble of wheels. The black police van with its barred windows rolled into the yard. It came to a halt and the driver got down in order to unlock the door at the rear. A second policeman emerged with Irene handcuffed to his wrist. He helped her down the step. Oxley was upset to see how pale and haggard she was. He watched all three of them move to the side door. Leaving his hiding place, Oxley rushed to the anteroom and stood behind the door with his gun in his hand. As soon as the newcomers entered, he slammed the door shut behind them and thrust the barrel against Leeming's temple.

'Release her at once!' he demanded.

'Jerry!' she screamed in surprise.

'Do as I say,' he shouted, moving the gun to point at Colbeck. 'Stand where you are.' He turned and punched Leeming. 'Hurry up!'

'Miss Adnam doesn't wish to go with you,' said Colbeck, calmly.

'Of course she does!'

'Why not ask her?'

Oxley swung round to her. 'What's he talking about, Irene?'

Irene shrank from him. 'Stay away from me, Jerry.'

'Don't talk nonsense. I've come to rescue you.'

'I know what you did to that woman you strangled.'

He gaped at her. 'Why on earth bring that up now?'

'Miss Adnam finally sees you in your true colours,' said Colbeck. 'I was able to tell her exactly what sort of a man you really were. Yes,' he went on as realisation slowly showed in Oxley's eyes, 'my name is Robert Colbeck and I was a good friend of Helen Millington. You'll be charged with her murder as well as with that of your other victims.'

Oxley was bewildered. Expecting to rescue

Irene from two New York policemen, he was instead confronted with the very man from whom he'd fled to America. It was only a momentary confusion but it was enough for Colbeck. Whipping out a truncheon from beneath his coat, he smashed it against the wrist holding the gun, forcing Oxley to drop it to the ground. Leeming tried to grab him with his free hand but Oxley reacted swiftly to push him hard against Colbeck. In the seconds that Colbeck was impeded, Oxley darted from the room and sped down the corridor towards the rear exit. As he came hurtling out into the street, he intended to race to the cab rank but the huge and intimidating figure of Captain Riley was blocking his way. Other uniformed policemen suddenly materialised out of nowhere.

Dashing back into the courthouse, Oxley rushed up a flight of stairs with no idea where they might lead. Colbeck pounded after him, discarding his hat on the way. Oxley reached a landing and ran along it until he found a second set of stairs. Conscious that Colbeck was gaining on him, he turned to fight him off but it was a mistake. As Oxley raised his fists to beat him away, Colbeck dived for the man's legs and brought him crashing to the floor. They grappled, rolled over and struggled hard to gain the advantage.

Oxley had a power born of desperation, punching, kicking out and biting for all he was worth. He managed to clamber on top of Colbeck and got both hands to the inspector's neck, applying pressure with his thumbs. Colbeck had a vision of Helen Millington in the same position, having the life choked out of her. Unlike her, however, he was no weak and defenceless young woman with wrists bound together by wire. He could fight back. Bucking and twisting madly, Colbeck put all his energy into a vicious right hook that caught Oxley on the ear and sent him sprawling sideways in a daze. Colbeck gave him no time to recover. Punching him relentlessly with both fists, he only stopped when Oxley was unconscious. As he panted away and felt blood trickle down his face, Colbeck looked at the man he'd been hunting for so long. Turning Oxley over, he pulled out the handcuffs attached to his belt and secured the prisoner's wrists behind his back.

It was all over. Helen Millington's killer had finally been caught.

Extradition procedures took less than a day to complete. Because Irene refused to stand beside Oxley in the courthouse, their cases had to be dealt with separately. Colbeck was very grateful for the help given by Captain Riley and his men. Having been drafted into the New York police for a morning, Leeming decided that he preferred life in plain clothes as a Scotland Yard detective. With their prisoners in handcuffs, they set sail for home on the *Etna*, another propeller-driven steamship. On their way, they promised to give Ireland a friendly wave on Matt Riley's behalf. Though the return voyage took longer, it seemed to be quicker because their mission had been accomplished. They reached Liverpool in the pouring rain but nothing could dampen their spirits. On the train journey to London, the detectives travelled in separate compartments. Leeming looked after Irene Adnam while Colbeck stood guard over Jeremy Oxley. Their prisoners were duly delivered into police custody.

'Congratulations!' said Tallis, shaking their hands in turn. 'This has been a signal triumph for all of us.'

'I don't remember that *you* came to New York with us, sir,' said Leeming, annoyed that the superintendent was claiming some glory.

'I was there in spirit, Sergeant. I also authorised the trip.'

'It was the commissioner who did that.'

'Why quibble over details?' asked Colbeck, stamping out the row before it took flight. 'The truth of it is that we all stand to gain from this escapade. First and foremost, two killers will now be condemned to death for their crimes and their victims have been avenged. Secondly, we've gained unanimous praise in the press.' He smiled at Tallis. 'I was pleased to see that *your* contribution was recognised, sir. You've earned their respect at last.'

'I'm not so foolish as to think that,' said Tallis, grimly. 'They'll praise me one day and stone me the next. However, that's in the nature of journalism and I have to endure it with my usual stoicism.' Sitting behind his desk, he eyed his cigar box as if about to attend a reunion with an old friend. He rubbed his hands together. 'Now, then,' he ordered, 'sit down, the pair of you. I want to hear the full details.'

As Leeming groaned inwardly, Colbeck came to his assistance.

'There's no need for the two of us to do that, Superintendent,' said Colbeck. 'I'm in possession of all the facts. Victor has been away from his wife and family for a long time. On grounds of compassion, I think he should be allowed to go home to them now.'

Leeming rallied. 'Thank you, Inspector.'

'Well,' said Tallis, grudgingly, 'as you're aware, I don't normally yield to any compassionate appeals but this is a special case. You've done sterling work, Sergeant. Because of that, we need detain you no longer. You may depart.'

'Yes, sir,' said Leeming, moving swiftly to the door before Tallis changed his mind.

'Thank you very much.'

After shooting Colbeck a look of gratitude, he went out of the room. Sitting down, Colbeck composed his thoughts. There was much to tell but Tallis would only get an attenuated version of it. Like the sergeant, Colbeck was also anxious to get home as soon as he could.

'This is truly splendid news,' said Tallis, grandiloquently. 'It wipes the slate clean of any mistakes we may have made during the investigation. I will have great pleasure in passing on the tidings to the Wolverhampton Borough Police and even greater pleasure in writing to the parents of Constable Peebles and to the young lady to whom he was betrothed.'

'I hope it will bring them a measure of satisfaction, sir.'

'With luck, it will take the edge off their sorrow.'

'It may be too soon to do that,' said Colbeck. 'Bereavement must run its course. But at least they won't be tormented by the thought that the constable's killers escaped justice.'

Tallis wriggled in his chair. 'Tell me all, Inspector.'

'Well, sir, it's rather a long story...'

It had been a good choice for a studio. Situated on the first floor at the rear of the house, it was a large room with a high ceiling. Madeleine set up her easel in a position where it caught the light pouring in through the two windows. Colbeck had singled the room out for her and – now that she'd actually tried to work in it – she saw that his judgement had been sound. There were immediate gains. She'd escaped the well-intentioned interference of her father and given him the freedom of their home during the day. Of much more satisfaction to her was the fact that she was in the house where Colbeck had been born and brought up. It was filled with mementos of him and with clear indications of his character. When Madeleine was working there alone, she somehow felt that he was beside her.

Her latest painting featured a locomotive that her father had actually driven. It enabled her to get expert advice from him but it also left her open to bitter reproaches when he felt she'd got a detail wrong. Working from sketches she'd made, Madeleine was now at the stage where the final touches could be applied. She stood back to study the painting with a critical eye. When there was a tap on the door, she barely heard it. It needed a second, harder tap to claim her attention. Madeleine opened the door, expecting to see one of the servants there. Instead, it was Colbeck, beaming at her with arms widespread.

'Do you remember me?' he asked.

'Robert!' She almost swooned as she went into his embrace.

'I called at your house but your father told me that you were here.' He looked around with approval. 'I told you this would make an excellent studio.'

'Oh, forget about me,' she said, pulling him into the room. 'You're safely back home in England, that's all I care about.'

He kissed her then stood back to gaze at her. 'It's a joy to see you again, Madeleine.'

'You look different.'

'I'm over two months older since we last met, that's why.'

'No, it's something else,' she said, scrutinising his face. 'You were so serious and preoccupied before you left, but not anymore. It's as if a great weight has been lifted from your shoulders.'

'It's more of a great cloud that's finally floated away. It's been hanging over me for far too long. In fact,' he went on, 'that's what I want to tell you about, Madeleine. This case meant a lot to me.'

She put a hand on his mouth. 'Say no more, Robert.'

'But you deserve an explanation.'

'You're home again – that's the only explanation I need. You left me for a long, lonely time but the Robert Colbeck I love has come back at last. One look at you has swept away all my sadness.'

'Don't you want to hear what happened?'

'Another time, perhaps,' she said, nestling against him. 'This is all I want at the moment.' Tears filled her eyes. 'I was beginning to think that you'd never come back.'

'Of course I was coming back, Madeleine,' he said. 'I had to honour a promise I made to you.'

'What sort of promise?'

He laughed. 'Don't you remember?'

'I'm too confused to remember anything just now.'

'Dear me!' he said, teasingly. 'I disappear for a couple of months and you forget all about me.'

'Don't be silly. I thought about you every single day.'

'Then you've probably already made the decision for me.'

She was baffled. 'What decision is that?'

'The small matter of a date for our wedding,' he said, kissing her again and lifting her up to twirl her in a circle. 'You're not leaving this house until it's fixed. I want to hear those banns being published and those bells ringing out in celebration. I've waited far too long for you already.' He pulled her close and rubbed his nose softly against hers. 'When will you become my wife?'

This Large Print Book, for people
who cannot read normal print,
is published under the auspices of

THE ULVERSCROFT FOUNDATION

35 $\frac{50}{}$